THE JUDGE

Peter Colt

SEVERN
HOUSE

First world edition published in Great Britain and the USA in 2024
by Severn House, an imprint of Canongate Books Ltd,
14 High Street, Edinburgh EH1 1TE.

severnhouse.com

Copyright © Peter Colt, 2024

All rights reserved including the right of
reproduction in whole or in part in any form.
The right of Peter Colt to be identified
as the author of this work has been asserted
in accordance with the Copyright,
Designs & Patents Act 1988.

British Library Cataloguing-in-Publication Data
A CIP catalogue record for this title is available from the British Library.

ISBN-13: 978-1-4483-1070-8 (cased)
ISBN-13: 978-1-4483-1069-2 (e-book)

This is a work of fiction. Names, characters, places and incidents are either the product of the author's imagination or are used fictitiously. Except where actual historical events and characters are being described for the storyline of this novel, all situations in this publication are fictitious and any resemblance to actual persons, living or dead, business establishments, events or locales is purely coincidental.

All Severn House titles are printed on acid-free paper.

Typeset by Palimpsest Book Production Ltd., Falkirk,
Stirlingshire, Scotland.
Printed and bound in Great Britain by TJ Books,
Padstow, Cornwall.

Praise for the Andy Roark novels

"Page-turning . . . the balance of plot and character is perfect"
Publishers Weekly Starred Review of *The Ambassador*

"A gritty whodunit that packs an unexpected punch"
Kirkus Reviews on *The Ambassador*

"Colt doesn't pull any punches and plays fair with the reader before the satisfying reveal. Fans of **Robert B. Parker**'s Spenser novels interested in a grittier private investigator will be eager to see more of Roark"
Publishers Weekly on *Death at Fort Devens*

"Excellent . . . balances a gripping plot with further development of Roark's character. **Jeremiah Healy** fans looking for a new Beantown hero will be eager for more"
Publishers Weekly Starred Review of *Back Bay Blues*

"A classical mystery with an honor-bound detective and a keen sense of place . . . Roark is genuinely likeable (not too tough, but not a patsy)"
The New York Times on *Back Bay Blues*

"Roark's skill at his job is displayed amid a gift for self-conscious mockery . . . There's plenty of room for detection and a blood-soaked finale"
Booklist on *Back Bay Blues*

"Entertaining . . . Like **Philip Marlowe** – or **Robert Parker**'s Spenser – Andy has a sharp eye for telling detail and male haberdashery"
Publishers Weekly on *The Off-Islander*

About the author

Peter Colt is a 1996 graduate of the University of Rhode Island with a BA in Political Science and a 24-year veteran of the Army Reserve with deployments to Kosovo and Iraq as an Army Civil Affairs officer. He is currently a police officer in Rhode Island. He is married with two sons and two perpetually feuding cats.

In memory of my Father-in-Law
David W. Bean 1938-2023
A good man, husband, and father.

For Cathy, Henry and Alder.

Acknowledgements

I just write the manuscript. In many ways I have the easy part. There are a lot of people who worked very hard to bring you the book. I would like to thank them.

The Volunteers: CME for reading the very rough manuscript and helping me fool the world into thinking that I can spell and have a working knowledge of English grammar. For TFA, who has let me bounce ideas off him for the better part of thirty years now. There is a small but dedicated squad of people who read early drafts and offer advice.

Fred Tindall who gave me a crash course in 1980's photography and how the blackmail photos could have worked. Any errors or omissions are completely my fault and not his.

The Professionals: My editor at Severn House, Rachel Slatter who offers advice and direction. I could not do it without her and her team, Tina Pietron, and Katherine Laidler. And the rest of the team at Severn House.

My agent, the incomparable Cynthia Manson.

The Family: My wife and boys who allow me to sneak away to the 1980's every night and write.

ONE

My left foot sank up to the ankle in a river of slush the type that Boston specializes in filling its gutters with from mid-December to mid-March. Fortunately, I was wearing a pair of duck boots from Bean's, and all I had to worry about was not slipping in it. It was the lull between Christmas and New Year's, the last few days of 1985. The nice shops on Newbury Street had swept the Christmas displays out of their windows in favor of ones advertising the commercial hopes and dreams of 1986.

Last night's snowstorm had left a few inches of the stuff on the ground. What in the early evening had made Commonwealth Avenue look like something out of a Currier and Ives print had by mid-morning turned into the gray-tinged, wet, slippery nuisance. That was the type of thing Boston provided for pedestrians to experience when the Bruins were the team to watch. It wasn't the Bs' fault; that was just how weather in New England worked.

I was dressed for the weather in jeans, a wool Pendleton button-down shirt over a long-sleeved T-shirt, and one of those rust-colored parkas from Bean's that are little more than a wool-lined, nylon version of an Army field jacket. I also had my .38 Smith and Wesson hammerless snubnose on my hip, holstered under my untucked shirt. It was loaded with five hollow-point rounds, and there were another five in a speedloader in my left pants pocket. If that wasn't enough, there was a lockback Buck knife in my right pocket. The knife was sharp enough to shave the hair off my forearm and broken-in enough that I could flick it open with a violent jerk of my wrist. I never left home without them.

If I thought I was going to get into some sort of trouble, I would carry a blackjack too. Today I was going to meet a prospective client, and somehow a blackjack didn't seem necessary. After all, I wasn't heading out to face the fashionable housewives looking for bargains on Newbury Street. I was on my way to meet my client at Jakie Wirth's. No self-respecting Bostonian would ever refer to it as Jacob Wirth's even if that is what it said on the sign above the door.

The sun was playing hide-and-seek behind large, pewter-colored clouds. It was bright enough that I had to wear an old pair of Army-issue aviator sunglasses. With my beard, moustache and longish hair that was three weeks overdue for a trim, I probably looked unsavory enough to scare off the Lord and Taylor set or any tourists who stumbled by.

Jakie Wirth's opened in 1868, making it the second oldest, continuously operating restaurant in Boston and therefore America. It was a Boston institution just like the Union Oyster House or Durgin-Park. Someone once told me the oldest restaurant in America was in Newport, Rhode Island, but I didn't believe them.

When I first started going there, the floors were covered in sawdust to soak up the spilled beer and blood from the occasional fistfight. As we grew more enlightened, the Department of Health decided that the sawdust had to go. At least they still had pickled eggs in a huge jar at the bar. Jakie Wirth's had been the first distributor of Anheuser-Busch beers. The Wirths were from the same town in Germany as the Anheusers. My mother was German, so I never missed a chance to go to Jakie Wirth's or the Wurst House in Harvard Square.

I knocked the slush off my boots and went up the steps into the restaurant. It had started life a few years after the Civil War had ended as a typical German beer hall. Now it was one of the best places in town to get your fix for wursts or schnitzel or beer that was imported from West Germany. It was close enough to the tourist attractions that a few of them made their way in.

It was also close enough to the New England Medical Center that it wasn't uncommon to see people in scrubs having a beer or hearty meal after a long shift. NEMC was both a world-renowned research hospital and a busy trauma ER. Its proximity to the Combat Zone probably had something to do with that. The Combat Zone was Boston's five square blocks of sin and squalor. After Scollay Square had been flattened to make way for Government Center, the burlesque shows, prostitutes and porno theaters had to go somewhere. That somewhere was wedged between Copley Square and China Town. The Combat Zone was under attack in a relentless campaign by the business owners in China Town who objected to the drugs, violence and seediness that the Zone was a magnet for. The Combat Zone was also being threatened by the real estate developers who wanted to tear down every bit of seedy red brick in Boston and replace it with antiseptic glass skyscrapers filled with offices and condos. I wasn't sure that was much of an improvement. Every year the Combat Zone gave up just a little more ground to decency and progress.

Even though the front of Jake's was plate glass, the interior always seemed dim. There was a beautiful dark wood bar that ran most of the length of the interior. The floor was wooden and had seen a lot of wear over the decades. Wooden tables and chairs were the seating options other than a stool at the bar. The décor was, not surprisingly, German beer hall. It was a little after eleven in the morning, which was too late for the morning drinking crowd and too early for the lunch crowd.

The bartender looked up from polishing a glass with a rag. Behind him was a portrait of Jacob Wirth himself in all his mustachioed glory. You'd be forgiven for thinking it was a portrait of the Boston Strong Boy, the prize fighter John L. Sullivan. The resemblance was close enough and the two were friends.

I was the only customer in the place. That wasn't a good sign because I was perpetually a few minutes late for everything. I walked over to him and was about to order in German when he said, 'Whadda ya want, kid?' In Boston-ese, calling someone above the age of twenty 'kid' can be a term of affection or derision. I wasn't sure which in this case.

'Bad Apfel.' It was chilly enough out that an apple schnapps seemed appropriate but not cold enough for a Slivovitz.

The bartender poured a belt of the sweet amber stuff into a tall, thin shot glass. I put a ten-dollar bill down, and while he was making change, I took a sip of the sweet apple schnapps. It went down easily, offering a pleasant warmth unlike the burn of something harsher, such as whiskey or bourbon. It was the perfect thing to have after coming in from the cold.

He came back with my change. Eyeing the empty glass he said, 'Kid, you want another?'

'Löwenbräu, please.' The nice thing about Jake Wirth's was the Löwenbräu was on tap.

'Sure.' He drifted off to get a glass and pull on the tap. He brought my mug, and I slid some bills across the bar to him including the tip. No one in the era of trickle-down economics was getting rich tending bar, especially at eleven in the morning. I took my mug and found a table in the back of the beer hall where I could sit with my back to the wall and watch the door. I took my sunglasses off and put them in the inside pocket of my parka. I took a couple of small sips of my beer and waited for my prospective client to appear.

Late morning in Boston while all the college kids were home on Christmas break and the tourists weren't braving the slushy cold meant that there wasn't a lot of foot traffic. The sunlight that was bouncing around the windows and melting ice outside didn't seem to make it far into the beer hall. Certainly not as far as my table. That was why I noticed the woman in the duffle coat. Though, in all honesty, I would have noticed her if she were wearing a burlap sack.

I watched her through the plate-glass window as she walked along in a matching white knit hat and scarf. Long, straight black hair spilled from under the hat, splashing on her shoulders. She should have walked by Jakie Wirth's at a little after eleven in the morning. There was no sensible reason to explain why she walked up the few steps from the street in her brown leather boots with a modest heel and into the beer hall. She walked through the door, paused, taking in the room, did a decent left face and went to the bar. No sensible reason at all. She looked too good to be in any bar at this hour.

The bartender went over with a hell of a lot more enthusiasm than he showed me. I didn't hear what they said, but he put down a shot glass in front of her and poured something in it that was too dark for Irish whiskey and too light for Scotch. Bourbon . . . had to be bourbon. The bottle didn't look like anything that my local packie carried, and if they did, I was pretty sure I couldn't afford it.

She slid a bill over to the bartender who seemed in no rush to take it. They chatted for a minute, their voices lost in the murmur of music coming from speakers high up on the walls. She looked around, raised the glass in a toast to no one and drank it.

The door opened, and a man walked in and joined her at the bar. While she was in her late twenties or early thirties, he was solidly in his sixties. She was chic in her boots and duffle coat. He looked as if he would be more comfortable at the Harvard Club. I should know, having spent a couple of nights there in October for a case.

She said something to him, and he nodded. He stood close to her; they were familiar with each other, but nothing in their body language spoke of any sort of intimacy. They didn't seem like lovers and they didn't seem like relatives, but they knew each other enough to stand close to talk in a place where the loudest thing in the joint was the ancient ceiling fans.

They chatted for another minute or two and then she got up, and instead of heading for the ladies' room as I expected, she stood in front of my table. She had a straight nose that was angular but stopped just short of being sharp. She had green eyes above prominent cheekbones, and they competed with the diamonds that sparkled in her earlobes. The diamonds didn't stand a chance.

I stood up because that was what a gentleman is supposed to do, and I wanted, hoped, she would be fooled into believing that I was a gentleman.

'Mr Roark?'

'Yes.'

'I'm Terry's friend.' Terry McVicker had been the one who had asked me to meet a friend of his at Jakie Wirth's at eleven-ish in the morning. Terry was a defense attorney who threw some business my way now and again. Other than his penchant for flashy-looking suits that reminded me of something Bozo the Clown might wear, Terry wasn't a bad guy.

He was a ruthless, mercenary lawyer who mostly defended drug dealers and drunks who got behind the wheel. But Terry also did a lot of pro-bono work that he desperately hoped no one would find out about. He didn't want to seem like the type of sucker to help people out just because it was the right thing to do. There's no percentage in that.

She nodded, and it struck me that her lipstick was a shade of red that reminded me of cranberries. When she spoke, her teeth were perfect little pearls that made me think she had braces as a kid. 'I'd like you to meet someone.'

She nodded at her friend, and he came over. For a man in his sixties, he seemed to be in good shape with a shock of neatly trimmed white hair and pale-blue eyes. He stuck out a hand and said, 'Mr Roark, I'm Ambrose Messer. I need your help.'

'Please sit down, Mr Messer and Ms . . .?'

'It's Judge Messer, and my name is Angela Estrella, his clerk.' She didn't offer to shake, and her tone let me know that she had no illusions about me being a gentleman.

'Ms Estrella. Your honor.' I gestured to the empty chairs they were standing behind. We sat down and there was an awkward silence. I have found that when people come to hire me, unless they are an insurance company, there is something embarrassing involved, and it always takes a minute.

'What can I do for you, your honor?'

'Um . . . Mr Roark, I'm in a bit of a situation.' He was neat and trim, and something told me that he hadn't been in a situation since he graduated from whatever Ivy League school he had gone to. He stopped for a second. 'Angela, would you mind getting us all a drink? I think I could use one, and if everything I've read about Mr Roark's profession is true, he won't object to one either.'

'No, I won't.' I wasn't really looking to tie one on at this hour, but if it would help Messer relax and feel comfortable around me, who was I to object? She stood up, her unbuttoned duffle coat flapping open to give a hint of a smart-looking tan suit and curves underneath. I watched her walk to the bar and briefly forgot about the man sitting across from me.

'Mr Roark, how long have you been a private investigator?' the judge asked.

'Seven years. Before that, I was with the Boston Police Department.'

'As a detective?'

'More like a punching bag.'

'A punching bag?'

'I was in Uniform for a few years, then ended up in the Special Investigations Unit.'

'Investigating what type of crimes?'

'Mostly undercover work in the Decoy unit.'

'What was that?' Angela was back with a tray of shot glasses with what looked like bourbon, or at least I hoped it was. It occurred to me that it could be rye, and I was not a fan.

'Basically, I would spend my tours on the street trying to get mugged. If someone tried it, then I'd arrest them.'

'That sounds dangerous,' she said.

I shrugged, hoping I looked heroic and self-effacing. I probably looked like I needed to see a chiropractor. 'It had its moments. It required more courage than brains, so I was overly qualified for it.'

'Here's how.' Messer raised his glass.

I raised mine and replied automatically, 'And how.'

After we drank our bourbons and he was fortified, Messer said, 'I'm being blackmailed.'

'OK.' I could have asked probing questions, but I had learned that clients won't tell you their story until they're ready. It didn't matter what the case was, everyone felt some embarrassment. Usually, they felt they should have known their spouse was cheating or their employee was stealing, or they didn't know how to tell you someone ran off.

'Mr Roark, I'm married. Gladys and I have adult children,' he said in a slow, measured tone. 'I know it was reckless of me . . .' He paused and sipped at his shot of bourbon even though there could only have been a few drops left.

'You had an affair with a younger woman and now she is threatening to expose you?' So much for waiting for the story. This one was as old as the hills.

'I had an affair' – he paused – 'with a younger man.'

'Oh.' Maybe not quite as old as the hills.

'Mr Roark. While times certainly have changed a great deal . . . well, I am a judge in Boston. I belong to a certain . . . less tolerant set.'

I could see his point. Boston was a very heavily Irish Catholic town – even in 1985, almost 1986, there were some things that were deemed unforgivable sins. Messer would have been better off if he liked whips and chains or had a slew of illegitimate children. There were some sins that the Brahmins and the Irish Catholics could agree were forgivable.

'I understand. Why don't you tell me what happened?'

The judge launched in. 'I don't travel often without Gladys. If I do, it's usually for a reunion or a judicial conference.'

'I see.' I nodded as though his travel habits had a bearing on his case.

'Last February, the conference was held in Miami.'

It must be nice to be a judge. Last year, the New England Association of Private Investigators held their annual conference in a Holiday Inn in Quincy. It wasn't even an open-bar event.

'I met Lee there. I saw him at the pool, and he was young, tanned and fit. Later, I ran into him one or two times, and then on the third and last night of the conference, I was getting a drink at the bar with an old friend. After our second drink, he got up to chat up a woman who he was making eyes at. Lee sat down next to me. We started chatting, and it turns out that he was from Massachusetts and was down in Miami on business.'

'What business did he say he was in?' I had taken out my notebook and blue felt-tip pen.

'Lee's an art buyer for an interior decorator. He was in Miami looking for tropical-themed art for a project.'

'What's Lee's last name?'

'Raymond. Lee Raymond.'

'How old is he?'

'Twenty-nine or thirty.'

'OK, go on.'

'We went our separate ways, and then, in April, I was at the club playing squash and bumped into Lee who was there too. We started to see each other when I could get away without arousing suspicion.'

'Where would you meet? Any place regularly?'

'Hotels, preferably discreet ones. Lee would get the room in his name, and I would meet him. Usually, they were out of town. Braintree or the ones off Route 128. Usually, they were big, anonymous places, the kind that cater to business travelers or conventions.'

'Did you ever go to his place?'
'No, he lives with his mother.'
'Or any place other than motels?'
'In October, we spent a weekend at an inn on the Cape. It was in Chatham.'
'When did the blackmail start?'
'Last month. When I got back to court after lunch, a courier had delivered a manila envelope. Inside were pictures of Lee and me together . . . intimate pictures . . . and a note.'
'How much are they asking for?'
'More than I am willing to pay.' He smiled, and for the first time, I didn't see the man worried about losing everything but got a flash of who the judge was when the screws weren't being put on him.
'Well, that would explain why I am here, but how much are they asking for?' I repeated. It had to be a lot because judging by the judge's head-to-toe Brooks Brothers attire, I was sure he had access to some money. That and I'd never met a poor judge.
'That's the funny part. They don't want money. They want me to throw a case.'
'A criminal case?' I asked.
'No, I don't handle criminal. I hear tort cases, civil liability, that sort of thing. They want me to rule in favor of a company that has been polluting several small communities.'
'That's it? No money?'
'No money. They just want me to rig the game in favor of Goliath instead of giving David a shot.' His voice wasn't bitter, exactly, more resigned.
'Is the case against the polluter strong?'
'It's too soon to tell. Class action suits like this tend to be an uphill battle; most of the big law firms won't take them on. There is more money defending the companies in question. That usually leaves the cases to smaller attorneys. It's a real struggle, but if they can win, it's usually lucrative.'
'And they can hold someone to account?'
'They can, but the cases tend to take a very long time and drain the plaintiff's resources, forcing them to quit or settle for a pittance.'
'Who are the players in this case?'

'Northeast Textile and Cordage, which is alleged to have knowingly dumped waste, a byproduct of processes of theirs, in an unsafe manner. Allegedly, it seeped into groundwater. This led to several people getting sick, and several children born with birth defects.'

'Allegedly,' I said.

'Allegedly,' the judge agreed.

'Are they asking you to dismiss the case outright?'

'No, they have made it clear that it should run its course and that I should find for NT and C.' He said the company acronym as though he were referring to a law firm.

'Why not bribe a juror?'

'It's a bench trial . . .' He must have thought I hadn't ever been near a courtroom because he followed up unnecessarily. 'Instead of a jury, it's just heard by a judge who renders a verdict.'

'OK, what can you tell me about the decorator that Lee works for?'

'Not much. He just said it was one of the bigger interior decorators in Boston.'

I spent the next several minutes asking the judge about the hotel in Miami, and the various other hotels he and Lee had frequented. I wrote it all down, including the inn on the Cape, but he couldn't remember it all and told me he would need to check his datebook.

Finally, he took a large manila envelope out of his coat and put it down in front of me. His hand rested on top of the envelope protectively.

'These are the photos that they sent. The note is inside too. Mr Roark . . . these are sensitive, personal. I can count on your discretion?'

'Of course, sir.' I didn't bother pointing out to him that a PI who was indiscreet was a PI who wouldn't be in business long. I couldn't blame the old boy for being nervous about the whole thing. He held eye contact with me, trying to decide if he could trust me. After a second or two longer, he lifted his hand off the envelope.

'Is there anything else you think you will need?'

'Your honor, I'll need to know a little bit about the case. Who the chemical company is and the like.'

'Angela will provide you with a synopsis and anything you need beyond that.'

'Thank you, sir.'

'Mr Roark, Terry McVicker thinks very highly of you. He said that you are tough and dogged.'

'Stubborn, more like.' I laughed. It was nice to be respected by people you respect.

'I took the liberty of bringing your retainer. Given the circumstances, I felt that cash would be best. I cannot stress enough to you how much I am counting on your discretion.' He must have been serious about my discretion because the white envelope he slid across the table had twice as much as I would have asked for, all of it in crisp hundred-dollar bills.

'Of course, sir. You can count on me.' I sounded just like all those times that I said yes to some dangerous mission in Vietnam.

'Good. If you need anything from me – more money or information, anything – please arrange it through Angela. Her card and number are in the envelope.'

'Yes, of course.'

'Thank you, Mr Roark. I trust you will be in touch.'

'Yes, sir. Through Angela.'

'Good day.' He stuck his hand out and I shook it. Then he was up, a trim, neatly dressed man walking out of one of America's oldest beer halls on a weekday morning in late December with an unbearable weight on his shoulders.

'He's a good man,' Angela said severely.

'I am sure he is.'

'He doesn't need anyone judging him for his private life.'

'Not my place. The man has hired me to help him and that is what I aim to do.' I probably sounded like a cheap imitation of the sheriff from every Western ever made, but I didn't care.

'Good. Call me if you need anything. Goodbye.' She got up without shaking my hand and followed in the judge's wake. I had the distinct impression that I had just been put on notice.

TWO

I took the two envelopes back to my office above the video store. The video store was relatively new. Half a year ago, it had been a pizza place, but then old man Marconi found out he had cancer. He sold out and went back to Italy to feel the sun of his homeland on his face. I couldn't blame him. He left me the old espresso machine that he had brought over from the old country. It now took up a substantial chunk of my office. I was at the point now where I was able to turn out something that didn't taste like a middle-school science fair entry gone wrong.

I left my coat on the rack by the office door and made my way into the inner office. There was a big wooden desk with a couple of chairs facing it and my comfortable office chair behind it. The espresso machine was on a table on the back wall, and the massive old safe that came with the office sat hulking alongside it. I threw the manila envelope on the desk where it landed with a slapping noise. I went to make an espresso, and while the machine was making noise, I counted the money in the envelope and transferred Angela Estrella's card into my wallet.

When the tiny scale model of a coffee cup was filled with the dark, bitter espresso, I took a pipe off the rack. I filled the bowl with a nice mellow mixture from Peretti's. I touched a match to the bowl and managed to get the whole thing going. Once I had the office filled with fragrant smoke, I sat back in my chair and opened the manila envelope filled with photos.

They were eight and a half by eleven black-and-white photos. The top couple showed the judge and a man who I had to assume was Lee Raymond. They were on a balcony of a hotel room that, judging by their wearing just shorts and the potted palm trees, must have been in Miami. In the photos, they were first laughing, then holding hands in another, and in a third, kissing. The photos were taken with a telephoto lens and, judging by the blurriness at the edges of the things in the picture, they had been blown up.

The Judge

The next few in the stack were taken in a hotel room. They were also black and white. The pictures showed the judge and Raymond in bed together. They were mostly of the two men in a variety of poses. The blow-ups left nothing to the imagination as to who was doing what to whom.

The rest of the pictures were more of the same; the only real variation was in the ones that were taken on the Cape. The curtains in the inn weren't the same industrial light-blocking, monolithic sheet of the hotels. Also, they were the only ones featuring a four-poster bed.

The note was typed on a sheet of plain white paper. It simply said, 'If you don't want the world to know your secret, the chemical company wins.' That was it. No request for money. No instructions beyond what was in the note. It was simple and to the point.

I picked up one of the less action-oriented pictures of Lee Raymond. He was a handsome man in his early thirties. He had dark curly hair; he was well groomed and not quite hairy enough to be swarthy. I flipped through the photos looking for tattoos or scars. There were no tattoos, and the only scar I could see was a small one shaped like a thumbnail under his right cheekbone. I jotted notes on a yellow legal pad while I went back through the photos. I put his photo aside. I wanted to copy it and get it cropped so I could show it around.

The next thing I did was write down everything that the judge had told me about how he'd met Lee Raymond. I wanted to know if he had stayed at the same hotel as the judge or if he was in one of the many other hotels in Miami. I was interested in the hotels and motels that he and the judge had stayed in locally. Maybe there was something of use to be gleaned from the registration?

I pulled the Yellow Pages over to me from their resting place by the phone. I flipped to the I section. There were about sixty or so interior decorators listed in the greater Boston area. I dog-eared the pages. I wasn't ready to start calling around just yet. It also occurred to me that if Raymond was the honey in this particular honey trap, then perhaps he had a record for hustling or running cons. That would mean a call to the Boston Police Department. There were still a couple of detectives around who thought well enough of me to help me out. I couldn't see any way that they could get pictures of the judge and Raymond without Raymond being in on it. After all, whoever was doing this probably wasn't in the same league as the KGB or CIA.

I was curious about Northeast Textile and Cordage, too. They were listed in the Yellow Pages. Their corporate offices weren't that far from my own. Did they have someone on staff ruthless enough to set up and blackmail a judge? Or was that the type of thing that you'd hire a specialist for? It seemed like something a lawyer or fixer might arrange. I flipped to the D section of the Yellow Pages but there was no listing for Dirty Tricks. I flipped over to the B section but there was nothing for Blackmail either.

Then I wrote down Angela Estrella's name on the legal pad. Below that, I wrote Gladys Messer's name and then question marks for their children. I crossed their names off. I couldn't see his own children setting him up like this. Blackmail wasn't a fast crime like knocking over a liquor store or snatching a purse. It required patience and intelligence, in the military sense. You had to know something about your proposed victim. I had to imagine that Messer was very discreet about his thing for men. It probably wasn't the sort of thing that he talked to the other judges or lawyers about. But someone knew about it. Knew enough to put the honey in the honey trap and leave it where the judge couldn't help but fall into it.

Someone close to the judge had to know about his secret. They had to be close enough to him to know how to exploit it. Whether they were the actual blackmailer or had just passed on the information remained to be seen. Somewhere the suit with the chemical company and the judge's private life, family, friends – somewhere it intersected. That intersection led to blackmail.

The only other thing I could think of was that someone mounted one hell of a surveillance operation on the judge. It wasn't like on TV. Surveillance, to do it right, required multiple cars, multiple people. It wasn't just Jim Rockford or Magnum sitting in a flashy car a few car lengths away with a cheap pair of binoculars. Most people barely look in the rearview mirror, let alone conduct counter-surveillance, but even so, if you didn't want to get caught, it usually required a few bodies. All but the most clueless would start to notice the same car or same person trailing behind them after a while.

Maybe it was another private investigator? Not everyone in the field was ethical, much less had a moral code. Some guys worshipped at the temple of the almighty dollar. It wasn't a way that I wanted to earn my money. The only one I answer to is my cat, Sir Leominster. For him, morality begins and ends with his food dish. He could care less how I earn my loot as long as the dish is full when he is hungry. He's a pragmatic sort.

My notepad was looking pretty bare. I might have to call Special Agent Brenda Watts over at the FBI and see if she or the Bureau had anything they could tell me about blackmail. I suspected that it was only of any interest to them if it was a multi-state affair or if national security was involved. In this case, neither seemed very likely. But I would take any excuse to call Brenda Watts and invite her to lunch at the Union Oyster House. Brenda was too smart to fall for my attempts to convince her that instead of platonic lunches at the Union Oyster House, we should upgrade to romantic dinners at the Café Budapest.

My stomach did a summersault to let me know that early-morning beers and bourbons needed to be countered by food. My breakfast had been some rather uninspiring yogurt, whole-wheat toast and a banana. I also wanted to stop at my branch of Old Stone Bank and deposit a good chunk of the cash that the judge had given me.

Outside on the street, the temperature was hovering a couple of degrees above freezing, which meant that tomorrow all the slush and water making its way on the pavement would freeze. Tomorrow morning promised a slew of bruises, broken bones and car accidents. The already congested traffic in and around Boston would only be that much worse, and winter had barely started.

I made my way to Faneuil Hall. This time of year, midweek, it wouldn't be wall-to-wall tourists looking for the Boston experience. As a rule of thumb, I, like most Bostonians, try to avoid Faneuil Hall. But today I was in the mood for chowder and maybe even oyster stew. Now, Boston is home to many, many fine restaurants, but none of them will treat you as poorly or cheaply as Durgin-Park.

I stepped off the street, out of the raw December wind and slush and into the maelstrom that was Durgin-Park at lunchtime. It was crowded – it's always crowded – and each seat at the communal table was full. Still, they managed to seat me after a short wait. Maybe it had something to do with not sounding like I was fresh off the bus from somewhere in the Midwest.

The waitress came and was so rude asking me what I wanted that had she been a man, we would have had a fistfight. Instead, I politely ordered the chowder and the prime rib with mashed potatoes and corn. You had to be half a masochist to appreciate the service at Durgin-Park. On the other hand, the food more than made up for the service.

'Want a drink?' she barked more than asked. I chalked it up to her looking like she had been an ambulance driver in World War I, even though she was at best ten years older than me.

'Coffee.' She grunted her acknowledgment and pivoted away to spread cheer and warmth elsewhere. Maybe if the Commonwealth ever brings back the death penalty, she can serve the last meal. Might help the condemned feel better about their fate knowing they'd never have to see her again.

My coffee came a minute or two before the cup of chowder arrived. The chowder was thick and had plenty of clams and diced potatoes with a pat of butter melting in it. I ripped the corner off the cellophane bag of oyster crackers and dumped some in. I have strong feelings about clam chowder. It has to be thick and stick to your ribs. There are some fine clam soups that call themselves chowder. Like the milk-broth version from Rhode Island that is too thin for my taste. Or the red version from New York that is basically clam minestrone. It tastes good, but I'll be damned if I call it chowder.

I ate my chowder and thought about the mechanics of black-mail. When I had consumed the layer of oyster crackers, I added another. In most cases, blackmail involved money: a payout or regular payouts. That meant a drop, a pickup and someone to follow or talk to or shake down for answers. This was neat and contained, like one of the box puzzles where the sides appear smooth, but if you push in the right place, it opens. I just couldn't see where to push, where to apply pressure other than Lee Raymond. To do that, I needed to find him. But something told me that the person who was the bait in the honey trap was unlikely to be the mastermind behind it.

I finished my chowder when Miss Personality came back and whisked my cup away abruptly. She came back and slammed a plate with a thick slice of pink-colored prime rib down in front of me. She slammed down a small dish of mashed potatoes on the table with enough force that I wondered how many dishes the waitresses broke a year. Next to that, she dropped another small dish with whole-kernel corn in it.

The prime rib was an inch thick and served in its own juices on a plate with a thin green border. A lot of people cop out when they describe how food is cooked and say it was cooked to perfection, but at Durgin-Park, the prime rib *was* cooked to perfection. There was no other way of describing it that would do it justice. The potatoes were good, and the corn was uninspiring. But the prime rib lived up to Durgin-Park's reputation for providing large portions of good food at an affordable price. That was enough to make up for the rude service, and that was why Durgin-Park was still around after one hundred and fifty years.

When Miss Personality came back and barked at me to see if I wanted dessert, I passed. She put the check down in front of me faster than Wild Bill pulling a six-gun. I dropped a twenty on the table. The tip wasn't bad; besides, at Durgin-Park you paid as much for the abuse as the food. The only other place in Boston that one could say the same was the Combat Zone.

Outside, there was a chilly breeze coming off the harbor. The salt air smelled fresh, and gulls wheeled overhead. It must have been high tide. I wasn't complaining. I crossed Congress Street and made my way through the red-brick no man's land of City Hall Plaza. I tried not to wince at the eyesore that passed for the architecture that defined Government Center. The whole ugly thing had been built on what had been Scollay Square, which had been the city's red-light district before the Combat Zone. Progress isn't always all it's cracked up to be.

I followed the Freedom Trail's red line on the sidewalk past the Masonic temple and into the Common. I cut through the

Public Garden and a few minutes later was in my local branch of Old Stone Bank. I walked in through large metal doors that were meant to deter anyone from breaking in after hours.

I waited in line for one of the two tellers occupying the six windows at the counter. I was going to deposit half of the money in the envelope and break the rest. Hundred-dollar bills aren't convenient for my lifestyle. It was rare that I had enough money to worry about the bills being too big.

I killed time in line thinking about the steps that go into setting someone up to be blackmailed. It wasn't just about baiting the honey trap; one also had to have access to it ahead of time. Hence, Lee Raymond always made the hotel reservations. He had to be able to get to the room and set up the camera. The camera or cameras had to be discreetly placed or camouflaged. They had to be able to view and capture the action. Unless it was a movie camera, a Super 8, someone had to snap the pictures. The cameras also needed the right lens or lenses. And the right type of film if they were shooting in low light. Those weren't the type of things that you'd just pick up at your local pharmacy. No, the blackmailer would have to go to a camera store for those sorts of things. That might help narrow my search down a bit.

Not only would the cameras have to be placed properly with the right lens and the right film, but someone would have to develop the film. That wasn't the sort of thing that you could just drop off and have done anywhere. Either you needed a photo developer who didn't care what he was developing or the blackmailer had to have their own darkroom. Either way, they needed to be developed. The pictures I saw obviously weren't Polaroids.

The cashier deposited half of the cash in my account and converted the rest into twenties and tens. I put the money away and decided to head to the Boston Police Department. I needed to know if Lee Raymond had a record, and I wanted to talk to a person rather than calling an overworked BPD detective who'd forget my phone call the second he hung up.

I made my way out into the post-Christmas slush and sun. I saw hints and remnants of the holiday that had passed. Bits of damp wrapping paper, ribbon fluttering from a trashcan, shards from a smashed glass ornament and one of the balls that had hung from the tree limbs all spoke of the holiday's faded passing. At least I had the Bruins to look forward to.

Police Headquarters was a gray, granite edifice that took up the corner of Berkeley and Stuart Streets, 154 Berkeley to be exact. It was several stories of imposing-looking architecture that was built in 1925. I went up the steps and stood in front of the desk sergeant. He looked at me suspiciously. I didn't hold it against him. Judging by the hash marks on his sleeve, he'd been a cop a long time and probably looked at his own saintly mother with suspicion. It's just how cops are.

'How can I help you, sir?' The words were polite and respectful, but the tone left no doubt that my very presence was an inconvenience.

'I'm here to see Sergeant Devaney if he's around?'
'What's your name?'
'Roark.'
'What's it about?'
'He asked me to come down.' It wasn't exactly the truth. Last time I had talked to Billy Devaney, he said, 'See you around.'

The desk sergeant was apparently satisfied by this, though, and picked up the phone. He stabbed at the buttons and spoke into it. He put the phone down and handed me a clip-on badge that said, 'Visitor.' He gave me directions to Devaney's office, but I was sure he really wanted to tell me where to go.

I made my way to Billy Devaney's office. The last time I had been to headquarters, it had been to see Captain Dennis Johnson about the murder of a Vietnamese man in Chinatown. The BPD, like the Yellow Pages, didn't have a section devoted to blackmail, but they did have a section that dealt with con games, and that would have to do.

Billy Devaney was sitting at his desk like a king on his throne. Instead of subjects, he was surrounded by files and paper. Instead of a jester, he had a gooseneck lamp. Instead of a scepter, he held a pastrami sandwich in one of his big, raw-knuckled hands. When I was a senior in high school, Billy was home from the Marine Corps and had taken exception to my dating his little sister, Patti. He bounced some of those big, calloused knuckles off my face a few times to illustrate the fact that he felt I wasn't good enough for Patti. I told him to pound sand, and when I came to, the only thing he seemed impressed by was how hard my head was. It was all a waste of time because Patti dumped me for a football player.

He looked up from his paperwork and fixed me with his pale-blue eyes. 'Roark, you shanty Irish piece of trash, what brings you in here?' It wasn't said mean-spiritedly; it was just that Billy was one of those miserable people who can't bring himself to speak nicely to anyone other than his mother. Even less so to someone he actually likes.

'Jesus, Billy, don't go putting on airs just cause your family's shanty was a little nicer than my family's.' And he was the type of guy that you had to speak to him the same way he did you or he would think you were buttering him up to take advantage of him.

'Every time I see you, I get indigestion.'

'That's not indigestion; it's just your body's way of letting you know you're a miserable Irish prick.'

'Ha, well, that's true. What brings you by?'

'Working on a case. I was hoping you could help me and see if a guy has a jacket?'

'You piker, I figured you weren't here to socialize.'

'Your personality isn't much to make me want to.'

'What's the guy's name?'

'Raymond, Lee Raymond. He's involved in blackmail but probably started out as a hustler or in the con game. Claims to be a buyer for interior decorators. Seems to prefer men to women.'

'A homo?' That was about as tolerant as Billy got.

'Or AC/DC, but in this case, he was with a man.' I told Billy as much as I knew or could describe about Raymond, and he wrote it all down.

'OK, give me a couple of days.'

'Billy, come on. Can you do better?'

'Sure, I'll drop the cases I'm on now, the ones the city pays me to investigate. I'll drop prep for the grand jury and forget about the cases that I'm so far behind on that if I stopped taking anything new, I could finish fifteen years after I retire.'

'Come on, Billy, how about a couple of tickets to the Bruins playing Montreal?' I said it 'Broones' so he would understand I was talking about the hockey team.

'Nosebleed seats? Naw, maybe I'll be able to take care of this by next week.'

'A few rows off the ice, so close to the boards you'll feel it every time someone gets checked into the boards.'

'OK, I think I can free up some time. Now I know what that goofy sister of mine saw in you.'

'How's she doing?'

'Her oldest is in high school and her youngest is in kindergarten, with a couple in between.'

'Tell her I said hi.'

'Sure, sure, kid. That's all I need is her pestering me about you.'

'Billy, the tickets are at home. I'll drop 'em off with the desk sergeant for you.'

'Sure, sure. Never understand what she saw in a shanty Irish piece of trash like you.'

'She do any better with the husband?'

'No, but she didn't do much worse either,' he said.

I nodded and said my goodbyes.

Patti was a nice girl, but Billy had done me a favor when he bounced his ham fists off my thick skull. I would have ended up married to Patti or a girl like her, living in Southie, working in a mill or construction, trying to figure out how to afford the next kid. I'd take Vietnam any day. It was dangerous, but I had been free. It hadn't been the same prison generations of my people had lived in: work at the mill, marry, have kids, die. No one in Southie commuted to the mill standing on the skid of a Huey mid-flight, heading into a hot LZ.

Leaving Police Headquarters, I began walking back toward Newbury Street. I wanted to take the picture of Lee Raymond to Artie Bogasian's camera store. Artie knew more about cameras and filming techniques than most professional photographers. Every now and then, when I needed to replace a camera, Artie managed to offer me something decent, usually used at a price I could almost afford. He could also copy and crop the picture of Lee Raymond so I could have something to show around that wouldn't earn me a distribution of pornography charge.

Artie was behind the counter helping a woman who seemed to be dropping off film from a Christmas get-together. I waited, looking at camera bags I didn't need and lenses I couldn't afford. Artie took the lady's film like some Don Juan receiving a token of his momentary beloved's affection. He held her hand and leaned in, briefly whispering something. Asking her to pose for him, no doubt. Artie wouldn't be the first photographic Lothario to ask women to pose for 'artistic photos.'

Artie did pretty well for a man in his mid-sixties. His eyes were brown, and they seemed to be quite the asset in his romantic adventures. He had a fashionably cut mane of dark curls that were showing a bit more salt than pepper these days. The curls offset his moustache, which was perfectly tended to and would have been the envy of a silent-movie villain.

The woman left, and I could swear that she seemed a bit flushed. Artie and his Armenian charm had struck again. I met him when he was working part-time for the police department taking crime scene photos. He liked me because I was one of the few people on the job who had heard of the Genocide. Whenever Artie had more than two beers or three cups of coffee, he became passionate about it.

He once told me that his mother and grandmother had survived the Genocide. He grew up in Worcester listening to stories about it, and it had left him with some pretty strong feelings about the Turks. Who could blame him?

'Andy, old friend, what brings you in?' Artie, to the best of my knowledge, had been born in Worcester, but he affected a certain amount of old-world charm in his store. If you came in around Christmas, he kept a bottle of Napoleon Brandy under the counter and glasses for his regulars. He'd wish you a Merry Christmas and have a snort with you.

'Artie, it's good to see you. I need some help with a photo. Can I borrow a pair of scissors?'

'Sure.' He handed me a pair from a cup of pencils and pens he kept by the cash register. I took out the tamest of the pictures, the one that offered the best look at Lee Raymond's face, and I cut it in half, removing the judge from the equation. I trusted Artie, but the judge was paying for discretion.

I handed him the surgically altered picture.

'Oh, he looks like he is enjoying himself.'

'I need copies with the face blown up and cropped so that I can show it around without causing too much excitement.'

'Sure, that isn't too hard. How many copies?'

'Four or five to be on the safe side.'

'I can have them for you next week.'

'How about tomorrow?' I slid a twenty across the counter to him. 'On top of your fee.'

'Tomorrow afternoon, say around four?'

'Sure. I can do that.'

'Working on a case?' Artie, like most people, thought that my job was a lot more interesting and glamorous than it really was. Movies and TV had left much of the general public with a romanticized point of view. It was silly, but more than one attractive woman had agreed to go to dinner with me because *Magnum P.I.* was on TV.

'Always. No one is getting rich out there besides the rich.'

'Blackmail case?'

'Yeah, something like that.'

'Because you're asking me to blow up a picture of some guy who is wearing a gold chain and smile and nothing else. Also, this picture looks like it has been blown up already – see how it is fuzzy looking at the edges?'

'Can you blow it up and crop it?'

'Oh, sure, that won't be a problem.'

'This guy was meeting his lover in a series of hotels. I was wondering if he would need any special equipment or film to take incriminating pictures.'

'Well, he wasn't using an Instamatic or a Polaroid. It depends.'

'On what?'

'The light in the room. Position of the camera, the film, the lenses, etcetera.'

'What do you mean?'

'Well, for one, if it was low light, then he would need special film and shutter speed. All depending upon the light in the room. It would be another thing altogether if he was using infrared.

Then, of course, I am assuming that he couldn't use the auto-shutter – too loud. Lastly, where was the camera hidden? Did he have a way of remotely taking the pictures?'

'I don't know. Do you have any ideas?'

'Let me think on it, and maybe I'll have something by the time you come in to pick up your prints.'

'How specialized is this stuff?'

'That depends on what it is. Some of it might not be that exotic or need that much in the way of training. Some of it is strictly for professional photographers – you know, National Geographic types.'

'I was thinking that if any of this was exotic or required a lot of training, then that might help me track the guys doing this down.'

'Maybe. Like I said, some of it is garden variety, some of it isn't. I need some time with the picture and to give it some thought.'

'Sorry, Artie, I'm getting impatient in my old age.'

'No worries. I'll have more for you tomorrow afternoon.'

'Thanks.'

I left Artie's shop. The temperature had come down a couple of degrees, hinting at a cold night. I decided it wouldn't be a bad idea to get some provisions. Sir Leominster wasn't a fan of going hungry and neither was I. Fortunately, there was a grocery store near the package store where I had planned to pick up a bottle of whiskey.

THREE

Sir Leominster met me at the apartment door when I managed to unlock it around an armful of brown-paper-clad groceries. I shut the door behind me and somehow managed not to trip as he rubbed up against my ankles. When he is hungry, he has two modes: overly affectionate or angry. I still hadn't decided which was worse.

His presence in my life had been the result of a girlfriend who thought we needed a pet. When she left me, she decided that I needed a pet. Actually, she said something akin to the fact that we were both miserable creatures and deserved to keep each other company. He lightened up a lot after it was just me and him, living the bachelor life in Back Bay. Maybe she was right?

I managed to deposit the groceries and, more importantly, the whiskey on the kitchen table without any further mishaps or attempted sabotage by the cat. What did he care if his food came in cans? I took off my coat and checked the answering machine. The message was from some Army types reminding me to send my money in for a reunion I was pretty sure I didn't want to go to. It wasn't their fault; they were all good people. I was just growing more antisocial the longer I lived.

I fished a can of cat food out of the brown paper bag. The can opener bit into the tin with an audible pop and a hiss of gas that smelled like rotting fish heads. The cat rubbed up against my ankles, purring loudly. I put his bowl of food down and watched him as he tore into the foul-smelling mess. I put the groceries away and, feeling accomplished, poured myself a whiskey.

The sky outside the windows was dark, and across the street was a brownstone indistinguishable from the one that I lived in. Some of the windows were lit, and lights from passing cars reflected off all of them. The temperature was dropping, and there would be ice everywhere tomorrow after today's thaw.

I didn't mind the cold – well, most of the time. The first winter home from Vietnam seemed like the coldest one ever. I had spent almost three consecutive years in Vietnam, and winter had snuck up on me. It felt like I started shivering in November and didn't stop until April. I briefly contemplated moving to Florida, but then I remembered that I burn easily in the sun. That and watching the Sox in Winter Haven couldn't compare to watching them play in Fenway Park. Though Fenway Park in July or August was almost as humid as Florida.

I sat with my whiskey at the table looking over the notes I had made about the case. I was trying to come up with some sort of investigative strategy. Mostly because I felt that phrases like 'investigative strategy' helped me feel more like a private investigator who knew what he was doing. Most of the time, I usually felt like a guy who bumped around a case until something shook loose.

I had started the process of trying to figure out who Lee Raymond was and where I could find him. I would start working the angle with the film and the cameras. That would mean slogging around the city and possibly the state looking for photographic puzzle pieces. I was also going to need a list of the hotels and rooms they visited. I might be able to jog a desk clerk's memory or get a name. Anything would help. Raymond had told the judge that he worked in interior decorating, so calling around to see if he actually did was another path to follow.

Either way, I also needed to find out more about the court case itself. It wasn't an accident that someone was blackmailing the judge, and it would stand to reason it was someone with a stake in the company.

By the time I was down to a finger of whiskey and some scribbled notes on a legal pad, it was apparent that unless Lee Raymond showed up soon, I would have to work both ends of the case. It seemed like a lot to contemplate, but you eat an elephant one bite at a time.

I sat back and lit a Lucky from the soft pack in my pocket. I had the sneaking suspicion that tomorrow I was going to spend a great deal of quality time with the Yellow Pages looking up local hotels, camera stores and interior decorators. I also wanted to learn more about Northeast Textile and Cordage. They were the beneficiaries of the blackmail, so that was another angle of attack in the investigation.

I made a list of further questions that I had for the judge. It included things like the names of the hotels he and Lee Raymond had frequented. The dates they had been there. If he had seen or heard anything unusual while he was there. The good news was that I was going to have to talk to Angela Estrella about my questions so she could pass them on to the judge.

The rest of the evening passed without much out of the ordinary. Dinner was reheated chicken and rice with green beans. I washed it down with more whiskey. There was nothing on TV worth watching; I felt uncharacteristically let down by TV38 and the Movie Loft. It was pretty rare that Dana Hersey didn't come through for me.

I opted instead for jazz from the local public radio station. I sat on the couch with my feet up on the coffee table listening to Coltrane. I lit a pipe and started reading Bernard Fall's excellent *Hell in a Very Small Place* about the siege of Dien Bien Phu.

It was odd to read about Vietnam from the French perspective. Many of the names and places were familiar even with a French accent. I had to admire the bravery of the French paratroopers and legionnaires while marveling at the hubris of their commanders. I wondered what it must have been like parachuting into the doomed base knowing that the most likely way out was death.

When I started to feel too maudlin, thinking too much about my time in Vietnam as opposed to focusing on the book, I put it down. Coltrane had given way to something I liked but didn't recognize. I had a bellyful of Vietnam, French accent or not, and opted for more whiskey. More whiskey and one of the many Inspector Maigret novels that I had kicking around the apartment. At least I was able to keep the French theme going.

The next morning, I woke in a tangle of sheets, half in and out of the covers. I somehow managed to be both too hot and too cold all at once. I had dreamed of Vietnam, but instead of my own experiences, I was jumping into Dien Bien Phu, dressed in a red beret and a trench coat. I landed under fire from the Vietminh, got out of my chute and ran to a nearby bunker. I skidded and slid into the bunker with no time to spare. But there waiting in the darkness, breathing in labored breaths, was a deer with its stomach torn open and its hoof blown away. It looked up at me with its big brown eyes and said, '*Sacré guerre*.'

I kicked off the sheets and decided that a run might do me good. It was too early to drink, which I generally avoided in the mornings unless I was on vacation or a bender. I hoped that dodging the patches of ice on the sidewalk while getting smacked in the face by the cold wind off the Charles River might push the thoughts of the deer into the recesses of my memory where it belonged. In Vietnam, a deer had the bad luck to step on a toe-popper mine I left on my team's backtrail. Then it fell on its side on the other toe-popper. The mines had been meant to wound the North Vietnamese Army on our tail. Instead, an innocent creature in the middle of a war zone was killed.

I wasn't sure why it bothered me so much, but for the last several months it had been on my mind. This latest French-speaking variant no doubt had to do with my reading about the French version of my equally doomed war. It was odd that I thought about the deer more than the men I had killed there. They had been trying to kill me, and I had been luckier or better skilled. I guess it balanced out, but the deer hadn't done anything to me.

Outside the apartment, the air was cold and made my lungs hurt with each breath. It tickled the back of my throat, and my ragged breath came out in clouds of steam reminiscent of a cloud of cigarette smoke. The cold also made me feel every footfall on the pavement, and by the time I got to the Charles River Bridge, the wind didn't disappoint. It smacked my face like a woman objecting to my making an ungentlemanly proposition.

I pushed along the bridge over into Cambridge, running parallel to the river. I was careful to watch out for patches of ice and careful crossing the streets. I had almost been hit by a car a couple of months ago on my morning run. I managed to make it back to my apartment without slipping on the ice or almost being hit by one of Boston's many stellar drivers. Miracles upon miracles.

Upstairs, I treated myself to a cigarette while making a coffee in the stovetop espresso maker. I used to have a percolator, but after old man Marconi introduced me to espresso, the stuff in the blue can brewed just didn't cut it anymore. I stretched out on the kitchen floor while waiting for the coffee to burble in its fancy Italian pot. Stretching after running, especially in cold weather, is important. I am sure that the physical fitness types wouldn't have appreciated the cigarette in my mouth.

When the coffee was ready, I went over to the phone. I fished Angela Estrella's card out of my wallet and dialed it. I listened to the ringing noise at the other end and then the sound of the phone being picked up.

'Hello.' She sounded a little out of breath.

'Hi, it's Andy Roark.'

'Oh, the boy detective,' she said with mock sweetness.

'No, that's Encyclopedia Brown.'

'What can I do for you?'

'I had some questions for the judge and need you to get them to him.'

'Can you write them down?'

'Sure, I'm mostly literate. Can you bring me some sort of summary of the case?'

'That shouldn't be a problem. I can swing by your office on my lunch break and pick up the questions.'

'Perfect.' I told her where my office was, and she said she would be by around quarter past twelve. Then she hung up. I went back to the kitchen for something to eat.

After a disappointing breakfast of yogurt and wheat toast, I showered. I dressed in faded jeans, a button-down shirt and one of those Norwegian sweaters that was blue with little white flecks like snowflakes woven in. The weather still meant wool socks and work boots.

I clipped my snubnose .38 in its holster inside my waistband. It was loaded with five rounds of hollow-point ammunition, and I dropped a speedloader with another five in the left front pocket of my jeans. I put the Buck knife in my right pocket. I topped it with my rust-colored parka from L.L. Bean, a wool scarf and gloves lined with rabbit fur. I grabbed my old mail carrier's bag with my pens and notepads and slung it over my shoulder. Then I was ready to go.

Outside, it was still cold, but the wind had eased up a bit.

Most of yesterday's snow was gone, and what remained was not the pristine white stuff that one pictures of winter in New England. But that was Boston for you. I made my way to the office by my usual route: down Commonwealth Avenue and through the Public Garden.

The weather hinted at more snow, and real cold was coming. Not the picturesque New England snow and hayride weather but the stuff that came roaring down from the great frozen north. Canada. That type of cold was pushed by angry Arctic air that made you want to open your freezer and stick your hands in to warm them up.

The walk was nice, if a bit chilly. The tips of my ears were only stinging a little bit when I got to the office. The video store was open, and there seemed to be a couple of people inside looking at the racks of video cassettes. I went inside the door to my building and up the stairs. I opened the office door cautiously; last spring, some angry Vietnamese gangster types had left a fragmentation grenade booby-trapped to the door for me. They also blew up my Karmann Ghia, which I was still annoyed about. I really liked that car.

There was nothing more harmful waiting for me than the smell of stale pipe smoke. After I hung up my coat and started the espresso machine to get it warmed up, I opened the window to air the place out a little. I didn't want Angela Estrella to have a reason to leave in a hurry. Watts had turned down my latest offer of a romantic dinner, and my last girlfriend hadn't worked out.

The radiator in the corner banged away as a result of the cold air flooding in. The espresso machine had come to life, and I was able to coax a reasonable demitasse cup of the stuff out of it. I wanted a pipe but decided to sit on the windowsill and smoke a Lucky instead while thumbing through the hotel section of the Yellow Pages.

The section itself was almost an inch thick and covered Boston and the surrounding communities. That meant that most of the hotels in the Route 128 corridor were in residence. None of them advertised for illicit rendezvous, but it figured that the judge would have felt more comfortable going with something bigger, more anonymous, like part of a national chain.

I flipped through it trying to get a feel for what was out there, the places the judge might have gone to meet with Lee Raymond. It was an exercise in imagination until I got the list of the hotels he went to. I found a number for Northeast Textile and Cordage where you'd expect it to be in the Yellow Pages. I picked up the phone and almost dialed them, but what was I going to ask the switchboard operator? 'Can you connect me with your blackmail division?'

I put the handset down. Maybe they weren't a big enough company to have a blackmail division.

I passed the time doodling in the margins of my legal pad next to the scribbled questions I had come up with about the case. They seemed like different versions of the same basic questions but just a bit rehashed. Most of the time, most of the cases I worked on, that was what detective work was, though: asking the same questions again and again in new ways until the answers started to make sense.

When I got tired of doodling, I turned back to the Yellow Pages. I started making lists of camera stores in the city. I added the ones in Cambridge for good measure. I wasn't sure what Artie would have to say on the subject, but Lee Raymond had to be getting his film and camera accessories somewhere. I hoped Artie could point me in the right direction. I was certain that the world of camera stores and photographic supplies in Boston was a pretty small one.

When I was finished, the two lists took up half a dozen pages of yellow legal pad. It wasn't a complete list by any means, but it was a start. This was always the problem when I began a new case that was more involved than divorce or workers' comp cases: I had to figure out where to start. Sometimes the cases seemed to have a thousand different starting points. Writing down questions and making lists seemed to give me focus.

While I was contemplating lists of questions, camera stores and discreet hotels, I heard the outer office door open. I got up and crossed the office and opened the door to the anteroom. Angela Estrella stood there, surveying my modest place of business. She was pulling off her knit hat with one hand and holding a large manila envelope with the other. 'You didn't spend a lot on an interior decorator, did you?'

'Nope, only the best that the Salvation Army had to offer.'

There wasn't much point in explaining that sometimes angry spouses or people who objected to my pointing out they weren't too injured to work liked to take their frustration out on my office furniture.

'The best . . .?' she said sarcastically trailing off. Her lower lip curled when she said it, and it made me consider all sorts of possibilities.

'Would you like a coffee?' I offered instead of answering her.

'Sure, that would hit the spot. It's cold out.' She took off the duffle coat she had been wearing the day before. Underneath, she was wearing boots with a pointy heel, blue jeans bloused into them and a turquoise sweater that looked to be cashmere.

'Dressed for court?'

She laughed. 'No, court is in recess for the holidays, so we get to dress down.'

'Aha, come into my office.' I held the door open for her and followed her in.

'Is that an espresso machine? I didn't think that was exactly what a PI would have in his office.'

'It was a parting gift from an old friend who was going home to Italy.'

'That was nice of him. It seems out of place, especially next to that giant safe. Did he give you that too?'

'No, that came with the office.'

'Can you work that thing?' she said, pointing to the espresso machine.

'I do all right,' I said, with more confidence in my espresso-making ability than history would warrant.

'Can you make the steamed milk too?'

'Absolutely. I even have some of those tiny scale models of real coffee cups that people drink out of.'

'Well, the tiny cups, then I am game.' She smiled, which I took as a good sign of the effectiveness of my boyish charm.

'OK, why don't you tell me about the lawsuit while I make us some espresso?'

'Cappuccino.'

'What?'

'It's called cappuccino when it has steamed milk in it.'

I knew that, I really did, but there was no way to point that out without seeming like I was a ten-year-old. 'Tell me about the lawsuit,' I said instead.

'Northeast Textile and Cordage has been around since the early eighteen-hundreds in one form of family-owned mill or another. By World War Two, they were known as New England Cordage and were making all sorts of webbing and straps that were used by the Army Air Corps. During the Korean War and the beginning of the Jet Age, they started to see that canvas straps were strictly Stone Age. Polyester and fiberglass were the thing.'

I was busy tamping ground coffee and filling the machine with water and couldn't see her face. She had a nice voice, and I could have listened to her read the tax code for hours on end. The machine made its collection of knocks, pings and hisses, eventually spitting out its dark brew.

'New England Cordage had decent capital and decided to invest in their future by buying out a small company in the Housatonic River Valley. It was called Northeast Chemical Processes. They were small, and their business existed mostly to service electronics manufacturers like Sprague. The bigger companies figured out that it was cheaper for them to just do the work in-house, and that put Northeast Chemical in a bad spot. They had one saving grace in that they were specialists in things like coatings and fiberglass technology. Some of their coatings were resistant to flames.'

'Never a bad thing.' I looked up at her and smiled the smile I reserved for pretty, smart women. I got the low-fat milk – it's supposed to foam up better – and poured some into the small metal pitcher that came with the machine. She waited politely while I foamed the milk with the steam from the angled metal valve. She didn't have much choice, as it was like listening to someone blow raspberries through a megaphone. When it was done, I poured the steamed milk on top of the cups of espresso and handed her one.

'Then New England Cordage bought Modern Textile Processes in Pawtucket, Rhode Island.'

'The town where the Sox have their minor league team?' That was the only reason that I had heard of Pawtucket at all.

'One and the same. It was a manufacturing hub: textiles, paper products, jewelry, things like that. Anyway, Modern Textile specialized in nylon and polyester-like fabrics. They had a small share of the market, but they too couldn't survive against bigger companies. They ended up getting bought out by New England Cordage.'

'How did they make money buying two losing companies?'

'Well, two ways. The first was making a type of fiberglass insulation that was coated with a proprietary chemical process that was flame-resistant. It was lightweight and could be molded. It was a hit in the aircraft industry, and later, when the world figured out that asbestos was killing people, suddenly New England Cordage, now named New England Textile and Cordage, had the answer.'

'That made them money?'

'Lots of money. That and one other thing.'

'What was that?'

'War. Your war.'

'Vietnam?' Terry McVicker no doubt used it as a selling point.

'Yep.'

'Don't tell me they made knockoff napalm.'

'No, flak vests.'

'No shit.'

'Shit. Yes, they made fiberglass flak vests. Probably saved your life.'

I laughed. 'Not me. I never wore them. Too heavy and not suited to my part of the war.'

'Maybe you should have reconsidered,' she said, pointing at the ragged end of my earlobe that an angry Vietnamese gangster had shot off last spring.

I didn't feel like getting into it. 'Tell me how this all ended up in court.'

'Well, for years NT and C were making these two products. They were making them in mills in Worcester, Pawtucket and Fall River. The process, like all of them, had a byproduct or two that couldn't be used in anything else. It was a liquid made with a bunch of chemicals that I couldn't pronounce even if I had it written out in front of me. Anyway, over the decades the liquid built up and was put in fifty-five-gallon drums. It wasn't a big deal; the mills were huge brick buildings and they just stacked them in the basement with all the other byproducts they didn't need anymore.'

'What happened to make it a big deal?'

'The competition was able to make the same products a lot cheaper.'

'Oh, I see.' I didn't, but I was pretty sure that my making decent cappuccino hadn't impressed her too much. I didn't want to convince her I was an idiot too.

'Oil, petrochemicals are a key component of synthetics. Bigger companies were able to negotiate better deals for the raw materials and oil, in this case. They were able to manufacture the products cheaper in non-union mills down south.

'Suddenly, they weren't making money hand over fist, but they were hemorrhaging it. When that happens, companies try to stop the hemorrhaging by reducing expenses. In this case, they closed a few of their mills, they laid people off and they emerged as Northeast Textile and Cordage after some unpleasant bankruptcy stuff. They sold off a couple of the mills and consolidated everything in Worcester.'

'So, they left the stuff and are getting sued by the new owners of the mills?'

'No, that would actually have been OK. They hauled all of the chemicals away because they didn't want to jeopardize the sale of the mills by leaving the mess. They were supposed to take the stuff to an industrial incinerator to dispose of it.'

'But they didn't.'

'Nope.'

'What did they do?'

'They started by burying the drums, but that took up too much space, so they dumped a lot of the waste out in some vacant land well outside of town. Really rural places.'

'And . . .?'

'Well, wouldn't you know it, someone bought the land and started building houses. The houses led to neighborhoods near where the stuff had been dumped. The residents there started to notice that they had higher-than-average levels of miscarriages and birth defects. No one put it together until people who had lived there since the houses were built started getting cancer. Most of them lived, but some got obscure types of cancer, not the stuff you get from smoking a pack a day. Some doctors started writing about it and then the lawyers got involved.'

'When was that?'

'That was in 1979.'

'And it's just going to trial now. 1986 will be here in a few days.'

'Nothing moves quickly through the legal system. It's a miracle that this has moved as fast as it has.'

'Six years is fast?'

'In the courts, especially a case like this, yes.'

'How much money is involved?'

'You mean how much can the penalty be if the defendant loses?'

'Yes.'

'It could be in the millions or tens of millions of dollars.'

I whistled. 'So, blackmailing the judge isn't a bad idea financially.'

'No, not for the defendant it isn't.'

'NT and C must be worried about losing the case if they are resorting to blackmail.'

'Sure, losing this case could cost them a lot of money in terms of the penalty, but also it could cripple their reputation. People might stop buying their products, and investors would probably stop investing in the company. Even more importantly, it would mean the owners couldn't sell the company.'

'That sounds bad.'

'Sure does.'

'You brought a synopsis of the case and the other things I asked for?'

'Yes.' She paused. 'Mr Roark, the judge is a good man, a nice man.'

'Andy. I am sure he is. It's my job to help him, not sit in judgment on his private life.'

'Good. He doesn't deserve this.'

'No, he doesn't.' I didn't point out that his wife might not agree with her.

'Will you be able to find out who is behind this?'

'I think so.'

'That's not the vote of confidence I was looking for.'

'There is a small pool of people who will benefit from the blackmail. There's also a limited number of ways the pictures could have been taken and developed. All of that narrows the search down. That increases my chances of finding the person behind it. If I can find them, then I can convince them to take the pressure off the judge.'

'How would you do that?'

'I'm not exactly sure yet, but blackmail is illegal in the Commonwealth. The threat of going to jail might be enough. No matter what, I will find a way to get the judge out of this mess.' I wasn't sure what that would mean, and I should have been leery of making promises like that. That's how I get myself into trouble.

'Good. He needs someone on his side. Someone good. Terry McVicker said that you're tough and discreet and smarter than you look.' She smiled as she said it.

'He's just partial to me because I picked up the tab the last time we had a drink.'

'Great,' she said with some exaggeration. 'I gotta run. Thanks for the coffee.'

'Cappuccino,' I said with a smile so she knew I was joking. 'It was my pleasure.' I walked with her to the outer office.

'Funny, this is my first time in a PI's office, and it's even seedier than I imagined.'

'But you have to admit you weren't expecting the espresso machine.'

'No, I wasn't. Call me if you need anything else.'

She had her coat on before I could act like a gentleman and help her with it. Before I could make a slightly suggestive quip she said, 'Thanks for the *cappuccino*, Roark.'

She walked out of the office, leaving behind the envelope and a faint trace of a perfume I couldn't name. I wondered if I was always going to be a half-step too late trying to impress her. I had faced tougher odds.

After Angela left, I sat at my desk and opened the manila envelope she brought. I thought about lighting a pipe, but there was still a faint trace of her perfume in the air and I decided the pipe could wait. Inside the envelope were several sheets of neatly typed paper which I shook out onto my desk.

The list of the hotels was about what I expected – large chains like the Holiday Inn, Howard Johnson's, the occasional Sheraton. All of them were outside the city proper on Route 128 or any number of the routes that connected the bedroom communities of Boston with the major highways. They were all large and anonymous, and one or two men checking in wouldn't attract any attention.

The judge had remembered the hotels and the inn they stayed in on the Cape. He also remembered the dates, or most of them. The bad news was that he had no idea what rooms he met Lee Raymond in. That wasn't surprising. Most people wouldn't remember their room number if it was stamped on the plastic tag on their key, much less months later. At least I had some dates, and later I would have pictures of Raymond that I could show around to the desk clerks. Who knows, I might get lucky, and he used his own name.

The synopsis of the lawsuit was a slightly beefier version of what Angela had told me. This one named the communities that were affected by the dumping. It wasn't good, but it wasn't on the scale of Love Canal either. The medical portion of it, especially the list of the children who were born with birth defects, was tough to read. The stuff about those with rare cancers was only marginally better.

The dumped chemical byproducts were traced back to the defendants because they'd packed them in old fifty-five-gallon drums that had originally contained chemicals sent to them by their vendors. It hadn't taken much detective work to figure out where the chemical waste that poisoned people came from. On top of that, they'd used an outside company named Commonwealth Trucking to dispose of the waste. According to the synopsis, Commonwealth Trucking filed for bankruptcy, and their assets were sold off in 1974.

There wasn't much more to be learned from the information that Angela Estrella had brought. I packed it all up along with all the photos, a couple of legal pads and some felt-tip pens into my battered postman's bag. It was time to head to the best resource I had as a private detective: the Boston Public Library.

I locked up the office and made my way out to the street. It was a little warmer than when I had walked over a few hours earlier. I knew it wouldn't last. Snow and more cold were coming. I could feel it, almost smell it in the air as I walked toward the Prudential Center. The Pru and the John Hancock building were in competition for Boston's most notable bit of architecture.

For my money, neither held a candle to the Boston Public Library in Copley Square. While the BPL was lower to the ground, it looked like a Renaissance cloister and had often been described as a 'Palace for the People.' It was a work of art in itself and that wasn't even taking the murals into account. If you have never been to the main branch of the Boston Public Library, you've missed out. It was a good place to do a little more research into Northeast Textile and Cordage until it was time to go see Artie.

FOUR

I spent a couple of hours in the reference section of the BPL looking up information about all the companies listed in the case summary that Angela Estrella had brought me. I wrote down addresses and phone numbers, trying to map out a path for the investigation. It was complicated by the fact that all the companies involved had either changed hands, been taken over by bigger ones or disappeared down the rabbit hole known as bankruptcy.

When my back started to feel stiff and I couldn't take the quiet anymore, I packed everything up in my postal bag. Outside, I shook out a Lucky Strike from the slightly battered soft pack. The sun had dipped below the skyline, and the chilly afternoon was shaping up to be a cold night. I made my way to Artie's camera shop by way of the police department, where I left Billy Devaney a white envelope with a pair of tickets for the Bruins' game, as promised, with the desk sergeant.

By the time I got to Artie's, the sky was that mix of purple and dark blue that immediately precedes full night. The streetlights were casting their harsh light over the city. Artie looked up from the counter and said, 'Hello, Andy. Cold out there?'

'It isn't too bad if you're from the Yukon.'

'Maybe you should invest in a hat.'

'I have one; I just need to invest in enough common sense to know when to wear it.'

'Here are your pictures,' he said, sliding a plain manila envelope the size of a *Reader's Digest* magazine across the counter to me. I noticed it wasn't in the usual brightly colored envelope with pictures of happy, smiling people advertising Kodak, Fuji or Agfa film.

I opened it and slid out a picture of Lee Raymond. Artie had done a good job, and it looked like Raymond was at the beach or some other place that didn't require him to be wearing a shirt.

'I tried to crop down to just his face but that was the best I could do.'

'No, this is perfect. Thank you. What do I owe you?'

When Artie told me, I slid the corresponding bills his way.

'Thank you,' he said, opening the register and putting the bills in. 'I've been giving some more thought to your questions about how he took the pictures.'

'I'm all ears.' The Army had spent some time showing me how to use a Nikon camera to take pictures of the Ho Chi Minh trail, but I knew what I didn't know.

'My guess is that he had help. Someone in another room. Either an adjoining room or one next door.'

'How do you figure?' Sometimes my Southie showed through.

'You can tell by the slight blurring around the edges of the original. It's faint but it's there. The camera was probably in a heating/air-conditioning vent. It would be easier in a room that's next door, sharing a central AC duct. Rent the two rooms and unscrew the vent cover in one room, use a long cable with a shutter release. It would look like a plunger or a syringe on a cable. Push it up against the other vent and wait.'

'Wait for what?'

'The action to start. Either they heard it or the guy in the picture signaled his accomplice somehow.'

'Are you sure? Wouldn't the slats from the vent show up in the pictures?'

'No, not if they were using a fifty-millimeter lens with a low aperture pushed right up against the vent. Up close like that, the slats would be almost invisible.'

'How would they get more than one picture?' I didn't know much about cameras, but I knew that they had to be advanced after each shot.

'Some cameras have an auto-shutter feature. You set it to auto, push the button to take a picture and it clicks away until the film is done. Like a submachine gun.'

'Ha! What do you know about submachine guns?'

'What? You think you're the only guy ever who was in the Army?'

'No, you just never mentioned it.'

'Korea . . . it wasn't a lot of fun.'

'No, I wouldn't think it was.'

'Andy, the auto-shutter would be loud – a mechanical clicking noise. Inside an air-conditioning vent, it would make a racket. My guess is that it was wrapped in something like a towel or in a bag. The guy also probably stretched nylon or pantyhose over the lens so there wouldn't be any reflection off the lens.'

'Like a sniper.'

'Well, he is a hunter of sorts.'

'Thanks, Artie, I appreciate the help.'

'Also, I think he would have bought film by the brick.'

'By the brick?'

'Yeah, this guy is probably taking a lot of pictures. Takes a roll with the camera on auto-shutter, pulls the camera back, reloads, resets, pushes it back in place and burns through another roll. He would probably burn through a bunch of film to get a few decent pictures. So, he would buy film by the brick, a dozen rolls bundled together in a four-by-three stack.'

'OK, what else did you notice?'

'He used glossy paper. Not pearl or flat. Flat would look . . . lackluster. Pearl is thicker, classier, but an unnecessary expense for this sort of thing. Glossy not only looks right but it really captures the' – he paused, trying to find the right words – 'the spirit of the moment.'

'Where would you get this developed? Private darkroom . . . shady camera shop?'

'Sure, either would work. Maybe your guy is a photographer. He might be a pro with his own set-up. He would have to have some basic knowledge of shutter speed, light, the right lens, etcetera. But none of this stuff is super exotic. It's a few notches above the average tourist running around with a thirty-five millimeter, but not many.

'They might have their own darkroom set-up. It wouldn't take much, and there are plenty of hobbyists out there. Or it could be a camera shop that doesn't care what you develop as long as you pay a premium. There are a few of those guys around. A lot of camera shops also rent out their equipment – enlargers, darkrooms, kit like that – after hours to bring in extra cash. Hell, even I do it.'

'Do you think you could write down a list of the shadier guys in your line of work?'

'Sure, no problem.' He took out a notepad and spent a few minutes writing down names. 'Here it is.'

'Thanks, Artie. This is all a big help. I really appreciate it.'
'Sure, glad to. Hey, I just thought of one other thing.'
'What's that?'
'If they are using a darkroom or renting a spot in a store, the paper is expensive. Most guys will take one piece of paper cut up into strips and do a bunch of test exposures to make sure their time is dialed in. It might not be of much use, but if you see a bunch of strips of photographic paper with gaff exposures and pictures, that could be something.'
'Thanks, Artie, I really do appreciate it.'
'Glad to help.'
'I owe you one,' I said, picking up the original and the enlargements of Lee Raymond and heading for the door.
'No problem. Let me know when you are looking for a new camera.'

I waved as I pushed my way out of his store and into the evening that had gone from chilly to cold since I had been inside. I made a mental note to pick up a bottle of decent hootch for Artie the next time I was around.

The Army had sent a bunch of us to a two-week course at Fort Holabird just outside of Baltimore. We were supposed to learn how to use cameras as Special Forces NCOs. Most of it was spy stuff that didn't apply to us, like how to emplace a microdot or spot one. We couldn't think of anything more useless in Vietnam where we all were headed.

It was a gentlemen's course, which meant that classes started at nine a.m., late by Army standards, and ended promptly at three p.m. every day. We felt that as newly minted Green Berets, it was our duty to patronize every bar in Baltimore that would take our money in an effort to win the goodwill of the local residents. Our second and equally important mission was to try to rescue the women of Baltimore from boredom by offering temporary romantic respite from the men of Baltimore. The end result was spending most days in class trying to overcome the effects of both and stay awake through some pretty technical lectures.

Months later, the joke was on me. I was new on the recon team, and we were laid up watching the Ho Chi Minh trail. Everyone was tense: we were almost on top of the trail, weapons at the ready. We were close enough to hear the chatter of the

North Vietnamese Army soldiers and smell the pungent fish sauce, nuoc mam, coming off them. They must have felt safe, confident, because the smell of fresh, burning tobacco smoke was wafting over to us.

I had a Japanese camera in my hands, my CAR-15 next to me. I was sweating, and it wasn't all the result of the oppressive heat and humidity of the Laotian jungle. We were close enough to the trail that the danger of being caught had gone up significantly. Even with camouflage, thick foliage and precautions, we were still at greater risk of being discovered. That would mean having to run and fight our way out.

We were there to gather intelligence, hence the camera, and if the opportunity arose, we might snatch a prisoner. That was the prize for MACV-SOG recon teams. A successful prisoner snatch meant that you had both the skill and moxie to pull it off. It was a technical triumph that was rewarded with a ten-day R&R. Most guys went to Bangkok, some went to Tokyo and everyone partied themselves into a near coma and back again.

The team was ten meters back, spread out pulling security. The One-Zero, the team leader, had motioned me forward with him. He handed me his camera and then pulled what looked like crude metal tubes, spot welded together to make some sort of plumbing tool out of his rucksack. It was a British STEN gun with the magazine of nine-millimeter bullets sticking out the side, the type with a full-length silencer. It was an innovation from World War Two, a cheap submachine gun that the island nation could crank out by the hundreds to arm themselves with. The silenced version was used by their Special Operations Executive, their secret commandos. While it looked as if it had been designed by a kid with an Erector set, it was still one of the quietest silenced weapons to be found. The crude metal stock and pistol grip could be unscrewed from the action and barrel, fitting nicely in the top of a rucksack. Perfect for a prisoner snatch.

We waited, sweat sliding into my eyes. The One-Zero motioned for me to take some pictures. I looked through the aperture of the camera and slowly pushed down on the shutter release, its click lost in the noises of the jungle and the trail. I slowly, quietly advanced the film and took another shot. We waited for a single

NVA to walk down the trail. Even two would be a possibility, but this seemed like a parade of NVA pushing heavily laden bicycles with a six-foot piece of bamboo affixed to the handlebars, so it was easier to balance their load. They were porters moving rice and ammunition down the trail. Then the deep-throated rumble of Russian Molotov trucks in the distance, coming closer. The trucks rumbled by one after another, moving down the trail, bringing weapons and ammunition from the Communist bloc by way of North Vietnam to the South. Trying to make South Vietnam into a worker's paradise, one bullet at a time. The trucks kept rolling, passing the smaller convoy of porters with their modified bikes.

After we had been there for longer than was advisable – but that could have been said of our time in Vietnam itself – the One-Zero motioned to me that we were going to crawl back to the team. I nodded and then we took turns slowly inching backwards, making sure not to leave the camera or my CAR-15 behind. We joined back up with the rest of the team. We stowed the camera and the STEN gun, then slowly started making our way back, deeper into the jungle away from the trail.

Later, sitting in the South Vietnamese H-34 Sikorsky helicopter, my back to the bulkhead, exhausted, I noticed the tape still on the muzzle of my CAR-15. I was a little disappointed. I hadn't fired my weapon; we'd had an uneventful recon mission. I was still untested and was keenly aware of it.

'Kid, don't lose sleep over it.' My One-Zero was from Worcester, Massachusetts, and it was nice to hear the familiar accent and slang. 'Any mission we don't have to shoot our way out of is a good one.'

'I know . . . I just . . .'

'You want to test your mettle. I get it. Don't worry, I guarantee you will get the chance. Missions like today's are the exception around here, not the rule.'

I leaned back against the bulkhead of the shuddering helicopter and thought about what he had said. I was eager to prove myself, to be worthy of being on a team, and coming home with the tape on my muzzle didn't seem to be the way to do it.

'Don't worry, kid. You'll get your chance.' I didn't realize how truthful his words were. It wouldn't be long before I would find myself shooting my way out of bad trouble and running for my life through the jungle.

A couple of days later, my One-Zero and I were standing in front of the CO. Usually in the Army, this meant that someone had done something stupid to get in trouble. He didn't seem angry and I hadn't been there long enough to screw up on R&R. He looked up at me and grinned. 'Roark, the S-2' – the intelligence officer – 'said you took some good pictures. He is very happy and so is Saigon.'

Outside, I said to my One-Zero: 'This is some sort of screwy war.'

'What do you mean?'

'Taking pictures is more important than being in combat?'

'They're all screwy.'

Sir Leominster was waiting for me at the door when I got home. He meowed at me and rubbed up against my legs while I took my coat off and hung it on the rack. The postman's bag went on the floor. I had no interest in going through any more of it tonight. I threw the mail that had been taking up space in the mailbox on the table.

I dug the ice tray out of the freezer and forced a few cubes out of the plastic tray into a tumbler that had been drying in the rack by the sink. I poured some Powers Irish Whiskey over the ice cubes and enjoyed the first sip of whiskey for the night, that warm feeling radiating from my center and the almost instant relaxing of my limbs. I pulled a Lucky out and lit it. The smoke would help with the stench of the cat food that Sir Leominster was meowing for. After that, I looked over at the machine by the phone, but there were no blinking lights.

I found some leftovers in the refrigerator and debated if it was worth heating them up or just better to eat them cold. I vaguely wondered what Angela Estrella was doing. Was she contemplating cold leftovers or was some guy, smarter than me, taking her out to a nice restaurant? I decided to heat up the leftovers, which gave me time to add a little more whiskey to my glass.

I contemplated what tomorrow's investigative efforts would be while waiting for my food to heat up in the oven. I wanted to go back to the library and do a little more research into

Northeast Textile and Cordage. I also wanted to start making the rounds of camera stores and hotels to see if anyone recognized Lee Raymond or anyone else who might have checked into an adjoining room at the hotel. I also needed to talk to Sergeant Devaney and see if Lee Raymond had a record or an address. But knowing that cheap Irishman, he wouldn't talk to me until after he had enjoyed the hockey game.

The hands on my Seiko dive watch came level to where I had set the bezel. My leftovers should be warm enough. I didn't mind leftovers. I had once tried some frozen meals that were supposed to be filling enough to satisfy a starving male. The convenience couldn't make up for the flavor. I turned off the oven and transferred the steaming pile of rice, chicken and broccoli onto the plate. I tipped the pan over the rice, coating it with any drippings from the chicken for a little flavor.

I took my leftovers to the couch with my glass of whiskey. The local news was depressing, and the national news wasn't much better. Both had stories about the upcoming New Year's Eve celebrations. The national news reminded me to make sure to tune in and watch the ball drop in Times Square. I couldn't say that I had much interest in any of it. When the news was over and the game shows and reruns of Barney Miller were done, there was nothing on the Movie Loft worth watching. TV56 was showing a movie about a cop in leather pants chasing a bike gang around Australia. I opted for a book, jazz on the radio and more whiskey. I think I made the right choice.

The next morning when I woke up, the sky outside the window was gray. White snowflakes whirled about like flights of starlings in the fall sky, doing their elaborate last dance before flying or hiding or whatever starlings do in the cold. I had slept well, and if I had dreamed about Vietnam or French-speaking deer, I couldn't remember it. I opted against going out to run in the snow flurries and contented myself with what I could do inside.

Sir Leominster watched me as I did a set of push-ups, followed by a set of crunches, followed by dips, hands braced on the coffee table, and then sit-ups. I finished one exercise and went to another without taking any time to rest. When I finished a set, I would do lunges into the kitchen, to the door and back into the living room, then another set of exercises starting with push-ups. I exercised listening to the news on the public radio station that had played last night's jazz.

The news was the usual depressing stuff, but that seemed to be the way of the world. By the time the news gave way to the sounds of birds chirping, marking the end of the news and the beginning of the morning classical radio program, I was sweating and my muscles ached pleasantly the way they do after a good workout.

The DJ came on with his deep, mellow voice that made me wonder if he liked to get baked before going on air. I would have loved to have heard his voice at the other end of the radio calling for help from Covey back in Vietnam. It would have been reassuring. I smiled at the thought of the possibly baked, public radio classical DJ calling in gunships for me in Vietnam. Sir Leominster just looked at me as if I had hit my head one time too many. He wasn't necessarily wrong.

I put the stovetop espresso maker on the burner after adding ground coffee and water. I found a soft pack of Lucky Strikes and shook one out, lit it and inhaled. There were few things better than the first smoke of the day. I put two slices of whole-wheat bread in the toaster. I hadn't given up on the self-improvement plan I had embarked upon a few months ago. I knew the whole-wheat bread was healthy because it ended up tasting like slightly charred sawdust smeared with butter by the time I ate it. The good news was that it made the faux French yogurt I had with it taste that much better.

I finished the breakfast that clearly wasn't the one that my heart desired. I wanted a cheese omelet, stuffed with corned beef hash, the kind from the can, on a plate crowded with rye toast and home fries. That was what I wanted, but I made do with sawdust toast and faux French yogurt. At least the coffee was good.

Later, after I had showered and dressed, I got ready for a day out and about. I gathered up my notebooks and pens, pictures of Lee Raymond and my case notes to date. I slid my little .38 into its holster inside my waistband and made sure I had a speed-loader of hollow points and my Buck knife too. I dropped my blackjack in my coat pocket for good measure. According to the news, it was getting rougher out there, and I didn't want to be left behind.

Outside, the wind was coming off the Charles River with enough of an edge to slip through my layers like a knife between the ribs. I had my nice wool scarf around my neck and, like all self-styled tough guys with long hair, didn't bother with a hat. The snow flurries had given way to the occasional pale flake drifting down here and there. I would have to go to the market later and would have to fight the bread and milk crowd. The Blizzard of '78 had so traumatized New England that even now, seven, almost eight years later, a few errant snowflakes could trigger a stampede to the market for bread and milk.

My slightly battered Ford Maverick was parked in its spot with the discolored asphalt. When the Vietnamese gangsters had blown up my beloved VW Karmann Ghia, the Maverick had been its replacement. It wasn't as pretty but with a 324 under the hood and a Holley carburetor, it was plenty fast. Out of habit, I checked around the car for stray bits of wire or anything to indicate that the gangsters were up for a second try.

Normally if I was going to the office or the library, I would walk. Trying to park in Boston was an essay in frustration, and I couldn't bring myself to pay to park in my own city. However, today I had camera stores to go to all over the city and surrounding areas. Add to that the hotels and motels off the highway, I had to cover a lot of ground today. Which, history had taught me, was better done by six cylinders than two feet.

The Maverick started with the customary throaty rumble that let me know that the Holley carburetor was doing its thing. My expectations were low, and I was just happy that it didn't explode. After my Karmann Ghia had gone to its fiery reward, I had gone to my friend Carney's garage to get something I could afford. Carney was a third-generation Irish villain in semi-retirement who ran a garage that specialized in clean cars and other things for Irish villains not in semi-retirement. His daughter got tangled up with a heroin dealer, and I helped him out. He had a soft spot for me ever since. It didn't hurt that he had been a paratrooper in the Korean War, where he'd picked up a couple of Purple Hearts.

The Maverick looked like a ten-year-old beater, painted a shade of blue that was so flat and boring it made the car almost invisible. No one looked twice at it. It lacked the style of my Karmann Ghia or Brenda Watts's Saab, but it made up for it under the hood. It had the other advantage that when it got dinged up a little driving in Boston, I couldn't bring myself to be upset.

My first stop was to Police Headquarters. I wanted to see if Billy Devaney, after enjoying the Bruins game, had found any information about Lee Raymond. He certainly wouldn't tell me anything before seeing the game. That was just his way. Billy was the type of person who felt that paying full price for anything was akin to being cheated. That even went for free tickets to the Bruins. If the Bs had lost, then I could count on little or no help from the ever-flinty Detective Sergeant Billy Devaney.

I circled the block a few times looking for a spot that wasn't taken up by a police car or so illegal that a Meter Molly would brave the cold to drop a ticket on the Maverick. There are few forces in the world more vengeful than meter checkers forced out into the cold. I walked the block and half to the entrance of Police Headquarters wondering if I should invest in a hat. The wool scarf, sweater and Navy surplus peacoat were just barely keeping up with the cold.

Inside headquarters, it wasn't busy but it wasn't quiet. There were a couple of people writing on clipboards, sitting on the bench in front of the desk sergeant. On another bench, asleep, sitting up against the corner wall, was a homeless guy who smelled as though he'd been dipped in cheap wine and pickled onions ten years ago. The steam radiators clanked and pushed their damp heat into the lobby. Off in the distance, I could hear people talking and the clanking of typewriters.

It was the same desk sergeant and he recognized me.

'Ah, the Seamus is back.' At least he didn't make any *Magnum P.I.* jokes.

'Yeah, is Sergeant Devaney around?'

'Sure, sure . . . hang on.' He picked up his phone and called Devaney, telling him I was there to see him. He put the phone down, handed me a visitor's badge and said, 'He's in his office. You know the way.'

Billy was sitting behind his desk, chewing on a cigar and looking a little worse for wear.

'Hey, Billy.'

'Oh, Jesus, Roark, you shanty Irish piece of garbage,' he croaked at me.

'What have I done now, Billy? Weren't the seats good? Right on the ice.'

'The seats were great. The game was great.'

'Then why the hostility?' I asked innocently.

'The beers were cheap, and I had too many.'

'The game wasn't that long. You couldn't have gotten too polluted.'

'It wasn't just the beer. Sully and me stopped for a taste after the game.'

'Oh, I see. A touch of the mother's milk not treating you kindly today?' I said, hamming up our mutual Irish ancestry. 'Mother's milk' meant Jameson's, and knowing him, a taste was most of a bottle between them.

'Something like that,' he said sourly.

'Did you find out anything about Lee Raymond?'

'Yeah, he's got a jacket. His name is Raymond Lee Keith. Goes by Lee Raymond, Raymond Lee, or Keith Raymond, you get the idea. He's a hustler by trade, usually takes his date's wallet and valuables, knowing that gentlemen of a certain persuasion tend to be reluctant to call the cops.' Billy had been a cop long enough and was Southie enough that his casual bigotry about gay men was second nature. His referring to them as 'gentlemen of a certain persuasion' with a sneer was as close to tolerant as he gets. I didn't like it, but putting up with it was part of the cost of the information.

'His record goes back to when he was a juvenile. He graduated to spending some time at the Plymouth House of Corrections and some time at MCI Walpole for an assault and robbery. Somewhere while he was a guest of the state, he took some art appreciation classes taught by those liberal do-gooders who go to prisons and try and reform the cons. He got out and decided robbing and hustling wasn't his thing anymore. The word is that he's into con games now.'

'He got any time hanging?'

'Yep, he's got five years left on a suspended sentence.'

'You got an address?'

'Not current but a couple of old ones, and his parole officer gave me his mother's address.'

Billy told me everything, and I wrote it all down in the notepad I kept in my jacket pocket. 'Thanks, Billy, I appreciate it.'

He nodded his head gingerly at me as if he had recently been clubbed in it. 'No problem.' He raised a limp hand in an almost wave.

When I got back to my car, there was a ticket on it despite my best attempts to avoid one. At least I could put it down as expenses.

The Maverick rumbled to life, and I nosed out into traffic. I headed out of the city onto the highways and routes that had hotels on the list that Angela Estrella had provided. I got on the highway and headed south out of the city. Traffic was light because all the commuters heading into offices had already traveled into the city. Traffic in Boston was rough, and to navigate it, one had to have the skill and experience of a big game hunting guide.

The hotels were as far south as Foxborough and then all along the Route 128 corridor and north of the city to the border with New Hampshire. I drove south to Foxborough, which is home to the New England Patriots and little else. I drove merging on to one highway, leaving another and eventually on to one of the state highways.

I was starting with the hotels that they had most recently stayed in. The inn on the Cape would have to wait. The first hotel was on the other side of the divided highway, so I had to loop around at the next light and double back. I pulled up the hill and past a Bennigan's restaurant. I wasn't sure how authentic the Irish cuisine was, but you could slap a shamrock on anything in this state and it would do business.

I parked the Maverick near the front door. The whole place was a brick, rectangular box with black plastic shutters and white trim around the windows. There were other decorative accents and moldings, all made of plastic instead of wood, all designed to make the hotel look something like a stately Colonial manor. The effect was about as useful as putting lipstick on a streetwalker.

I walked inside, and the lobby was furnished in the generic

but not unpleasant way that the big chain hotels were, the idea being that travelers were comfortable wherever they went because it reminded them of where they had been. There was some sort of Zen principle to it, but I wasn't there for philosophizing.

I stopped at the front desk and the clerk looked up. She was around my age and pretty. She smiled a bright but cheerless smile. The nametag on the front of her shirt said, 'Jessie.' 'Hi, Checking in?'

'Actually, no, I was hoping to talk to someone about a confidential matter.' There are different schools of thought about approaching people you want information from. Some guys try the bribe early. Others go Jim Rockford-style and try some sort of half-assed con. While I have done both, sometimes the best strategy is just being honest about why you are there.

Her smile froze and then she said, 'What is it?'

'I'm a private detective from Boston.' I showed her my license. 'I have a client who stayed here a few weeks ago. He was a guest of a guest. Now he is being blackmailed.'

'Now you're trying to find the guy.'

'Exactly.'

'This isn't some sort of dodge to get information for a divorce case, is it?'

'If this turns into a divorce case, then I've done a really bad job.'

'What are you looking for?'

I took out one of the cropped pictures that Artie made and slid it across the counter to her. 'This man stayed here November sixth. He would have checked in sometime in the early afternoon and would have left that night. He might have been using the name Lee Raymond, Raymond Lee, Raymond Keith, Keith Raymond or some combination thereof.'

'I wasn't working then,' she said doubtfully while looking at the picture.

'Do you think you could check the register?'

'Mister, I don't know. The company has policies about this sort of thing, and my manager is kind of a stickler for the rules.'

'Please, a good man is being blackmailed, put through hell . . . all for making a bad decision.'

'I don't know.'

'Please, it won't take you long to check, and it can stay between us.' Sometimes people needed that little extra push, either that they were part of a conspiracy or that you would keep their part in it secret.

She looked at me and then opened the hotel register. 'Yep, here he is. Lee Raymond. Checked into room three ten.'

'Great.' I wrote it down. 'Can you tell me is there a room on either side of it that would have been booked at the same time?'

'Sure, right here, room three twelve.'

'Who booked it?'

'He did. Two rooms, Lee Raymond.'

'Is that common, a man renting two rooms at the same time?'

'Mister, there's nothing common in this line of work.'

'Don't I know it. Listen, do you think the person who was working that night might talk to me? I can make it worth their time.'

'I don't know.'

'Why don't you give her a call and see if she'll talk to me?'

'It's not she; he's a he.'

'OK, see if *he* wants to make a little dough talking to me and a little something for your trouble too,' I said, sliding a portrait of Andrew Jackson across the counter to her. When I first started in this business, you could get away with a Lincoln or a Hamilton . . . inflation, I guess.

She took the twenty and it disappeared in a pocket of her slacks. She picked up a phone, and I walked a few feet away to give her some privacy and a sense of ease. I walked back after she hung up.

'Darren is going to be here in ten minutes. You can wait over there,' she said, pointing to some wing chairs in a little lobby area.

The chairs were someone's idea of what would be found in an upper-crust home, and looked more comfortable than they actually were. I picked up a copy of this morning's *Boston Globe* that was lying neatly re-folded on an end table. There wasn't much news that was good, other than that the Patriots had a shot at the Super Bowl.

A few minutes later, the lobby door opened and in walked a thin man in his mid-twenties. He was wearing stonewashed jeans,

The Judge

Nike basketball sneakers and a Patriots team jacket. He stopped at the desk and Jessie waved me over after a minute.

'Jessie says you've got some questions about one of our guests.'

'Yeah, I'm interested in a guy who rented rooms three ten and three twelve on the same day. He goes by Lee Raymond.' I showed him the picture of Raymond that I was carrying.

He took it out of my hand. 'He might look familiar.'

'How about twenty-dollars familiar?' I said, holding up a bill.

'Sure, he does. He rented both rooms. Had a guy with him.'

'Older gentleman in his sixties?' I asked.

'Sure, him too, but they were shacking up. But he was with another guy. Younger, in his forties maybe.'

'Were they shacking up too?'

'No, their relationship was all business.'

'How could you tell?'

'The way that they talked to each other. You know, polite but not warm and not like lovers do. No, they were more like coworkers.'

'Why did they stand out to you?'

'Well, for one, the guy in the picture and the other guy, it wasn't like the way he talked to the older dude. They had some luggage, a couple of camera bags, two duffel bags. Nothing crazy. Then later I saw this guy.' Darren held up Lee Raymond's picture. 'He was with an older white guy. Looked like someone's granddad. They were clearly very close, intimate; you could tell.'

'How?'

'I saw them in the hallway when I had to check in on another room on the third floor. They were in the hallway going somewhere. He put his hand on the old guy's arm or in the pocket of his sports coat. He whispered in the old guy's ear, and he blushed. Giggling on the elevator. With the not-as-old guy, it was like they were discussing math class or something.'

'OK, can you show me the two rooms?'

'I don't know, man.'

'I just need to see something, then I will split. There's another twenty in it for you.'

'OK, let me check and make sure no one is in them and grab the key.' He walked over to the girl at the counter, and when he returned, it turned out that I was uncharacteristically in luck.

'Not occupied. I grabbed the passkey from Jessie. C'mon.' I followed him to the elevator, and we rode up.

'So, you're like a real private investigator?'

'Yep, licensed and everything.'

'What's it like?'

'It's nothing like it is on TV.'

'No car chases and gunfights?' he asked in mock disappointment.

'No, those are pretty rare.' Though I had been on a streak in the past year. 'Mostly, it's a lot of waiting and watching. Talking to people and sometimes taking pictures of people lying.'

'Lying?'

'Sure, lying to their wives, husbands, employers, the insurance company – take your pick. If it weren't for people lying, most of us would be out of work.'

We arrived at room 310. 'Here it is,' Darren said.

'OK, open it.'

He knocked on the door even though the room wasn't booked and waited a half-beat, then opened it.

It was a standard hotel room with standard hotel furniture. To the left of the door was a bathroom; to the right, a closet with the type of hangers that had a ball and socket instead of a hook. I shook my head at the thought of people stealing clothes hangers; then again, people would steal dust bunnies if they could be resold. In the room proper was a queen-sized bed, a low bureau, a TV on the bureau, a small table and two chairs. There were the standard large windows and floor-to-ceiling drapes. It occurred to me that the fake shutters outside were of an unusually large scale to fit the windows.

What I was looking for was high up on the wall above the TV. A vent. A vent for the heating and cooling system in the wall that room 310 shared with room 312.

'Let's take a look at the other room.'

'Sure. There's no rush.'

'Huh?'

'We're here and the room isn't being used,' he said suggestively.

'Yeah, unfortunately, I am in a rush,' I said, not unkindly.

'Well, your loss.'

'Usually is,' I said for want of anything actually clever to say.

'Come on, cowboy,' he said with an air of long-experienced disappointment.

He went through the habit of knocking again and then let us in. Room 312 was a mirror image of 310, and this time I knew what I was looking for. I dragged a chair over to the side of the low bureau and the vent. I stood on the chair so that the vent was at eye level. The screws holding the vent in place were black, and there were faint scratches showing the bare metal beneath. They had been unscrewed with something that didn't quite fit the screw holes. A coin, a knife or one of the screwdrivers on a Swiss Army knife. The vents didn't match directly up but were offset by a couple of feet, most likely so that there was some sort of privacy. With the vent removed at my end, a camera could have been pushed the few feet into place by the other vent, and based on the drag marks in the dust, it had. It would have worked just as Artie said.

I hopped down and dragged the chair back to the table.

'Find what you were looking for?'

'Yes, thanks.'

We rode down in the elevator in relative quiet. I was happy to put another piece of the puzzle in place. It was a feeling that was always satisfying. The doors opened and we were in the lobby. I handed Darren a twenty-dollar bill. 'Thank you.'

'Come back anytime.' He was being more than just polite.

I nodded and left business cards with him and Jessie at the counter in case anyone remembered anything. I then went out to the Maverick. There were a lot more hotels on the list, and there was only so much daylight.

The Maverick started with its customary throaty rumble, and we got back on the highway to continue on our tour of local hotels, while Jim Carroll's voice came out of the radio singing about his sister Miranda.

The tour of hotels continued like the first. There were two more with staff who remembered Lee Raymond and a distinguished older gentleman or some variation of that description. One of them remembered a man in his forties with Raymond too. The best description I got was 'brown hair, average-looking.'

The longer ago the hotel stay was, the less detail people remembered. Raymond or one of his aliases had rented adjoining rooms in all of them. They all had air vents that connected the rooms.

I passed out business cards and spent a few hundred dollars of expense money and all day to confirm that. I was, however, lucky enough to get an address for Raymond. The problem was that the address was the same as a theater in the Combat Zone that showed X-rated movies. Last summer, I spent a lot of time in the Combat Zone looking for the runaway daughter of a friend. I knew that there were no apartments in the theater. It still made sense to check it out; maybe he had worked there at some point. Maybe we knew some of the same villains. The Combat Zone had more than its share of them, ensuring that the drugs, pornography and prostitution all kept turning a healthy profit. It seemed like a logical place for a blackmailer to be associated with.

I was only propositioned one other time, but she had done it with so little enthusiasm that I almost wondered if it was a new service that the hotel chain was offering.

By three in the afternoon, I was piloting the Maverick back into the city under a sky that was taken over by darkening clouds. I was hungry and there was more talk on the radio of snow. Mercifully, traffic wasn't too bad. It moved fifteen miles an hour below the speed limit into town, but it moved.

I pulled into the parking lot behind my office just as the first snowflakes danced around like pale fireflies on the wind. Upstairs, the office was booby-trap-free, and I hung my coat on the rack. I started the espresso machine and packed a pipe with a nice blend of Turkish and Virginia. I was hoping the caffeine and nicotine would convince my hollow stomach to go a couple of hours longer without food. I wanted to update my case notes. I had to figure out if it was worth a trip to Chatham and the romantic inn to see if they could tell me anything. That would be tomorrow or another day.

I had the pipe lit and drawing nicely by the time the espresso burbled into the tiny cup. Outside, the tiny firefly snowflakes increased in number and size. I was struck by the snow swirling outside contrasting with smoke from my pipe swirling around inside. Maybe I shouldn't skip meals; hunger made me overly philosophical.

Lee Raymond had picked large, anonymous hotels, usually chain hotels. He didn't try to cover up that he was renting two adjoining rooms, and no one thought it was suspicious. More likely, no one cared. It wasn't like the front-desk people were paid enough to care that much. It was also interesting that a couple of them noted that Raymond had been with an average-looking man with brown hair, in his forties. That could be almost anyone.

Was Raymond being sloppy by not trying to cover his tracks? Or maybe that was the advantage of blackmail: the victim was probably too cowed to come looking for you. I couldn't imagine Raymond giving up his leverage over the judge after the case was over. Also, based on what Artie told me about the technical challenges of taking the pictures, I didn't think this was Lee Raymond's first rodeo.

I cleaned up the office and packed my case notes in my postal bag. It was time for dinner and a drink. Outside, the snow was swirling, coming down against the light from the streetlights. It wasn't fully dark but more the time when day has given over but it's not quite night. The French have a term for it, but they have a term for everything.

The snow was light and fluffy. I used my gloved hand and coat sleeve to brush it off the Maverick's windshield and assorted windows. The car started easily, but I gave it a minute to warm up. The romantic in me wanted to walk home, to enjoy the snow falling on the Common and Garden. Or to enjoy the snow falling through the trees on the walkway in the middle of Commonwealth Avenue. Unfortunately for the romantic in me, my stomach was a realist that rumbled to let me know that I missed a meal already.

I drove carefully through the early-evening traffic. The roads were slick, and the city hadn't bothered to send out the plows or sand the roads yet. An inch of snow wasn't much to get the Department of Public Works excited. I stopped on the way home to get a pepperoni pizza from Athena's Pizzeria.

Athena's was a Greek pizzeria, and while their pie couldn't compare with old man Marconi's, he had moved back to Italy and they were here. Inside, it was warm and the jukebox was playing 'Runaround Sue.' I wasn't partial to the song, but it wasn't my nickel. At the counter, I ordered a large pepperoni with black olives. I asked them to sprinkle garlic powder and red pepper flakes on it. The dark-haired kid with glasses and pimples wrote it all down. I handed him a ten, and he told me it would be fifteen minutes. I went next door to the packie to get a six-pack of Löwenbräu. I liked whiskey, but beer went better with pizza.

On the way back to get my pizza, I unlocked the Maverick and put the six-pack Löwenbräu in its brown paper bag on the floor in front of the passenger seat. I locked the car and went back into Athena's to wait for my pizza, which ended up riding home on the passenger seat. There were some advantages to not having bucket seats. I drove home tantalized by the smell of the pizza that filled the car. I was looking forward to a nice quiet night on the couch with my dinner and the cat.

FIVE

The helicopter touched down on the red clay earth of the firebase, as it had thousands of times before. The mission was over, and we were sweaty and alive. The tape was shot off the muzzle of my musket. I hopped off the bird and noticed my white breaches were picking up the red clay dust. My jungle boots had been replaced by crude leather shoes, and I held a tricorn hat in my free hand.

It took me a second to realize that I was dressed like a Colonial militiaman from the Revolutionary War. While I was contemplating this odd turn of events, the distinctive whistle of incoming artillery followed by the explosive crumps of it landing nearby caught my attention. I ran to the nearest bunker. I noted the French tricolor flag flying over another.

I managed to dive into a nearby bunker, half blown in with the dust and gravel from an exploding round. I sat up, dimly aware that I had lost my hat and that my pants would always be stained by the red clay dust. I still had my musket in hand, which was some comfort.

In front of me, playing cards over an old wooden ammunition crate with a flickering candle on it were two familiar figures. One was my old point man Ger, his head cleaved from the machine round that had killed him on our unlucky last mission. Next to him, reclining on a chaise lounge, was the deer, its legs and abdomen torn apart from the toe-popper mines I had left on our backtrail.

They were speaking in French, and then they both took notice of me. Ger smiled at me, which looked funny because the only intact part of his head was his mouth. The deer turned to me and said something in French I couldn't understand. Then he said in heavily accented English, 'Great, the Americans are here.' He was not happy about it.

I woke up, curled under the blankets. It was gray outside, with snow still swirling around outside the window. It was the type of cold that made you want to stay under the covers for a long time. Sir Leominster was curled up on the pillow beside me, pressed into my neck in a warm ball of itchy fur. My .38 was on the bedside table next to an empty glass that had three fingers of whiskey in it when I finally turned off the TV and went to bed last night.

I got out of bed and went to the bathroom to scrub the taste of old cigarettes and whiskey out of my mouth. I wish there was something to scrub away the bad taste the dreams left. In the end, I settled on just getting on with my day.

After working out, breakfast and shower, the snow hadn't lessened any. It wasn't that there was a lot of it coming down or that it was even accumulating, it was just that it kept swirling around and around. I didn't fancy a drive out to the Cape in this type of weather and didn't feel like getting blown all over the narrow highways on Cape Cod.

Fortunately, there were plenty of camera stores in town and in Cambridge that I wanted to check out. I could spend a productive day in the city endangering my life on the narrow byways and one-way streets of Boston instead. The swirling snow wouldn't make any of the other drivers any better, but at least the city looked a lot prettier.

The T was probably the smarter way to go given how bad it is to find parking in Boston. It's even worse when there's snow. Locals move their cars and clear out their parking spots, then put anything they can in the cleared spot as a space saver. Trashcans, traffic cones, folding beach chairs, even a child or two. In Boston, while not written into the law, the space saver is universally understood and respected. Ignoring the space saver or taking someone's spot after they have shoveled it out can lead to serious consequences. A fistfight at a minimum, and I am sure that there is at least a murder or two every winter over them. Boston is still a bare-knuckles kind of town.

Despite the obvious advantages of the T, though, I didn't relish the thought of being stuck in a subway car all day. Plus, I would be transferring all over the city and it would take forever. I would just have to accept driving in the weather, the bad drivers and the dangerous parking situation while checking out camera stores. Maybe that's why I get paid the big bucks.

I decided to head out of the city and work my way back in. The parking in Cambridge wasn't much better than in Boston, but there were only a few camera stores on the list. Harvard University was the big business in Cambridge, and I didn't think that Lee Raymond was doing his illicit photo development at the Harvard Cooperative, affectionately called the Coop. That left a few smaller camera stores, and then I would head south to check out a couple, then back into town. At least I didn't have to worry about Artie's store. He wasn't the type to have anything to do with blackmailers.

I eased the Maverick out of its parking spot and onto the city's slick streets, fishtailing a little as I turned onto the street. I went down to Mass Ave and turned left onto Harvard Bridge. Driving over the Charles River at five miles per hour below the speed limit, I could appreciate the beauty of the swirling snow.

I was born and raised in Boston, South Boston to be exact, and my world had been limited to the several square blocks of Southie that I was raised in and destined to live and die in as well. I tried to escape the life destined for me and generations of others in Southie, of growing up, working in the mill and dying of either alcohol or violence, by going to college. I had failed out, and Uncle Sugar offered me a devil's bargain to escape. The Army and Vietnam. I had my hair shorn off and was given a tour of the South. To a boy from Southie, everything below the Mason–Dixon line was new and foreign.

Then I landed in Vietnam, and for the first time in my brief life, I found myself in a place that was truly exotic. The country I flew over was lush and green. The earth was red, and the heat was intense. The country smelled foul, like rot and decay. Sometimes sweet. The food was spicy, like nothing I had ever experienced, and while I loved it, I often felt like it was trying to kill me from the inside out. In the space of weeks, I went from being a kid from Southie whose life was predestined to being worldly. It wasn't just Vietnam but the people I met in Special Forces.

Driving over the bridge, watching the snow whirl around us, frosting everything in its path, I was struck. Suddenly, my home had the veneer of being exotic. It looked peaceful and pretty, unlike the Boston that I knew. It was neat to see the very familiar transformed.

I made my way to the camera stores that weren't in Harvard Square. If you aren't from around here, you could be forgiven for assuming that Cambridge consisted of Harvard Square and everything else was some other town on the fringe of Boston. No one working in the camera stores in Cambridge recognized the picture of Lee Raymond, and most of them didn't keep any record of renting out their equipment.

Crossing the bridge back into Boston didn't yield any better results. The best I came up with after spreading the judge's cash around was a few maybes. Maybe he looked familiar, maybe he might have been in a few months ago, but no one definitively could say they had seen Lee Raymond. I left business cards, and in some cases cash, all around Cambridge and Boston with little to show for it except a gas needle that was just that much closer to E.

I had spent most of the day fishtailing through the streets and alleyways of the greater Boston area. If I was going to do my due diligence, then I would have to start looking at the suburbs. Clubs, too. I thought I heard Artie mention that there were photography clubs. It was nearing mid-afternoon, and it was going to be dark by the time I got anywhere outside of the city. Also, I didn't know where I was going. I could waste time trolling through suburbia, but a few minutes spent with the Yellow Pages could save me hours on the road.

That decided it: I would go to the office. I had eaten a burger and some fries from one of those roadside places that serve them in a Styrofoam clamshell box. It had temporarily plugged the hole in my stomach, but now my eyelids were drooping, and an espresso sounded like just the thing.

I pulled in behind my office building and parked the Maverick by the spot vacated by Marconi's Pizzeria's old dumpster. It could rain for a hundred straight years and not get the grease spot clean. At least the snow had given it and the whole city a veneer of class. I locked the Maverick and made my way up the back stairs to my office.

I hung my coat on the coat rack and fired up the espresso machine. I checked the answering machine, but no one had called to tell me that they knew where Lee Raymond was. The only message was from the retired sergeant major who was responsible for the reunion I didn't want to go to. It wasn't that I didn't want to see the guys; I was just too aware of how many of the guys I wanted to see wouldn't be there.

When the machine burbled, I poured out a small cup of the dark, bitter, overly caffeinated stuff. I packed a pipe and managed to get it drawing nicely with only three matches. I opened the office window enough to let out some of the smoke and let in only every fifth snowflake. I took out my lists of stores and the yellow legal pad I was taking notes on. I wrote out a summary of my unsuccessful day. After that, I got out the Yellow Pages and started working on tomorrow's foray into suburbia. I might even make it out to the Cape to check out the B&B in Chatham. After that, I would wind my way back to the city, stopping at the camera stores in the 'burbs.

I made a note to circle back to the library to check out the lawsuit, and I should see if I could talk to Lee Raymond's parole officer. I was pretty sure that blackmail wasn't in keeping with the terms of his parole. Not even in the Commonwealth would that fly.

My pipe had gone out and the espresso had been a memory for almost an hour. I decided it was time to go home. It was not quite dusk, and Sir Leominster would worry if I was late. Worry about his dinner, that is. I packed my postal bag, put on my peacoat, locked the office door and left for the night.

Outside, the snow was swirling around, but the storm was definitely letting up. I unlocked the Maverick and slid my postal bag across the seat. The engine started with a slight hesitation and then a throaty roar. Then there was a flash, and the night roared back at me. The back windscreen shattered, and I dove across the bench seat for the passenger door. There was another roar and the sound of metal striking metal. I was dimly aware of the cold air pouring in through the obliterated back windscreen and the sound of the ocean in my ears.

I tried to open the passenger door, but it wasn't working. I reached up and pulled up the lock and then pulled on the handle. I wriggled out of the car like an overgrown worm, shoulder rolling on the hard pavement, coming up with my .38 in front of me. A .38 is a good gun, small and compact, but going up against someone with a shotgun, it is a bit outclassed. It was better than no gun, though, and I was in no position to argue as I scanned the alley.

There were footprints in the snow a few feet from the back of the injured Maverick. I followed them and ended up out on the street in front of my building. The prints were lost in the foot traffic from the people leaving their office jobs and going home or heading for the T. I realized that I was holding the gun out in front of me when one sharp-eyed office-type gasped. I stuck it in the pocket of my peacoat and went back to the Maverick to inspect the damage. Off in the distance, growing closer, I could hear sirens wailing.

The back windscreen was in pieces, like ice crystals, all over the back seat. It wasn't just the shotgun pellets that had shattered it, but the muzzle blast from the shotgun had seemed like a giant ball of flame, making me wonder if it was a sawed-off. There is a lot of blast coming out of a shotgun and even more so if the barrel is cut down. The roof of the Maverick had some gouges in it. What stood out most was the dented trunk, with holes from the buckshot. One of my taillights had been shot out and, while the car was still running, it looked a little rough.

I turned the engine off, leaving the key in the ignition. I lit a cigarette and sat down on the bumper to wait for the police. I wouldn't have to wait long. Lately, lots of cars in Boston were getting blown up and lots of people were getting shot, all courtesy of an ongoing Mob war. I wasn't a part of it, and I didn't want to be mistaken for being a part of anything so clichéd. My car was just another in a long list. I was getting sick of people taking out their anger at me on my rolling stock.

The first cops on the scene were young and jumpy. They were still riding high on the adrenaline dump from going to a 'shots fired' call. It made them twitchy, and that scared me. I spoke slowly to the more reasonable-seeming one while holding my hands up in front of me at chest height. 'Officer, I'm a licensed private investigator. Someone just shot my car.'

He and his partner walked up to me with their hands on the butts of their holstered revolvers, their eyes taking in the alley and my car but somehow never actually taking them off of me. 'We got a call for shots fired and a man with a gun.'

'I'm a licensed private investigator. Someone shot my car, and I chased after them. I have a permit for my revolver, which is in my right pocket.' I said it slowly the way you might talk to a dog that is unsure if it wants to snap at you or wag its tail. Only most dogs don't carry guns. I didn't want to survive Vietnam only to get shot in an alley in my hometown a decade later.

'You got a gun on you?'

'Yep, I used to be a cop. Now I'm a . . .' I am not sure he heard any of it.

He barked, 'Hands!' It clearly wasn't a suggestion. I raised mine above my head. He moved in and I felt rough hands grabbing mine, spinning me around, pinning me against the car. I was quickly and efficiently handcuffed and felt him pat me down.

'It's a snubnose thirty-eight in my right coat pocket.' I felt his hand fishing around in my pocket and then taking my gun.

'You got a license?'

'Yep, in my wallet, back pocket.'

I felt him fish it out and heard him say to his partner, 'Run him.' Then more hands liberating my knife and speedloader of .38s.

'Mister, if you're lying, you are in a world of trouble.'

'Uh-huh,' I said drolly. I thought about saying something sarcastic, but I didn't feel like dealing with the resulting punches.

A few minutes later, his partner came back to assure him I checked out. The first cop took the handcuffs off, and I rubbed my wrists. 'What happened?'

'I was leaving my office, heading home. I got in my car, and someone shot at it. Probably with a sawed-off shotgun.'

'You got any enemies? Anyone with a grudge? Anyone who'd want to kill you?'

'Jesus, sonny, you don't have a notebook big enough to write down all the people who'd want that shanty Irish piece of trash dead.'

'Hello, Billy,' I said to my old neighbor Detective Sergeant Billy Devaney.

'Evening, Andy. Oh, that's a shame about the car getting shot.'

'Coulda been worse. Had one blown up once.'

'Just once?'

'Well, you know, underachievers,' I said with a shrug.

'You feel like telling me anything about who might have decided to shoot at you tonight? Not that you're worth the price of the rounds.' Billy was as charming as ever.

'No, idea. As you said, there's a bit of a list these days.'

'Anything to do with the case you're working on?'

'Honestly can't say.'

'Can't or won't?'

'Pretty much the same thing.'

'If you're thinking that you're going to go get in some sort of retributive gun battle, do me a favor and do it in another town. I don't need the ass ache.' He didn't mean to be an asshole, he'd just been one for so long that he didn't know any other way.

'Sure, sure. Can do, anything to help.' I was making hollow promises, but Billy wasn't expecting anything better.

The younger cop brought my gun, bullets and knife back, handing them to me in an awkward pile. I took them and put everything in their respective places. The cop looked a little uncomfortable. They were used to having a monopoly on who could carry a gun in this state. Anyone without a badge doing it tended to make them a little nervous.

'Roark, I'm serious, don't go shooting up my town, or I will pull your license so fast your head will spin.'

'Roger that, Sarge,' I said with palpable sarcasm. Both Devaney and the young cop looked as though they wanted to punch me in the face. Instead, Devaney said, not unkindly, 'Try not to get killed, Roark. My kid sister would be all broken up over it. Even after all these years.'

'I'll do my best,' I said to his back as he walked away.

Eventually, the other cops had enough information for their report, and they too left the alley. I was able to find an old towel in my office, wiped the glass off the back seat of the Maverick and managed to get a slim majority of it in a trash-can.

The kid in the video store was able to scrounge up a piece of clear plastic that had been used to wrap some promotional item in the store. I had half a roll of duct tape in my office and was able to make a half-assed rear window. It was like looking through a cataract, but it was better than nothing. A couple of strips of duct tape went on the roof and that was as good as it was going to get tonight.

I made it home without anyone else trying to kill me, not including the people who shouldn't drive in anything more than a snow flurry. Bad driving was too random to count as an actual attempt on my life. Sir Leominster was waiting, and it was nice to be home.

I settled in and poured myself a tallish whiskey. I called Angela Estrella.

'It's Roark,' I said when she answered.

'Any progress?' she asked in lieu of an actual greeting.

'Some. Someone tried to shoot me tonight.'

There was a sharp intake of breath on her end. 'Are you OK?'

'Yes. Sadly, my car isn't. It took the brunt of it.'

'Did you get them?'

'No, they got away. But I spent today and yesterday going around to hotels and camera stores showing everyone Lee Raymond's picture. I was leaving my office when someone unloaded a sawed-off twelve gauge into my car.'

'Raymond?'

'Probably, or his partner in crime. Either way, I would call this progress.'

'You have a funny sense of progress.'

'Someone at one of the hotels or camera stores must have contacted Raymond.'

'Sure, one of the people you talked to might be an accomplice of his.'

'I handed out my cards everywhere, and they have my office address and phone number on them.'

'They wouldn't be of much use if they didn't.'

'No, they wouldn't.'

'I'm surprised you don't have your home number on them to give out to women in bars.'

'Now you're just teasing me,' I said.

'Probably am,' she said. 'I'll call the judge and let him know about this development.'

We said our goodbyes. I put the phone down in the cradle and went to freshen up my tall glass of whiskey, which had gotten noticeably shorter during my conversation with Angela Estrella.

I was about to start thinking about dinner when my phone rang.

When I picked it up, Special Agent Brenda Watts of the FBI said, 'So, someone shot up your car. Why am I not surprised?'

'Hi, Brenda. I'm fine. How are you?'

'I hear that you are unhurt and that for once you managed not to shoot anyone.'

'By the time I bailed out of my car, he was gone. He blended into the evening foot traffic in front of my office. It didn't seem like a good idea to start ripping rounds off.'

'I'm surprised you didn't just pick someone at random and shoot them.'

'Brenda, come on. I'm not that trigger-happy. Besides, I'm the victim in this.'

'Ha! From what I hear, your car was the victim. You were just shooting adjacent.' After my last car was blown up, Brenda tried to say I was blown up. I had pointed out that I was just 'explosion adjacent.' Now she was using my own joke against me.

We talked for a few more minutes so that Brenda could reassure herself that I was actually all right. Her feelings for me were a mix of equal parts annoyance and frustration with a dash of near-maternal concern thrown in. Sadly, her feelings, as she had made clear on the occasions I had been brave enough to bring it up, were strictly platonic. She had also quite correctly figured out that I was a bad prospect, romantically speaking. It was my loss.

After she had hung up, I decided that I was too hungry to wait for the oven to get warm enough to heat up last night's leftover pizza. I would compensate for the cold pizza by having more whiskey on the rocks. I was good at adapting to adverse situations.

I took my dinner and drink over to the couch. The Movie Loft on TV38 was playing a movie I wasn't that interested in. However, WLVI TV56 had John Carpenter's *The Thing*.

It was at the beginning when the Norwegian helicopter is chasing the husky across Antarctica, with a guy shooting at the husky from the open rear door with a fancy German rifle. I was hooked. It was a Bell Jet Ranger, not a Huey, but it was still cool. It was about as different from my experiences in a helicopter as it could be, but it was still enough to grab my attention. It probably didn't hurt that it had started snowing outside.

Later, after the movie ended, I crawled into bed, glad I wasn't trapped out in the ice and snow of Antarctica with a hungry alien.

The next day, with the pale winter sunlight shining on it, the Maverick looked even worse than the night before. Bits of broken glass that I had missed glinted in the back like chips of ice. It started right up and drove as well as it always did, though. I drove it to Carney's shop, over by the Charles Street Jail.

Carney had sold me the Maverick when my beloved VW Karmann Ghia went to its fiery end. I was hoping he could work his magic on the Maverick. It was a good car that performed well without standing out. There was a lot to be said for being anonymous in my line of work.

When I wheeled the Maverick into the shop, Carney came over. He is a big man, more Scots than Irish, with big, scarred hands with prominent knuckles. He still wore what was left of his blonde hair in a high and tight, and even at rest, his face looked mean – 'piss mean,' as a drill sergeant of mine had once said. I didn't know many people who had fought with Carney. One look at him was usually enough to convince even the toughest of guys not to bother.

He let out a low whistle. 'Jesus, Andy, ya ever think of taking the T? You are rough on cars.'

'It's not me, I swear.'

'No, just people who don't like you.' He was looking closely at the cluster of holes, dents and raw metal in the trunk. 'Looks like a twelve gauge. Jealous husband?'

'No, a blackmailer.'

'Really? Huh.' Carney was the epitome of a man who'd seen too much, and that didn't leave enough room for shock or surprise. 'So whaddaya need?'

'Can you fix it?'

'Sure, gonna take a few days.'

'Can you give me a loaner?'

'Sure. I have something that I think will work. Wait here.'

I waited, listening to the sounds of work from the bays where Carney's mechanics plied the legitimate side of his business. He did good business servicing the cars of the regular people who lived in Back Bay. It was also a great way to wash the money he made on the side. I didn't ask too much, and I didn't want to know much. There were men who did what he did in every city in America, in the world for that matter. He wasn't actually in an organized crime family or a gang, but rather he was a vendor providing a service. He had his rules about how he conducted his business, and he had his code. I could live with it. Hell, who was I to judge? My hands weren't exactly clean.

He pulled up in a silver Ford Escort that was so plain it made my eyes hurt. Ford sold them by the score, and they were everywhere. They were just what America wanted in the Reagan era: small, efficient cars with good gas mileage that were about as exciting as a bowl of cold oatmeal.

He got out of it and handed me a set of keys. 'It's a work of art.'

'Sure, Picasso would be proud.'

'No, under the hood. It's got some pep, but the only thing that stands out less would be a taxi. Perfect for tailing people and easy to park in this town, too.'

'Well, that's something at least.'

'It's fast when you need it to be, and no one will look twice at it. It's perfect for you, Andy.'

'Are you trying to sell it to me or loan it to me?'

He just laughed and handed me the keys. 'Try it out for a few days. If you like it, we'll talk,' he said jokingly. 'No, I'll have the Maverick ready for you in a few days.'

'Thank you.' I liked the Maverick. I had gotten used to its throaty roar and horsepower to spare. It had a little style too, unlike the Escort I was in, which was about as exciting as a breadbox on four wheels.

I pulled out of Carney's and onto Charles Street. I wasn't sure where I was going. Part of me – the part that had run recon in Vietnam – wanted to go back to every place I had visited in the last two days and get some answers. I wanted to shake everyone I had talked to until someone gave me a line on Lee Raymond. The problem was I had talked to thirty or forty people. They may not have said anything to Raymond but to someone who knew him. I also spread my business card around. That was the problem with advertising that you were looking for the bad guy. Sometimes they find you first.

I drove over to the Public Library and found parking four blocks away. By Boston standards, that was almost right out front. I still had a few things about the case that I wanted to look into, and the walk over helped me put them in order in my head. I still had more questions about NT and C. Also, I was unlikely to be shot at in the Boston Public Library, and now that I was driving Carney's version of Wonder Woman's invisible jet, I already gave myself better odds at seeing another day.

I climbed up the steps and went into the warm, quiet building. The reference section was where I left it. I found a spot to drop my bag and my peacoat, on the collar of which I couldn't help but notice some small flecks of auto glass. The reference section had volume after volume of records of incorporation. I took the years that were relevant to the many permutations of NT and C. I settled into my seat with my legal pad and a blue felt-tipped pen. It took me a couple of hours and a headache, but I found something.

A law firm that had handled one of the corporate filings of NT and C when they swallowed up another company had an address at 17 Bowdoin Street. I didn't recognize the name of the law firm, but I knew the address. That was where my old friend Danny Sullivan had his office at the time the documents were filed. Now, that might be a coincidence, except for the fact that Danny was a Mob lawyer. It made me wonder: who really owned the trucking company that had hauled the waste away? It also made me wonder: who had really invested in NT and C?

Maybe it was time to reacquaint myself with my old friend. We had grown up together in Southie, gone to high school together, and we were close. His daughters called me Uncle Andy. I hadn't spoken to him since November of 1982 when a case he had set me up with went badly awry, and I had almost been killed. Correctly or not, I blamed him and threatened to kill him if he crossed my path again. I had calmed down a little since then, which was good because I was going to have to talk to him.

I packed up my legal pad and pens and headed out to the silver breadbox on wheels. I didn't like the bucket seats in the Ford Breadbox as much as I liked the bench seat in the Maverick. I couldn't imagine putting a pizza on the passenger-side bucket seat and not having it slop onto the floor. That and I couldn't see myself sliding easily across the bucket seats if someone happened to be shooting up the Ford Breadbox. On the other hand, there were so many of them on the road that it was nearly invisible. I would just have to be careful about parking it in a big parking lot, as I might confuse it with one of the many other Breadboxes parked there.

Out of an abundance of caution, I stopped to pick up a sandwich on my way to the office. I didn't want to lose my edge because I was faint with hunger. No one seemed to be following me, and the tasty, tasty turkey melt on seedless rye with Russian dressing would keep me well fed.

I parked a couple of blocks from my office building and decided to go in the front door. I slipped the .38 in my outer pocket and kept my hands in my peacoat pocket for more than just warmth. I had kept an eye on the plate-glass windows and crossed the street unnecessarily a couple of times to make sure that no one was tailing me. It was all stuff I had learned from watching Michael Caine in spy movies on the Movie Loft.

No one was waiting for me in the hallway or upstairs in my office. Satisfied that I was alone, I slipped the .38 back into its holster in my waistband. I sat down at my desk and alternated between eating the sandwich and writing case notes. I managed to do both without slopping too much Russian dressing on my chin or my notes. I don't know why Russian dressing gets everywhere and mayonnaise doesn't. One of life's persistent mysteries, I guess.

Everything I heard and saw of Lee Raymond's record to the half-assed-at-best attempt on my life told me that he wasn't the mastermind behind this whole scheme. That made finding Danny's address in the filing papers all the more significant. If Danny had been involved with anything to do with NT and C, then that guaranteed Mob involvement. Which would point to someone else pulling Lee Raymond's strings. I was sure that the Mob wouldn't mind having a judge under their thumb.

It would also make sense that the Mob would use a hustler like Raymond who seemed to be doing life on the installment plan. There were certain taboos in mafia culture, and being the male version of the honey trap wouldn't work for their rank and file, no matter what they were into in private. Raymond was both a hustler and had the right predilections for the job.

I picked up the phone and called Devaney at headquarters. It rang and rang; I hung up after listening to it ring six or seven times. I thought about calling Watts, but I wasn't sure that would have had anything to do with the case so much as my liking the sound of her voice. I called Devaney again, and this time he answered.

'Devaney, Detectives.' He said it like he was angry at the phone for ringing.

'Billy, Andy Roark here.'

'Hi, Andy. I'm assuming this isn't a call to ask how my health is, seeing as you only call when you want something.'

'Well, seeing as you're still sore at me for asking your kid sister out almost twenty years ago, I try to limit my calls.'

'You're just using your friends at the BPD so you don't have to do any actual detective work.'

'More or less,' I said. There was no point in trying to convince him otherwise.

'Well, at least you're an honest piker. What do you need?'

'I was hoping you could tell me who Lee Raymond's parole officer is.'

'Anything in it for me?'

'I'll go away and not bother you.'

'Sold. Give me five minutes so I can pull his file. I'll call you back.'

'Sure, sure.' He hung up without saying goodbye, but at least I was spared the inevitable half-joking, half-meant insult. He called me shanty Irish trash not because he thought he was better than me, but because he felt I was never good enough for his kid sister. He felt the need to remind me of it to this day. My phone rang five minutes later. Devaney was true to his word.

'Devaney, you shanty Irish prick,' I said by way of greeting.

'Who is Devaney, and what is a shanty Irish prick compared to other pricks?' Angela asked, half laughing.

'Sorry. I was expecting a call from someone else.'

'A shanty Irish prick, apparently.'

'Actually, yes. A detective sergeant on BPD. We grew up in the same neighborhood.'

'Oh, that explains everything,' she said sarcastically.

'I was asking him for information about Lee Raymond's PO.'

'PO?'

'Parole officer. They usually know more about a criminal than anyone.'

'Ah, that makes sense. On another note, what are you doing tomorrow night?'

'I didn't have anything planned. Are you asking me out?'

'Sort of. The judge and his wife are having a party. He wants to talk to you but wants to be discreet.'

'And tomorrow night?' I asked pointedly.

'He's throwing a New Year's Eve party. He figured you could come as my date.'

'Well, that is very cloak-and-dagger of him. What is your real date going to say to being displaced by the likes of me?'

'I didn't have a date. I usually don't for these things.'

'Oh.' I said it because I genuinely didn't know what to say. I wasn't sure how it was possible that a woman like Angela would be single.

'I don't suppose you have a tuxedo. It's black tie optional.'

'A tuxedo, no.' Who did she think I was, James Bond?

'A suit. Even someone like you must own a suit.'

'Sure, I picked one up from the Salvation Army last year. The pants almost cover my ankles.'

'Great,' she said unenthusiastically. 'Pick me up at seven.'

She told me her address and waited while I wrote it down. Then she hung up.

My phone rang again a few minutes later. This time it was the shanty Irish prick.

'Your guy's PO is Joe Pinto. I know Joe; he's a straight shooter.' Devaney recited his number, and I wrote it down underneath Angela Estrella's address.

'Thanks, Billy.'

'You're welcome. Now fuck off and let me do my job.'

I picked up the phone again and called Joe Pinto. His phone rang several times and then was picked up by someone else at the Probation and Parole Office. I left a message explaining who I was, why I was calling and where I could be reached. POs were a funny breed; they weren't law enforcement but they weren't exactly for the defense either. I knew some who were just punching a time clock, and I knew others who were really trying to help their people. This meant that sometimes they would talk to me, sometimes not. I was hoping that Joe Pinto was different.

I killed a couple more hours by going to see my barber to get my hair and moustache cleaned up. It wasn't an actual date, but I still wanted to look good. When I left the barber's, he had done a good job of trimming my hair while still leaving it on the long side. My moustache had been neatened up too.

I then steered the silver Breadbox toward Bowdoin Street. Parking was a mess, but I was lucky enough to find a spot for the Breadbox not too far from Tremont Street. The bar I was looking for was on the corner of Beacon and Bowdoin. It was a bar two blocks from Danny's office that he liked to stop off at before heading home to Maryanne and the girls. Danny and I used to meet there regularly to hang out or, if I was working a case for him, to talk about it. Maryanne liked me, but she was always trying to introduce me to nice girls I was supposed to fall in love, settle down and start families with. That was not the plan I was following.

It was four thirty when I pushed through the door. It wasn't crowded yet, but the 'sneak out of the office a few minutes early' crowd was claiming territory. I thought that I would get there before Danny, who was never one to leave the office early, but he was sitting at the bar. Even with his back turned to me, his shoulders a little more slumped and a little heavier, I knew it was him. We had known each other for more than twenty years.

I slid up and sat down on the stool next to him. The bartender drifted over just as Danny looked up in the mirror and recognized me. He paled a bit under his beard. To be fair, he might have been under the impression that I was there to hurt him.

'Löwenbräu, please, and another for him,' I said, pointing to Danny's almost empty glass.

'Jesus, Andy . . .' he started, his voice a bit on the high side.

'Relax. I am here to talk.'

'You said you'd kill me if you saw me again.' His face was a little fuller, and his beard and moustache were still red and neatly trimmed. Other than the small burst veins in his cheekbones and dark circles under his eyes, he hadn't changed much.

'Well, I was angry at the time. You almost got me killed.'

'Andy, I told you, I never meant for that to happen.'

'I know. Water under the bridge.' I waved my hand magnanimously.

'Really? You're over it.'

'No, but I can see that it wasn't what you intended.' I didn't bother telling him that I had other old friends who had actually tried to kill me. The drinks came, and he picked up his unpronounceable Scotch and took a big sip. I pulled on the long neck of the Löwenbräu.

'It wasn't. Andy, you're my oldest friend. I could never.'

'We covered all that three years ago. You made a choice. It almost got me killed. You have some freight to carry on this one. It got a man killed, but he made his bed.' Also, he was going to kill me at the time of his demise, but there was no point letting Danny off the hook, especially as I needed information from him.

'Oh, OK.' He turned back to his drink and then his IBM-like brain kicked in. 'Andy, why are you here?'

'I'm working on a case. A judge is being blackmailed in a civil case involving a company that dumped waste illegally. While looking into it, I noticed that the law firm that did some legal work for them had a name I didn't recognize but an address that I did.' I paused both for dramatic effect and to take another sip of beer.

'You know I can't talk about any legal work I've done. No lawyer can talk about their clients.'

'Danny, you put a chain of events in motion three years ago that meant I had to shoot a man . . . kill a man. He was there to kill me, and he was there because you or your clients sent him. In the history of people who "owe me one," you are at the top of the list.' I watched his shoulders slump and the false hope that I might have come by to renew our friendship slip away. 'Now, I am not looking to send anyone to jail or hurt anyone. I just want to help my client.'

'Andy, you know the people I work for.'

'I do, yes.'

'They won't talk to you, and if they have a money-making scheme, they won't stop it. Not even for you.'

'I just want to talk to someone who can make decisions. Reason with them.'

'Andy, you don't reason with these people. You don't talk to them. They run a lucrative empire. If you get in their way . . . they kill you. That's it. No finesse, no discussion.'

'Well, buddy boy, that is why you are going to convince them.'

'No, uh-ah, no way.' He looked queasy just thinking about it.

'You're their counselor, counselor. Give them good advice. If not, I will become very, very bad for their business. You know I can be irritating.' I fished my wallet out and threw a twenty on the bar. 'Nice talking to you. I'll be waiting for your call.'

I left him at the bar feeling more like a bully than proud of myself. Danny wasn't tough; he never had been. But there was a lot riding on this. A decent man was being squeezed. A community of people who were poisoned were counting on the system to make it right. Those were reasons enough to put pressure on my one-time friend. For once, he could feel what it was like to be the one getting squeezed.

SIX

I wasn't lying to Angela about having a nice suit. I had, however, been joking about it coming from the Salvation Army or being ill-fitting. It was from Brooks Brothers and was dark but not quite navy blue. It was wool, double-breasted. Instead of a shirt and tie, I chose a turtleneck in a darker shade of blue. I thought it made me look like a well-dressed man out of a movie from the 1930s. I was certain I would be the only one at the party with a gun and knife on him. The whole ensemble was well suited to the last few hours of 1985. It had been a tough year, and I wasn't sorry to see the last of it.

I parked the Ford Breadbox in front of Angela Estrella's apartment. Hers was a brownstone not too far from the Harvard Club. I waited on her steps with the collar of my peacoat turned up against the wind and my scarf folded under my chin. I pressed her doorbell, and a minute later she buzzed me in. I walked up the stairs to her second-floor apartment where she was waiting by the door, which she had opened a crack.

'You made it on time.'

'I did. I even wore a suit.'

'Good, nice to see you can take direction. Come in.' She opened the door and stood back. She was wearing a black cocktail dress that matched her dark hair and eyes. The dress was more suggestive than revealing, but it was enough to make me contemplate what was underneath?

I followed her into her apartment, which didn't seem much bigger than mine, but hers had a fireplace, and I would have killed for one. The couch was a shade off white and, like the couple of chairs, lamps and other furniture, it was modern and tasteful. There were framed prints, mostly modern art, on the walls. There was a rug on the floor that reminded me of a sheep's fleece, and if there was a dust bunny in the place, I would be shocked.

'What do you think?'

'Of the apartment or the dress?'

'Both.'

'You look stunning,' I said truthfully. 'The apartment looks very chic.'

'Do you spend a lot of time in chic places?'

'Ha, no. My job is not glamorous, and the places I go, even less so.'

'I can imagine. Give me a minute.' She disappeared and reappeared a few minutes later with fresh lipstick on and a thin wrap for her shoulders.

'Give me a hand with this,' she said, pointing to her coat, which I held for her while she slipped into it. She slipped the wrap in her pocket. We went out, locking up and making first-date type of small talk. We headed south out of the city on Route 3. His Honor lived in Duxbury, which was about forty-five minutes or several hundred thousand dollars a year out of the city, depending on if you were driving to it or trying to move in.

The Ford Breadbox certainly didn't have much going for it in the cool department, but the heater worked, which made the ride cozy. The advantage of not actually being on a date was that there was no pressure on either part.

'How did you end up as a clerk for the judge?'

'It's kind of a long story that's not so long.'

'Try me.'

'My family is from Portugal. There weren't a lot of opportunities there, and my father moved here in the early fifties. He and my mother and my older brother Gustavo.'

'Where here?'

'Fall River. There were jobs in the mill, and there was a strong Portuguese community. He and my mother moved here, and I was born shortly after, and my two sisters followed along. Growing up, we lived in a three-decker.' Three-storied houses, built around the mill towns, were as common as pine trees in Canada. 'As a kid, I didn't know that we were poor. We always had food and clothes, toys at Christmas and birthdays, but there wasn't anything extra. Gus went to work in the factory when he was sixteen. I did well in school and wanted to go to college, but there was no money. The two big career fields for girls in my neighborhood were the mills or getting married and having kids. Neither appealed to me.'

'So you moved to the big city?'

'No. I went to work in the mill. On weekends, I waitressed and saved my money. I also managed not to get married or pregnant. When I was twenty, I had enough money saved up to move to Boston. I worked waitressing and went to Bunker Hill Community College. I got my associate's degree a couple of years later and applied for a job in the clerk's office. A few years after that, I ended up working with the judge.'

'Been with him ever since?'

'Yes. He's been a mentor to me. He encouraged me to go back and get my bachelor's degree. There were times when he would slip a little extra cash into Christmas cards or find ways to help me get a little extra overtime so that I could get through school. He's been really good to me.'

'He seems like a nice man.' This definitely didn't seem like the right venue to bring up the judge's infidelity.

'He's more than that . . . he's decent – a decent man. I saw living in Fall River, in the mill town, as a dead end. Life there, in my community, didn't offer much for women other than pregnancy and a mill job, and if you were lucky, maybe you'd marry a guy who wouldn't knock you around too much.'

'That sounds like the same kind of neighborhood I was running away from in Southie. Except in my case, it wasn't college but an Army recruiter.' That wasn't exactly true. I had tried a semester at the University of Rhode Island, but it didn't take.

'Your neighborhood was a dead end too?'

'Sure, graduate high school if you were lucky, get a job in the mill, get drunk on the weekends with the guys, meet a girl and start a family. Or go into a life holding up liquor stores and doing small-time crime. It was the same trap as yours just with corned beef and cabbage on the table, is all.'

'I saw it as a one-way ticket to misery.'

'Me too.'

'Was that how you ended up in Vietnam?'

'More or less. My father was a paratrooper in World War Two. He didn't talk much about it, but I know that he wanted a life for himself outside of Southie and working at the mill. When my turn came, the Army seemed like the only real option. I enlisted and then volunteered for Airborne School and then Special Forces.'

'Geez, a real live tough guy. How long were you over there?'

'Three years, give or take.'

'You liked it that much?'

'It wasn't that I liked it, but I felt like for the first time in my life I was doing something that mattered. Something important.'

'Fighting and killing?'

'Yes. My country was at war, and that was the only thing I had to offer. I was good at it, and I was with the finest soldiers in the world. It was like being an Olympic athlete. Also, I worked on small teams; the guys were like brothers to me. I never had that before.'

'Why did you leave the Army?'

'I only wanted to stay in if I was in Special Forces. Big Army is chickenshit. If I stayed in Special Forces, I would have stayed in Vietnam and I would have been killed.' As the recon missions wore on, I found that I was taking more risks, and it was only a matter of time before my luck ran out. An officer I worked with used to talk about 'Roark's luck.' I was smart enough to know it was finite.

'Most likely.'

'One day, Sergeant Major Billy Justice pointed out that I was running low on my nine lives.' Actually, he had found me at the Recon Club and bought me a Chivas and beer. Then he suggested that I was getting burned out on a team, and maybe I should consider being a Covey Rider. Covey Riders were experienced team guys who ended up flying with Air Force Forward Air Controllers, helping direct teams on the ground when they were in trouble. It was still plenty dangerous, and Billy made it clear that it wasn't exactly a suggestion.

'So, you came home.'

'Eventually.'

'Then what?'

'I joined the cops in Boston and went to night school to get my degree.'

'What was your degree in?'

'Political science.'

'Well, that's almost useful for a private eye.'

I would have shot back some sort of pithy reply, but we had

arrived. Duxbury – or, as it is known by us peasants, Deluxe-bury – is a town that sits smack in the middle of the South Shore. It is shoehorned by Marshfield to its immediate north and Plymouth to its immediate south. The water views and beaches are all of Plymouth Bay, and what used to be the first Colonial farmland was also home to some of the oldest old money in New England.

I wasn't sure when the Messers had first arrived in Deluxe-bury, but judging by the judge's house, their money was old and there was plenty of it. It wasn't exactly a mansion, but the pile of yellow-painted clapboard and black shutters with matching trim was perched on a hill at the end of a very long driveway. I counted four chimneys and lost count of the windows at the front of the place. Each window had a little electric light like a candle giving off a warm glow. There was still a wreath on the door, and I am sure if I had been here on Christmas Eve, there would have been real live carolers too.

Cars seemed to be parked at the side of the driveway, and we found a spot behind a nifty-looking Audi. Most of the other cars were Mercedes or Jaguars. There were a couple of Lincolns and Cadillacs smattered in with them, but they were more the exception than the rule. The Ford Breadbox looked decidedly exotic with its affordable price tag next to all the other high-tone cars.

We walked up the driveway and the steps to the wide covered porch. By covered, I mean that the columns holding up the overhanging roof three floors up kept the snow off. The place made me instinctively want to find the back or side entrance.

Inside, after we had left our coats on hangers on one of those hotel-style rolling racks, we found the bar. White wine for the lady and Scotch and soda for me. Fortified, we went looking for the judge so that we could have our clandestine debriefing. We walked through the groups of lawyers, judges, court folk and the country club set, and I was struck by the oak paneling being hidden by copious amounts of artwork. There was something about the place that reminded me of the Harvard Club in Boston. If I had the same feelings of not belonging here as I did there, I didn't notice, but that had something to do with Angela hanging on my arm.

We eventually found the judge in a large room with a huge fireplace, complete with a roaring fire and a Christmas tree that looked like an understudy for the one in Rockefeller Plaza. Once we had circumnavigated the room, we ended up standing next to the judge by the fire. He saw us and nodded, then said something to the distinguished-looking couple he was talking to. Even if the room wasn't quite the size of an airplane hangar, it would have been impossible to hear what he said over the din of the revelers.

He broke away from the couple and made his way right to us. He gave Angela a fatherly peck on the cheek and shook my hand.

'Mr Roark, it was good of you to come on short notice.'

'My pleasure, Your Honor.'

'Let's find a place to talk away from the din.'

He led us out of the noisy throng, and after a few twists and turns, we ended up in a much smaller book-filled room that was clearly his home office. There were a couple of Rowlandson prints on the wall, and most of the books on the bookshelves were law-related. The centerpiece was a framed movie poster of *Inherit the Wind* with Spencer Tracy scowling down at us.

The judge saw me looking at it. 'Do you like it?'

'Yes, I remember the movie. I saw it on TV, or maybe we saw it in high school.'

'It changed my life.'

'Really, how?' I had liked the movie but hadn't found it life-changing, but I was certain that the judge would say the same of *The Green Berets*. Spencer Tracy and John Wayne were in different leagues, though I loved Tracy in *Bad Day at Black Rock*.

'I was a lawyer for a large local company. I can't tell you which one, but they were substantial. It was my job to protect them from litigation, which in those days was mostly from other companies. Class action suits were unheard of. I toured their factories and saw the conditions their workers worked in.

'They weren't horrible, not like a POW camp, but they were bad enough. I saw a lot of people who were toiling, mostly immigrants – Irish, Italian, Portuguese – struggling to earn a living. Sometimes they would get hurt at work, and then it was public assistance at best for them. It was a living, but it wasn't a calling.

'Anyway, one night I was sitting in the theater, watching Spencer Tracy talk about the pretty rocking horse, and how it was pretty on the outside, but the wood had rotted, and the thing fell apart. That spoke to me. I knew then that it couldn't just be about enriching myself but that I had to find a way to do good.'

'By being a judge?'

'It took some years, but yes. I felt that I could judge things through a more compassionate lens. That I could . . . I could do some good from the bench.'

'I see.'

'This isn't just about someone blackmailing me, Mr Roark. Someone is trying to subvert the course of justice, the law itself. People have been hurt, and the court is their last recourse. If I let this happen, then everything I believe in is at stake.'

'I understand that, sir.' I did. My job might not be much, my life might not be much, but I believe in right and wrong. I could feel his anguish at having to choose between his moral code and a scandal that would no doubt ruin him.

'I'm not saying that I've made a decision in the case, but a judge, any judge, must be able to render a decision free of duress. If we do not have that, then our whole system is broken, and we might as well live in a banana republic.'

'Believe me, sir, I get it.'

'Angela tells me that someone tried to kill you.'

'Yes, two nights ago, someone emptied a sawed-off shotgun into my car while I was sitting in it.'

'You weren't hit?'

'No, the car heroically took the brunt of it.' I smiled what I thought of as my most charming smile at them. 'By the time I bailed out of the car, he was gone.'

'Mr Roark, I think we should go to the authorities. I don't want you to be hurt on my behalf.'

'Sir, you pay me to take risks. I know what those risks are, and frankly, the minute I walk away from a job because it's dangerous, I might as well walk away from all of them. It's the nature of the beast.'

'OK, thank you. Why did someone shoot at you?'

'Well, I have been shaking the trees looking for Lee Raymond, which, by the way, is not his real name. His real name is Raymond Lee Keith.'

'Oh.'

'Yeah, it doesn't sound as nice. Let's just call him Lee Raymond. Anyway, I talked to a friend of mine in the photography business. He laid out how Raymond was able to take the photos. It required adjoining rooms and an accomplice. Anyway, I went to the hotels and the camera stores flashing his picture around and leaving my card all over the Commonwealth.' Well, not the whole Commonwealth, but I wanted the judge to feel he was getting his money's worth. 'A couple of nights ago, someone was waiting for me in the alley behind my office.'

'Raymond?'

'Or his accomplice.'

'Surely in your line of work, you've made enemies. Could it be any of them?'

'None of them have tried to kill me lately, and the timing is awfully coincidental.'

'So, you think it was Raymond.'

'Most likely. However, there is one other wrinkle.'

'What is that?'

'I've found a link, a tenuous link, to organized crime.'

'The Mafia? How are they involved?'

'One of the companies involved in the shipping of waste from NT and C used the services of a Mob lawyer I am acquainted with.' I didn't feel like going into my history with Danny Sullivan.

'Mafia involvement seems . . . a bit much.'

'I know and agree, but there is a connection, and I wouldn't be doing my job if I didn't look into it. There could be any number of reasons why they might want to pressure you. They also have the resources to run a complicated operation like this.'

'Complicated how?'

'I don't think it was an accident that Raymond was at your hotel in Florida. It also wasn't an accident that a very private part of your life was targeted. Someone had to know about how to use the cameras – in this case, one that was muffled – in an air vent with pictures taken on an auto-shutter. That meant they had to scope out the hotel rooms well in advance to know which ones would fit the bill. Adjoining rooms and a vent that looked out on the bed. The photos had to be developed somewhere, and someone had to front all of the money for the rooms, two per meeting.' I refrained from saying rendezvous because the judge already had a pained look on his face.

'I see. I suppose that when you break it down like that, it does seem a bit complicated.'

'The Mob might not be involved, and I will keep trying to track Raymond down. I have left messages with his parole officer and hope to meet up with him soon. After that, I have a few other angles that I can pursue.'

'You will be careful. I would feel awful if you were hurt on my behalf.'

'Of course, sir. Careful is my middle name.'

'Sure, that's how you got your ear lobe shot off,' Angela said sarcastically but not harshly.

'I can't complain about someone else's bad aim.'

'Well, don't run into anyone with good aim,' she said.

'Sure, I'll do my best.'

'I should get back to Gladys and the guests. Please stay and enjoy yourselves.' He excused himself and stepped back into the fray.

'Do you think the Mob is actually behind this?' Angela asked me.

'I don't know. It's too soon to tell, but I bet they wouldn't mind having a judge in the palm of their hand.'

'But he isn't a criminal judge.'

'No, but if they are involved with NT and C, they might have money at stake, or maybe they don't want anyone looking too closely at NT and C's finances. This might be a pretty convenient turn of events for them.'

'OK, that makes sense.'

'Someone put Lee Raymond in the judge's path, and he couldn't work the camera and be in the photos too . . .' I trailed off. Her face wore a pained expression, and I was being overly clinical about someone she cared a great deal about. 'I'm sorry, sometimes I don't think before I say things.'

'You didn't say anything you shouldn't have. It's just tough to see him go through this. He is a good man. When I told him you had been shot at, he wanted to release you from the case.'

'Well, that is nice of him, but . . .'

'I talked him out of it. I told him you were pretty tough and that you wouldn't walk away from a case just because someone shot at you.'

'He needs my help, and I'm not the type to cut and run when things get dicey.'

'I know. I spoke to Terry McVicker about you, remember? He said you were – and I quote – "a genuine badass."'

'He just likes me because I pick up the tab more often than not.'

'I don't think that's it,' she said smiling at me. The room felt a little warmer.

'Want to get a drink and see what's going on with the party?'

'No,' she said, stepping closer to me and putting her arms around my neck, pulling my mouth down to hers. We kissed, reminding me of something that I hadn't felt since I was a teenager. A sort of breathless anticipation of what was about to happen next.

After a time, she stepped back, literally keeping me at arm's length. 'That was nice.'

'Yes, it was.'

'Now we should rejoin the party,' she said, taking my hand in hers.

Beyond the open door, the din had risen, fueled by the judge's open bar and the arrival of a regiment of friends, colleagues and hangers-on. Instead of leading me back to the party proper, however, Angela led me over to the coat rack. 'Roark, let's get out of here.'

'Change your mind about rejoining the party?'

'It's a lady's prerogative.'

'Who am I to argue with a lady?'

SEVEN

Nineteen eighty-six was shaping up to be a good year, I thought, letting myself back into my apartment in the late morning. Sir Leominster met me at the door and meowed accusingly. He didn't approve of my staying out all night. Not on moral grounds but because it meant that his breakfast was delayed. He was a pragmatic cat whose chief passion in life came in a can and smelled like the hold of an old fishing boat.

We went back to her apartment, and she made us Martinis. She made them dry, and by dry, I mean splashing vermouth over ice cubes, swirling the shaker then dumping out the vermouth. She then added vodka and shook the shaker until it was coated with frost. She poured the drinks into appropriate glasses. We sat on her couch drinking, chatting about our childhoods, and making out while the TV played with the sound off. Dick Clark was freezing his ass off in Times Square, and we eventually made our way off the couch and into the bedroom after the second Martini disappeared. We never did see gravity work its magic in Times Square.

At some point, she got up and turned off the TV, and then came back to bed, her chilled skin against mine.

'Roark, are you awake?'

'Yes.'

'I don't do this all the time.'

'Do what?'

'Hop into bed with guys I barely know.'

'Usually, by the time most women get to know me, they want to hop out of bed.'

'I'm serious.'

'Me too. I have lousy luck with women.' There had been a few disasters lately.

'Ha! Something tells me you do all right,' she said with her head on my chest.

'Um, a gentleman never tells. I am OK at meeting women. They just don't seem to end up staying around.'

'Your winning ways?'

'I am not necessarily easy to live with, and a lot of them find my job romantic or interesting until the reality of it hits them.'

'Well, I have no interest in living with you if that is any consolation. As for your work, it doesn't seem very stable.'

'It isn't. The hours are usually long. Sometimes I get banged up or sometimes I am quiet. On occasion, women have seen me in confrontations. It is a turn-off. It looks great in the movies, but in reality, it's ugly and mean.'

'Not the stuff that most women care for.'

'Exactly.' I glossed over the stuff about the nightmares or the fact that part of me never left Vietnam. That sometimes I got in a funk because I couldn't understand why I was alive and better men than me weren't. Men that I called my brothers. That didn't seem like the stuff to talk about the first time in bed with a woman I liked. There was enough awkwardness with new lovers; no need to bring the war into it.

'Well, you make up for it by being tall enough and handsome in a slightly battered-looking way.'

'That is exactly what I go for.'

We drifted off to sleep, and in the morning, I woke up alone in her bed. I pulled on my pants and found her in the kitchen making coffee.

'Hi.'

'I thought you might want some coffee,' she said, pointing to one of those drip machines that was making weak, brown, coffee-flavored liquid.

'I wouldn't say no to a cup.' She was staring at me and I said, 'What, do I have something on my face?'

'No. No, sorry. I just don't think I've seen someone with as many scars as you have . . . with scars from being shot.'

'Some of it's shrapnel. I did three tours in Vietnam . . . it took its toll.' I didn't bother pointing out the one caused by white phosphorous.

'The one on your arm is newer.'

'Last spring.'

'Working on a case?'

'Yes. I got lucky.' I had jumped off a ship before a Vietnamese gangster could blow more holes into me with his submachine gun.

'Jesus.'
'You said something about coffee.'
'Oh, yes. Of course.'

I fully appreciated the fact that she was wearing just a Red Sox T-shirt that was a little too big for her and a little too small for polite company. After coffee and toast, we reached that almost awkward lull in conversation that signaled it was time for me to leave. She kissed me at the door, and I went down her steps into the cold morning air of the new year.

Back at my apartment, after Sir Leominster's culinary requirements had been met, I checked the flashing light on the machine. There was a message from my old friend Chris. Chris and I had met in Special Forces training. He was going through the course to be a medic, and we were separated only to link up again in Vietnam. A year ago, when I was out in San Francisco working a case, he and some of his biker buddies came and saved my ass. His buddies by providing some muscle, and Chris by treating a bullet wound in my arm. The nice thing about having an SF medic who earned his way by treating biker gang members' wounds was that the police never were involved in my shooting.

His slightly drunk voice down the line from San Francisco to wish me a happy New Year. He called to check on me most holidays. We had lost a close friend from Special Forces training while we were in Vietnam, and I think he was worried that I would be next.

There was another message from the sergeant major asking if I was going to the reunion. Telling me I should send my check in soon as time was running out. The sergeant major was persistent; I had to give him that. He probably thought that I'd be at home nursing a hangover.

I showered and spent the rest of New Year's Day lazing about my apartment. I alternated between reading about Dien Bien Phu, and, in keeping with the French theme, reading a Maigret novel. I was tired and felt a little worked over, so the time on the couch listening to jazz was a nice break. I could go back to being shot at tomorrow when it wasn't a holiday.

That night in my dreams, I was in the bunker with the blown-apart deer. My dead friend Tony walked in with his face that was half normal and half shot to pieces. He had died when the VC sappers attacked the camp at Nha Trang. Chris and I had lived, neither of us ever understanding why. Tony said something to the deer, and then to me he said, 'He doesn't even play belote.' The deer threw his cards down in disgust, and I woke up.

I bundled up in thermals and a sweat suit, a wool watch cap on my head, and went for a run to clear my head. I had enough ghosts taking up real estate in my nightly dreams without Tony and some French-speaking deer that I had inadvertently killed too. The exercise and the cold wind off the Charles did their job, and by the time I was home and showering, my mind was back on the case.

When I got to the office, the light was flashing on the machine. The first message was from an old SF buddy asking if I was going to the reunion. The sergeant major had probably put him up to it. He was shaping up to be a formidable adversary.

The second message was from Joe Pinto, finally returning my calls. He didn't say much more than that he was getting back to me and he'd try again later.

The last was from a guy telling me that he had information about Lee Raymond. He would meet me at an address on Mass Ave near Melnea Cass Boulevard at twelve thirty. The voice sounded muffled, like in the old movies when they try to throw someone off by holding a handkerchief over the handset. It sounded hinky. It was, however, the only thing that looked like a lead that I had. I guess I had a lunch date.

I called Joe Pinto back, and for once was rewarded by his answering the phone. 'Probation, Pinto.'

'It's Andy Roark, thank you for getting back to me.'

'You're the PI looking for information on Raymond Lee Keith.'

Thanks to *Magnum P.I.*, everyone called private detectives PIs now, but, in all fairness, I have been called a lot worse. 'Yep. I know him as Lee Raymond.'

'Uh-oh, that doesn't sound good if he's using another name. Has he done anything to violate his probation?'

'Um, he seems involved in extortion. Does that count?'

'It most certainly does. How can I help you?'

'I was trying to find an address for him. Place of employment, someplace he's living, a relative who might know where he is. That sort of thing.'

'Yeah, well. He hasn't checked in for a few months.'

'Wouldn't that violate his probation?'

'No, he's not on monthlies anymore, and his behavior has been good.'

'OK, so how long has it been?'

'Six months or so. He was doing well, and then I got sick. Honestly, though, I have a lot of cases, and he wasn't a troublemaker. You know what I mean?'

'Sure, sure. I get it.' Pinto was buried up to his neck in cases, and a guy who was working and not getting jammed up with the cops could skate under the radar for a while.

'Let me grab his file. Hang on a minute.'

I waited, listening to the sounds of him opening and closing a filing cabinet.

'OK, I'm back.' He read off addresses for a hotel in Quincy, a warehouse down by the harbor and a gallery that Raymond had worked at. He also gave me the name and address of an aunt who lived in Brockton.

'He has a pretty long record. Do you know who his lawyer is?' I asked.

'Yep. Looks like he's had a couple of lawyers.' Pinto read off a few names, but I only recognized one of them: Terry McVicker. Was Terry involved or was it a coincidence? The criminal court system in Boston was a small community, and you tended to run into the same lawyers on cases.

'OK, thanks, man, I appreciate it.'

'No problem. Do me a favor, will you? If you come across him, let me know where he is.'

'Sure,' I said, knowing that if I found Lee Raymond, there were probably a few other discussions that we were going to have first.

I decided to check the addresses in town and then head to Quincy and Brockton after meeting with the mysterious caller. I navigated the Ford Breadbox through the streets, down toward the waterfront. Not the part that was being gentrified for the yuppies, but the part that was still a working port out by Castle Island. Recently, the whole thing was renamed the Paul W. Conley Container Terminal. I wasn't going to the terminal itself, but the warehouse I wanted was near enough to it.

The warehouse had a small parking lot for visitors. There was a bigger parking lot for the workers on the long side of the building. The bigger lot had mounds of dirty snow where it had been plowed. I went in the visitor's entrance and found myself inside a small office where a woman was sitting behind a desk with a phone pressed to one ear and one of those thin cigarettes they market to ladies burning between her brightly painted lips. She looked up at me over the rims of her half-moon reading glasses and held up her index finger. Her hair was a dark shade that I was guessing came out of a bottle, because I am pretty sure that she had been born when being a 'flapper' was all the rage. She hung up the phone and looked up.

'You Tony's guy?'

'No.'

'You're not the guy Tony was supposed to send over?'

'Nope.'

'Who are you?'

'Name's Roark. I am a private investigator. A guy who used to work here applied for a job, and they hired me to do a background check on him.'

'What's his name?'

'Raymond Keith.'

'Yeah, he used to work here.'

'Was he a good employee?'

'Nope. He was just here because he needed a job, and his PO sent him here.'

I smiled at her. 'I take it he wasn't management, then?'

She snorted. 'No, honey, he was a con. They work cheap and don't complain much. The owner likes that.'

'He got any friends who still work here?'

'No. He worked here almost ten years ago. We have a lot of turnover.'

'He left an impression.'

'He was good-looking, and guys just out of the stir aren't too picky about the bed they stay in, if you know what I mean.' She smiled the weary smile of someone who had been taught by the world to take what little joy she could find wherever she could find it and not ask too many questions.

'I get you.'

'Look, he was good in the sack if you don't mind being tossed around. Other than that, I can't say much that's good about him. Tell your client not to hire unless they don't mind being stolen from or getting conned.'

'There were problems?'

'Only if you call taking off with the petty cash a problem.'

'Did the owner report him to his PO?'

'Sure. He called right away. Called the cops too.'

'What happened?'

'Nothing. Cops said the owner couldn't prove who took the cash.'

'That's the theft part. What about the con?'

'That was my own stupidity. He said he needed money to help his mom out.'

'I see.'

'Yeah, sure. You got any more questions?'

'No. Thanks.'

'You're welcome, hon. Now I gotta figure out where Tony's guy is. Bye.'

'Bye.'

Outside, the sun was shining, and bits of ice and snow were melting. It sounded almost like a mountain stream, except this was Boston down by the port, and the smell of diesel reminded me of where I was.

I got back in the Breadbox and headed back into town. Steely Dan was on the radio, singing about a girl who didn't know who Aretha Franklin was. I threaded my way through the late-morning traffic, back from the working man's part of Boston and into the exact opposite. The gallery was on Newbury Street, sandwiched between a gourmet food store and a travel agency that had never heard of economy class.

I parked the Breadbox a few doors down and walked back. I saw a woman walking a tiny dog, wearing what looked like a cashmere sweater. She was a vision in Lord & Taylor with Audrey Hepburn sunglasses and didn't give me a second look, much less a first one. I pulled on the heavy glass door of the gallery, and it wouldn't budge. Then I noticed an intercom set next to it.

I pushed the button, and it made a godawful noise that was a

cross between a beep and a screech. A disembodied voice came over the intercom and said, 'Deliveries are in the rear.'
'I pushed the button again and the voice said, 'Yes.'
'I'm not here to make a delivery.'
'Are you here about business?'
'Yes. I'd rather not discuss it over an intercom.'
The door buzzed, and I pulled it open. Inside, it was warm and smelled faintly of jasmine. The gallery seemed to specialize in a mix of paintings of seascapes without people, all in simple black frames, paintings that looked like but weren't quite Impressionist paintings, and statues from Cambodia or Thailand. I stopped for a second, struck by the fact that they had traveled all the way from my war to be here in Boston.
'Do you like them?' a man with an educated voice asked me.
'Yes. Cambodian?'
'You know your statues. Yes, from the Angkor dynasty.' He was almost my height but slimmer. My good suits came from Brooks Brothers; his were from a tailor. He took in my peacoat, fisherman's sweater underneath, jeans and duck boots. 'You aren't here to buy anything, are you?'
'Unfortunately not, but they are fantastic.' They were. I had seen some in my time in Vietnam and on R&R in Thailand, but at the time I was too young to appreciate them.
'Well, why are you here if not about the art?'
'I am a private investigator.'
'Everything here has provenance and was acquired legally,' he said defensively.
'Relax. That isn't why I'm here. I am flattered that you think I would know enough about any of this to investigate it.'
'Why are you here, then?' he repeated.
'I was hired by a company to do a background check on a man who used to work here.'
'Keith Raymond?'
'Yes, how did you know?'
'There isn't anyone else it could be. Would you like an espresso? We have a machine in the back. It's like coffee but stronger.' He smiled, but there was no joy in it.
'Yes, please. I'd love one. I have an espresso machine too.'
'I'm sorry, Mr . . .?'

'Roark. Andy Roark.'

'I'm Leonard Dupuis.' He stuck his hand out and we shook. 'I appear to be both pretentious and making assumptions about class.' His smile softened a little, and I liked him a lot more.

'No worries, I am from humble, almost Dickensian origins.'

'Come with me.'

I followed him to the back of the gallery, past a pretty young woman sitting at a Louis XIV desk, manning the phones and looking like she was also on display. We went past an office and into a small break room. He set about making us each an espresso.

'Why are you looking for Keith, Mr Roark?'

'He's involved in a scheme.'

'Of course he is; that's all he's involved in.'

'You hired him?'

'Yes. It was a moment of charity I'll regret. His probation officer said he had an interest in art. He convinced me to hire him with the idea that a diamond in the rough like Keith could better himself if exposed to some culture. Get out of his life of crime and have a future.'

'It didn't work, did it?'

He shook his head. 'Sadly, no.'

'Did he steal from the gallery?'

'No.' He handed me a tiny cup of espresso. 'He was a diligent pupil. He soaked up everything I had to teach him. Share with him. Not just art, but manners, how to act around the wealthy. I gave him a crash course in culture.'

'What happened? Did he con you?'

'No, not directly. He was cleverer than that. He would accept gifts from me, use my car, but nothing outrageous.'

'Mr Dupuis, what did he do?'

'He started to have relations with my clients. He used me to gain access to them so he could be a gigolo.'

'Oh. Men or women?' I asked indelicately.

'Whoever wanted to give him nice things. I found out later that he got ahold of several blank checks and made off with tens of thousands of dollars.'

'Let me guess. No one wanted to involve the police?'

'Exactly. These were people I have known for decades. They trusted me with large sums of money, they let me into their homes, and Keith used me to get close to them. I was mortified – beyond mortified. I lost a few very lucrative clients – more than clients, friends.' There was no mistaking the bitterness in his voice.

'I see. When did you see him last?'

'Two years ago.'

'You don't happen to have an address or an idea where he might be?'

'No, last I heard, he was in Florida, living the good life.' His voice was more brokenhearted than angry.

'Thank you, Mr Dupuis. I am sorry to bring up such unpleasant memories.' I gave him my card, but I knew that he wasn't going to call me about Lee Raymond. I finished my espresso.

'Mr Roark?'

'Yes.'

'Where did you develop an interest in Angkor statuary?'

'I spent some time in Southeast Asia.'

'I suspected as much. If you find him . . . please don't . . . don't hurt him.' Was it possible the man had feelings for the hustler?

'I'll try not to.' It wasn't much of a promise, but it was all I had to offer the brokenhearted.

I threaded the Breadbox back through town. Newbury Street was nice and clean, and the area was dripping with class and money. I drove down Mass Ave, noting that the cars grew older and more beat-up the closer I got to my meeting with my anonymous caller with a line on Raymond. There were no Audis, BMWs or Mercedes-Benzes to be seen down here. I drove past the building, circled the block and parked a few doors up. It was a habit left over from the cops, where you never pulled up in front of the address you were dispatched to.

I walked down the block and couldn't help but notice the litter. It was mostly fast-food wrappers and empty beer bottles, but I wouldn't be surprised to find a needle or two lying around. I was always struck by how half a mile in this city could mean such a difference in neighborhoods.

I walked up the three short steps to the three-story brick apartment building, which had some overgrown shrubs like a barrier between it and the sidewalk. It had probably been a fancy modern building when it was built in the 1920s. Now it had faded, and whatever paint was last slapped on it was peeling off. I tried the front door, which was unlocked, and I went in.

I was standing in a small vestibule with a door to my front and half a dozen mailboxes to my right. They had all been pried open long ago, but now there was a pile of junk mail on the floor. The door in front of me was unlocked too. It's nice to be expected. I unbuttoned my peacoat so I could get to the .38 snubnose on my hip. I didn't want to scare anyone by walking around with it in my hand, though something told me that this place was as abandoned as any place Scooby-Doo and the Gang ever went.

I pushed the door open and found myself in a stairwell with the stairs going up against the wall in one long flight. To my left was a doorway, missing a door that should have opened into a hallway, which I went into. There was light coming from the far end. There was an apartment on either side of the hallway, each with a door at either end of the hall near the corresponding stairwell.

I went down the hallway, trying each door handle as I went. My eyes started to adjust to the dim, dusty light. Each door was locked, and the handles rattled but didn't budge under my hand. At the end of the hallway was the back stairwell. There was a back door and steps leading down to the cellar. Based on the stench coming up from the cellar, there was a lot of trash rotting away down there. I opted for the stairs up to the second floor.

These stairs were more like a series of half flights that switched back on themselves to save space, unlike the grand staircase in front. The second floor had the same layout as the first floor, with an equal number of equally locked doors. I went to the landing and walked up the long front staircase that some long-ago architect must have thought gave the place a classy look. The stairs felt a little rickety under foot, and the railing at the top of the landing was too low and too shaky to meet current building codes by a long shot.

I made my way down the third-floor hallway with the same results as the first two floors. My reward at the back stairwell was a mountain of old trash bags that gave off a nauseating smell. I turned and walked back to the front stairs. At least they would

The Judge

bring me out closer to my car. I was starting to feel like someone was playing a joke on me or maybe trying to get me out of the office so they could snoop around. It wouldn't be the first time.

The hairs on the back of my neck stood up, as they had done so many times in Vietnam. He must have oiled the hinges. I never heard a door open, and if he had been surer-footed, I wouldn't have heard his foot scrape on the floor. I pivoted in time to realize in the dim light that he was swinging a baseball bat at me, and I was able to jump back out of the way of it.

He was right-handed and clumsily swung it backhanded toward me, missing me again. He kept swinging back and forth while I backpedaled down the hallway. I was running out of room, and going for my gun would leave him an opening to knock my head out of the park. He swung again, and when the bat ended its arc, I leaped forward and shot my hands under his arms, my body crashing into him and my hands wrapping, fingers interlocked, around the back of his neck, pulling down while pushing my face into his collar bone and neck.

A bunch of us Recon men had been on R&R in Thailand, and early on in the trip, we saw a GI pick a fight with a local man. The local was thin, slightly built, and had to be sixty. He had taken the GI to pieces, quickly and viciously. We spent the next few weeks learning a little Muay Thai boxing in the mornings when we woke up and needed to work the hangovers away. It wasn't enough to make any of us proficient, but we had learned some new, very dirty tricks. Mostly enough to be a danger to ourselves. But it was new and different from the Karate and Judo we usually practiced. When we made it back to CCN, we would practice sometimes, usually little more than drunken shenanigans.

I had my would-be batter in the classic Muay Thai clinch. He was big, bigger than me and strong, but he was heavy, and he was getting winded fast. He tried to shake me off, but I locked my elbows into my ribs and dropped my center of gravity. I heard the bat hit the floor and felt ineffective blows landing on my back and shoulders.

When I had my legs firmly under me, I delivered a series of strikes with my right knee, raising it, pivoting at him, jamming my knee into the cluster of nerves in his thigh. It wasn't an end to the fight, but his leg stopped working right after the first one. Now he was having a hard time pushing me or getting me off of him. I took a half-step back, dropping my hips lower, pulling him down by the neck, and then drove my knee into his floating ribs, again and again.

His bad breath came out in gasps with each knee strike. I could feel sweat on the back of his neck. It was time to end this fight. I eased up on my grip, and he automatically started to pull his head back. That is when I pulled down on the back of his neck, pushing his head down as I snapped my knee up into his face. When I felt his nose flatten into mush, I let go of his neck. Between my knee strike and his automatically jerking his head back, he rocked back on his heels.

I had tried to pull the knee strike a little. I didn't want to knock him out. I needed to know why I had been set up. The problem with my plan was that he wasn't clued into it. Instead, he took a shuffling step backward and hit the wooden railing at the top of the landing. We had, in the melee, gotten turned around. He was a big, heavy-set man, and the railing gave way with a snap. For a micro-second he teetered, windmilling his arms, and then he fell.

I heard him hit something – a dull, wooden, thwocking noise. Then he impacted on the ground-floor landing.

I looked over the broken railing, trying to catch my breath, and he was on the floor, looking like a ragdoll that had been tossed by a kid who didn't want it anymore. 'Gravity,' as one of my instructors in Airborne School had told us one day, 'is a motherfucker.' By the time I got down to the first-floor landing, he wasn't breathing or moving; he was just lying in a puddle of blood.

I was able to pull the door open enough against his body to squeeze through into the vestibule. I slipped on the pile of junk mail, doing my own pinwheeling of arms in a sick imitation of his last seconds. I stayed upright, leaving some bloody footprints on the pile of mail. Outside, I took a couple of deep breaths and stopped to light up a Lucky Strike. Then I went down the street to the phone booth. I was going to have to call Devaney and try not to end up in a jail cell.

EIGHT

When Devaney walked into the interrogation room that the detectives had left me in for a couple of hours, he was angry. I know that because he said, 'Andy, I am really fucking angry with you.'

'I know, Billy. Usually, when your face is that red, it means you've been in a bottle for the better part of a day. Or you're really fucking angry with me.'

'This is no time to crack wise, Andy. You killed a guy. Then, even worse than that, you called me. You could have called nine-one-one or even the complaint desk. You could have run away. No one would have known but, no, you called me. I don't even work homicide, but I am stuck with this one, because you called me. Your old friend, Billy Devaney. Why would you do that to me?'

'Billy. The guy was swinging at me with a bat. I already told the other two that. I also told that kid who didn't seem to be old enough to get into the Police Academy that. He was swinging at me, after luring me there and ambushing me.'

'So what? The way I feel about what you've done, I might be half sorry he didn't connect with your head.'

'Billy, it was self-defense, and even if it wasn't and you got stuck with this as a homicide, you would have actually solved this one.'

'You're not funny, Roark.'

'Who was the guy?'

'You tell me. You were the one meeting him in an abandoned building.'

'I got a message on my machine telling me, if I wanted information, to meet in that building. I went.' I explained the set-up with the locked doors and the trash in the stairwell. 'He came out swinging and I didn't have time to grab my gun. We ended up tussling, and he ended up going over the railing.'

'Through – he went *through* the railing.'

'Fine. He ended up going through the railing. It was self-defense. Who was he?'

'A leg breaker named Lonnie Cusick.'

'Lonnie? Who the hell names their kid Lonnie?'

'I don't know. He just got out of prison a couple of months ago. You owe money to anyone? Been betting and losing?'

'Ha. No, you know I don't have enough money to lose it betting.'

'He used to collect for the Mob. He specialized at breaking legs with a baseball bat.'

'Sounds like a real charmer.' Then something occurred to me. 'Say, you don't know who his lawyer is?'

'Terry McVicker repped him on his last case. Got him a pretty good deal on an ADW charge. He pled to simple assault but ate the parole violation and served two of his remaining five.'

'Terry McVicker, huh?'

'You know him?'

'Yeah, good guy,' I said, lost in thought. Terry's name kept coming up, and I was beginning to wonder if there was anything more to it. Lately, I'd been having a bad run of luck with my friends turning out not to be so friendly. 'Billy, are they gonna charge me or what?'

'Nah, they found the bat with his prints on the scene. The footprints in the dust on the floor fit with what you told us. And given his criminal record and history of violence and all that. Plus, that you had a gun and didn't try to pop the guy all kind of backs up your story.'

'Oh, and what doesn't?'

'The fact that you're an asshole who'd dump a homicide on my desk when I don't even work homicide.'

'Yeah, well, what can I say? I knew you'd make sure there wasn't a miscarriage of justice.'

'Come on, let's get you out of here.' He walked me out of the interrogation room and down to the entrance. 'Here you go,' he said, handing me a bag. My revolver, speedloader and Buck knife were inside. I hadn't been booked, and they hadn't taken my wallet, belt and shoelaces, but they drew the line at interrogating me while I was armed.

I had been driven over in a squad car, and no one seemed to

be in a rush to give me a ride back to my car. I put my gun and everything else in their usual places, then went to flag down a cab. Sitting in the back of the cab, starting to feel the spots where Lonnie had connected with me, something occurred to me. He didn't match the description of the man who had been seen with Raymond at any of the hotels.

The Breadbox was where I had parked it and seemed mercifully intact. I didn't want to have to explain to Carney how I got one of his criminal works of art stolen. I drove back to my apartment listening to George Thorogood and the Delaware Destroyers sing about the depth of their osteo malfeasance.

When I got back, Sir Leominster was waiting with his usual demands for food and attention.

'You could have come and bailed me out at least,' I said as I opened a can of his favorite cat food. Ignoring the smell of low tide in Boston Harbor coming from his dish, I went over to the answering machine to check the blinking light. There was a message from Angela Estrella that wasn't all business and might have made me blush a little. The sergeant major from the reunion committee was fulfilling his promise of calling me daily until I got back to him.

The last message was from Danny Sullivan. 'You've gotten your wish. A guy wants to meet you at Copley Place tomorrow. Be in front of the Sharper Image at noon. Andy, he's important; don't keep him waiting, and try not to be a wise ass.'

Well, that was progress at least. I poured myself a drink and was going to call Angela back but my phone rang. When I answered, Watts was on the other end. 'I heard you had a fight with a Mob leg breaker.'

'Yeah, someone lured me to a building, and a guy with a baseball bat was waiting.'

'So, you killed him?' It was one of those questions that wasn't much of a question.

'He was trying to bash my brains in.'

'Well, at least you didn't shoot him.'

'No, I wasn't trying to kill him. I really wanted to talk to him.'

'But?'

'Gravity is a motherfucker,' I said.

'Ha. I'm glad you're OK. Listen, he worked for some dangerous people.'

'Anyone in particular?'

'Mostly people from your old neighborhood.'

'That makes sense. We tend to stick to our own.'

'Just be careful.'

'Thanks. I will.' That probably explained Danny's timely call. He also worked for some dangerous people. I wondered if they were the same dangerous people.

Next, I finally managed to call Angela and have a conversation with her that her parents most definitely wouldn't have approved of. We agreed that we should go out for dinner at some point. Both of us were fully aware that the meal was just a formality. After we hung up, I realized that I hadn't eaten in hours and had drunk two glasses of whiskey. I remedied that situation by making a grilled cheese sandwich with a couple of slices of ham and a fried egg in it. It wasn't the healthiest dinner I've ever had, but after the day I'd had, I wasn't taking any chances on boring, healthy food.

The next day, at exactly eleven fifty-nine, I stepped onto the escalator on the ground floor of Copley Place and rode it up one flight. I had my .38 snubnose in the pocket of my peacoat and my custom Browning Hi-Power on my hip. I had an extra magazine for the Browning in my other coat pocket. I wasn't planning on a gunfight at the city's fanciest shopping mall and convention center, but if I had to have one, I wanted to use a gun with decent sights. The snubnose was an intimate weapon meant for close up. The sights reflected that philosophy by being a trench from the rear of the gun to the thin blade in the front.

When the escalator came to the top, I saw three men standing in front of the Sharper Image. Two were clearly muscle, wearing dark clothes: matching slacks, sweaters and leather jackets that came down to mid-thigh. They both had dark hair, one longer than the other, and based on their postures, each had a substantial amount of metal under their arms.

The man standing between them was strictly management, upper management at that. He had salt-and-pepper hair, worn on the long side, slicked back but not quite reaching his collar. His coat was blue cashmere, and if I wanted one, it would probably cost me a few months' rent.

I assumed his hands were expertly manicured. He wore glasses perched on a nose that had been broken once. I wasn't much taller than him, and his goons were substantially taller than both of us. When I was standing in front of him, he appraised me with dark eyes.

'You Roark?'

'Yes.'

'I'm a friend of Danny Sullivan's. He asked me to speak with you.'

'I appreciate it.'

'I assume you're armed.'

'Yes.' This was all so damned civil that I was beginning to wonder why all my meetings with gangsters couldn't be like this.

'I don't care about that, but I have to have Mike check you for a wire.'

'Sure. No problem.' I wasn't looking forward to it, but life is about compromising. One of the two men stepped forward. He quickly and discreetly patted me down for a wire. It took seconds, and if anyone noticed, no one let on. That was the advantage of living in a major metropolitan area: everyone conveniently sees nothing. He stepped back and nodded. 'I'm surprised that you agreed to meet with me,' I added.

'Normally, I wouldn't under any circumstances, but Danny was quite insistent. He said that you are quite stubborn.'

'I'm sure he didn't use that exact turn of phrase.'

He motioned with one manicured hand, and we started walking. Copley Place is made up of a series of walkways with stores on the outside and a large atrium in the center. There is a lot of white marble and a beautiful water effect to go with the high-end stores and restaurants. I was more of a Jordan Marsh at Downtown Crossing kind of guy.

'No, he didn't. He said you're the type of stubborn son of a bitch that it's easier to give him what he wants because he won't go away and he's too hard to kill. Then he pointed out some of the people who tried. The list was quite extensive.'

'A man has to stand for something,' I said by way of a reply.

'And those principles bring you into conflict with dangerous men?'

'Yes, they do.'

'And you are not the type to back away from a fight?'

'Not in recent memory, no.'

'OK, Mr Roark, can I assume that our discussion will be discreet?'

'Within reason, yes.'

'Within reason?' He raised an eyebrow at me.

'I have a client. I will have to share certain aspects of my investigation with him.'

'That seems reasonable. I would appreciate it if you don't share what we discuss with your friend in the FBI.'

'Sure, that seems reasonable.' I felt safe to make assurances because I was certain he wasn't going to implicate himself or his crew in anything.

'OK, Mr Roark, ask away.'

'Back in 1978 or 1979, Danny or someone using his office drew up letters of incorporation for a waste haulage company. Later, that company would end up dumping toxic waste from a local company called Northeast Textile and Cordage.'

If any of this meant anything to him, he didn't show it. 'You think my organization is involved?'

'We *are* here having a pleasant walk and discussion.' It was pleasant in Copley Place; pretty women on their lunch breaks from their office jobs were walking around. Well-dressed, polite businessmen too. We had one well-dressed goon ten feet in front of us and one ten feet behind.

'Go on. I sense there is a theory coming.'

'NT and C are now being sued. The trucking company involved also has ties to your organization, and it would benefit you if the lawsuit went away.'

'Ah, and how would we do that?' His accent had some Ivy League paved over the North End, not unlike the Army steamrolling my Southie accent.

'Blackmail.'

'Ah . . . I see.' He smirked at me like the guy who knows the punchline to all the jokes. 'And who are we supposed to be blackmailing? A judge? A juror?'

'Something like that.'
'Ah, I see, and you are going to save them?'
'That is what I am being paid to do.'
'At any cost?'
'Well, there are things that I won't do.'
'That, Mr Roark, is the difference between you and the people I deal with.'
'And who is that?'
'The same type of people Danny Sullivan keeps out of prison. You, however, knew that or we wouldn't be talking.'
'Are you trying to tell me that you aren't blackmailing anyone involved in the case?'
'I am.'
'Huh.' I gave my best imitation of a Gallic shrug.
'Mr Roark, have you noticed that there is a bit of a turf war going on in this town? Cars blowing up, people getting shot, bodies turning up or not turning up.'
'I have noticed something like that, yes.' I had to assume that he wasn't counting my old Karmann Ghia in that.
'An Italian outfit, a throwback to a past era, is fighting with an Irish outfit, an upstart, over control of the rackets in this town. They are fighting for a franchise. They are fighting for the right to distribute cocaine and other narcotics, to offer protection, to loan shark, that sort of thing.'
'Sounds familiar.' The ongoing Mob war was common knowledge in the city. It had to be with the number of cars being blown up.
'You're right that we invested in the trucking company, and we invested in the company they were hauling waste from too. You probably don't think of those as traditional investments for, uh, um, entrepreneurs such as I represent.'
'No, not really.'
'Well, the short version is that there is a great deal of money out there that's earned but can't, for a variety of reasons, be accounted for. However, there's no point in making money if one can't spend it or if spending potentially lands you in prison. Failing businesses help take that money and give it a new lease of life.'
'Money laundering.'

'Yes. My family and I invested in a number of failing companies in order to enter into short-term, mutually beneficial business arrangements. We also offered similar opportunities to other like-minded entrepreneurs.'

'I would think a lawsuit would draw unnecessary attention to your arrangement.'

'Not really. There are several layers of insulation, and some time has passed. There is little to connect those businesses with my organization. If there are criminal charges to be faced, our partners, those whose companies we invested in, would much rather be compensated for any inconvenience than implicate themselves in a criminal conspiracy.'

'Or potentially face the consequences for ratting on you?' I asked indelicately.

'Yes, that too,' he said, smiling faintly. 'The fact is that most of the companies that we, uh, invest in are thankful for the loans. They are usually having credit and/or liquidity problems. Sometimes it is temporary, sometimes not. In those cases, they find it in their best interests to not discuss the source of the non-traditional loans.'

'How profitable is it?'

'For my organization?'

'Yes.'

'Very. We are able to, um, ensure that we have a clean flow of revenue, and our friends pay us a fee for helping them do the same.'

'I think I went into the wrong line of work,' I said, whistling softly.

'Oh, yes, Mr Roark, it is quite lucrative for my organization. Our friends like it because we offer discretion and very, very low risk for all involved.'

'Blackmailing to try to throw a trial is a risk?'

'Yes, it is. The companies we deal with are carefully chosen. They appreciate the service we provide. Our friends certainly don't want to encourage undue scrutiny. Besides, blackmail is coercive; it breeds resentment.'

'Which might give someone an incentive to cooperate with the authorities.'

'Exactly. Besides, there are enough lawyers and judges with

gambling problems or other expensive habits. They always need money and look to the people who lend it to them favorably. There is no need to blackmail anyone. At least not for what my organization does.'

'What else does your organization do?'

'We have a very diverse portfolio and try to stay under the radar. I will say that it is my goal for my family to give up the more hands-on elements of our business. I think providing financial services is less risky and just as profitable.'

I was pretty sure he meant protection, gambling, prostitution and drugs. 'You don't happen to know a man named Lonnie Cusick, do you?'

'No. Should I?'

'He was hired muscle, a leg breaker that someone sent to beat up or possibly kill me yesterday.'

'No, that is not how we do things. Leg breakers, blowing up cars – that all draws the attention of the police, the FBI. That is for the guys who think it is the mark of success to have a lot of money in garbage bags in the basement. What happened to Mr Cusick?'

'He's dead.'

'Did you kill him?'

'No, gravity did him in . . . I just get credit for the assist.'

He winced. 'That is unfortunate for him.' We had arrived back at the Sharper Image. 'I hope that I have satisfied your curiosity, Mr Roark.'

'You have. Thank you. I appreciate your taking the time to see me.'

'I trust Danny's judgment. He said that you are a tough son of a bitch but that your word is ironclad.'

'I have my moments.'

'If it were me, Mr Roark, I would look at who else might profit from this blackmail.'

'That is more or less the plan. Thank you.'

'Goodbye, Mr Roark. I hope our paths don't cross professionally.'

'No worries. I don't make enough money for you to consider investing in me.'

He smiled and moved off with his matching goons. I wondered

where the unconventional banker had earned his degree. I shook my head and contemplated what had been my strangest business meeting to date. I rode the escalator back down to the street level and headed out into the early-afternoon sunlight.

I stopped at the first pay phone I came across and called Terry McVicker's office. He was in District Court, so I descended into the T for a ride over to Government Center. His secretary knew me and told me where to find him. By a stroke of luck, he was walking out as I was walking in. Terry's one of those guys who's forty but looks thirty, fit with brown hair and eyes to match. He is one of those guys you hope you'll run into at office parties or things like that because he is good company.

'Andy, how are you?' he asked.
'Good, I was hoping to run into you.'
'You got lucky. My arraignment just wrapped up.'
'Anything good?'
'No, drunk driving.'
'Your guy innocent?'
'Hell, no! If he was, he wouldn't need me.'
'Wanna grab a bite?' I asked.
'Sure. You buying?'
'Why not?'
'I did just send a case your way.'
'That you did.'
'Good, then someplace good. If I leave it up to you, you'll be your usual cheap self and we'll end up at Brigham's.'
'No, we could go someplace classy like the Burger King at the bus station.'
'The hell you say. Locke-Ober's.'
'Fine, but only out of recognition of the business you have thrown my way over the years.'

Locke-Ober's wasn't cheap, but it was the fourth-oldest restaurant in Boston, and I did have a paying client. Lunch could legitimately be put on the expenses part of the judge's bill. Up until 1970, Locke-Ober didn't allow women to dine there, and for a time it was a haunt of the legal profession because men of a certain age mistook sexism for discretion.

If you've never eaten at Locke-Ober's, I recommend it. It's

one of a handful of iconic Boston restaurants like Durgin-Park, Jake Wirth's, the Union Oyster House and the ever-romantic Café Budapest. While every other restaurant is trying to chase the current culinary fad – sushi, nouvelle cuisine – the aforementioned restaurants do what they have been doing so well for so long: offering good food and a good atmosphere.

Dining at Locke-Ober's was like eating in a museum that specialized in nineteenth-century European antiques, but with a menu that was as timeless as the décor. Inside, the wood was deeply stained, dark and ornately carved. The lighting was soft, and the chairs were dark wood and red leather that contrasted nicely with the tablecloths which were the color of newly fallen snow. The silverware was actually silver, and the whole effect was that of dining in some long-dead nobleman's chateau. On a good night, you could find Teddy Kennedy holding court at the bar.

Terry must have spent lavishly here often enough because no one complained about my lack of a tie. We were seated at the edge of the room, which suited my needs. The waiter came, and Terry ordered a Martini. I opted for a beer. The waiter returned with our drinks and asked about appetizers. Terry ordered something that sounded a lot like bone marrow with mushrooms on toast. I ordered the escargot.

'You're going to eat snails?' he asked with a look of bemusement.

'Yes, snails that are drowning in butter and garlic.'

'But they're still snails.'

'Tasty, tasty snails.'

The waiter came back for our lunch order. Terry ordered the sole with mashed potatoes and creamed corn. I ordered the filet mignon with mashed potatoes and sautéed mushrooms. When the waiter drifted away again, Terry looked up from his Martini and asked, 'To what do I owe the pleasure?'

'The case you put me on to.'

'Yeah, for the judge. How is that going?'

'Um, fits and starts.'

'How can I help?'

'Do you know Raymond Lee Keith or a guy named Lonnie Cusick?'

'Sure, they're occasional clients of mine.'

'Occasional?'

'Well, when they can afford me, they're clients. When they can't, they either go bargain basement or the public defender.'

'I see. When was the last time you represented either one?'

'I dunno. It's been a couple of years. Why? Are they in trouble again?'

'Cusick attacked me yesterday with a baseball bat.'

'Shit. You didn't shoot him, did you?'

Why does everyone ask me that? 'No, I don't shoot everyone I run into, but if he owes you money, I'd forget about it.' I explained about my run-in with the late Lonnie Cusick.

'Oh, that's bad.'

'Better him than me. He called to lure me there. A few days ago, someone shot my car with a shotgun.'

'Cusick?'

'I don't know. Could have been, but I can't say for sure.'

'Who then?'

'My guess is Raymond Lee Keith. He is involved in the case, very involved, and I had been asking around about him. Shortly after I started, my car was shot, and then the next day, I ran into Cusick.'

'Didn't someone blow up your old car? You must have a tough time getting insurance. I could see Lonnie shooting your car, but Raymond . . . he's not a hard guy. Not the type to go for violence or use guns.'

'Murder is in the hearts of all men.'

'Sure, sure, Shakespeare.'

'How about blackmail?'

'More like it. He is more of a thief, a con man. He's not muscle.'

'Didn't he have a felony assault and robbery beef a few years ago?'

'A misunderstanding.' Even at lunch talking about an old client, Terry was trying to minimize his client's culpability. He waved his hand dismissively in the air, his class ring catching the light. He was one of the few people I knew who didn't go to West Point who actually wore a class ring. 'If he'd had me representing him instead of his cut-rate type, he never would have eaten that charge or done that type of time.'

'Who represented him last?'
'One of your people.'
'My people?'
'Shanty Irish, Johnny O'Day.'
'We aren't exactly the lost tribe of Derry.'
'Ha! Anyway, in the last couple of cases, O'Day represented both of them.'
'He any good?'

There was a pause as the waiter brought Terry his fancy toast with bone marrow and my escargot. I watched Terry tear into his toast while I waited for my snails in their molten butter and garlic to cool enough to attempt to eat.

'No, he's not good. He probably could be, but he mostly just continues cases, and then, when the DA gets sick of it, they come to some sort of plea.'

'That doesn't sound like a great *legal* strategy.' I put extra emphasis on the word 'legal.' I had worked for enough defense attorneys to have picked up some of what goes on.

'That depends on what you are there to do. If you are trying to provide your client with a rigorous defense, then no, it isn't great. On the other hand, if you are trying to run up billable hours and avoid going to hearings, it is a pretty sound strategy.'

'I get the billable hours part, but how does it help the defense?' I popped a hot, buttery, garlic-laden escargot into my mouth and chewed with great satisfaction.

'Ugh, how can you like that? I pour salt on things like that in my garden.'

'If the ones in your garden were broiled in butter and garlic, I would eat them too.'

'I believe that. Anyway, it is a solid but not particularly gifted strategy because DAs are at heart bureaucrats with fancy degrees. They have a caseload that they need to move, and cases that hang around too long start to stink.'

'So, he kicks the case down the road and racks up the bill, and in the end, the DA is more likely to agree to a favorable deal?'

'You missed your calling,' he said with a laugh. 'That's exactly it. The only problem is that sometimes the deal isn't going to get any better or his client sits in jail a few months longer than he needs to.'

'Why do people hire him?'

'Well, some think or hear that he is a good lawyer and may retain him. You know, the kind who hears it from a cousin or a friend. In other cases, he might be court-appointed. Sometimes his name is the one someone's finger lands on in the Yellow Pages.'

'Hasn't anyone called him on it?'

'Like who?'

'I dunno. A judge or the Bar Association. Don't you guys have an ethics commission or something?'

'Sure, but he isn't actually doing anything wrong. Not only that, but who is going to complain?'

'Remind me not to hire him if I get jammed up.'

'No, you'd hire me or maybe your old pal Danny Sullivan.'

'I might be able to afford you . . . I don't have the type of money that hires a guy like Danny.'

While we were talking, we managed to finish our appetizers, order a second round of drinks and have our small plates replaced with our entrees. My steak was a perfect medium rare, and the sautéed mushrooms were delicate and flavorful. The mashed potatoes were what mashed potatoes should be. You have to get up pretty early in the morning to screw up mashed potatoes. I looked over at Terry's flat slab of white fish. I am sure that it was as excellent as sole could be, but I'd never know. I watched him eat creamed corn with the same sentiment that he had as he watched me enjoy my escargot.

'What about the clients?' I asked. 'They're criminals; most of them sound like they've been in and out of trouble. Don't they realize he's screwing them?'

'Some get it, but what can they do? By the time they get out and get back in trouble, they just get another lawyer, the ones that figure it out. Remember, if these guys were geniuses, both the cops and the lawyers would be out of business.'

'That's true. I don't remember there being a lot of James Bond supervillains when I was in the cops.'

'Some of his clients keep hiring him because they think he is a good lawyer.' Terry snorted. 'Can you fucking imagine that? He does the bare minimum, kicks the can down the road, and they thank him for it. They thank him for keeping them locked up longer.'

'Who represented him last?'
'One of your people.'
'My people?'
'Shanty Irish, Johnny O'Day.'
'We aren't exactly the lost tribe of Derry.'
'Ha! Anyway, in the last couple of cases, O'Day represented both of them.'
'He any good?'
There was a pause as the waiter brought Terry his fancy toast with bone marrow and my escargot. I watched Terry tear into his toast while I waited for my snails in their molten butter and garlic to cool enough to attempt to eat.
'No, he's not good. He probably could be, but he mostly just continues cases, and then, when the DA gets sick of it, they come to some sort of plea.'
'That doesn't sound like a great *legal* strategy.' I put extra emphasis on the word 'legal.' I had worked for enough defense attorneys to have picked up some of what goes on.
'That depends on what you are there to do. If you are trying to provide your client with a rigorous defense, then no, it isn't great. On the other hand, if you are trying to run up billable hours and avoid going to hearings, it is a pretty sound strategy.'
'I get the billable hours part, but how does it help the defense?' I popped a hot, buttery, garlic-laden escargot into my mouth and chewed with great satisfaction.
'Ugh, how can you like that? I pour salt on things like that in my garden.'
'If the ones in your garden were broiled in butter and garlic, I would eat them too.'
'I believe that. Anyway, it is a solid but not particularly gifted strategy because DAs are at heart bureaucrats with fancy degrees. They have a caseload that they need to move, and cases that hang around too long start to stink.'
'So, he kicks the case down the road and racks up the bill, and in the end, the DA is more likely to agree to a favorable deal?'
'You missed your calling,' he said with a laugh. 'That's exactly it. The only problem is that sometimes the deal isn't going to get any better or his client sits in jail a few months longer than he needs to.'

'Why do people hire him?'

'Well, some think or hear that he is a good lawyer and may retain him. You know, the kind who hears it from a cousin or a friend. In other cases, he might be court-appointed. Sometimes his name is the one someone's finger lands on in the Yellow Pages.'

'Hasn't anyone called him on it?'

'Like who?'

'I dunno. A judge or the Bar Association. Don't you guys have an ethics commission or something?'

'Sure, but he isn't actually doing anything wrong. Not only that, but who is going to complain?'

'Remind me not to hire him if I get jammed up.'

'No, you'd hire me or maybe your old pal Danny Sullivan.'

'I might be able to afford you . . . I don't have the type of money that hires a guy like Danny.'

While we were talking, we managed to finish our appetizers, order a second round of drinks and have our small plates replaced with our entrees. My steak was a perfect medium rare, and the sautéed mushrooms were delicate and flavorful. The mashed potatoes were what mashed potatoes should be. You have to get up pretty early in the morning to screw up mashed potatoes. I looked over at Terry's flat slab of white fish. I am sure that it was as excellent as sole could be, but I'd never know. I watched him eat creamed corn with the same sentiment that he had as he watched me enjoy my escargot.

'What about the clients?' I asked. 'They're criminals; most of them sound like they've been in and out of trouble. Don't they realize he's screwing them?'

'Some get it, but what can they do? By the time they get out and get back in trouble, they just get another lawyer, the ones that figure it out. Remember, if these guys were geniuses, both the cops and the lawyers would be out of business.'

'That's true. I don't remember there being a lot of James Bond supervillains when I was in the cops.'

'Some of his clients keep hiring him because they think he is a good lawyer.' Terry snorted. 'Can you fucking imagine that? He does the bare minimum, kicks the can down the road, and they thank him for it. They thank him for keeping them locked up longer.'

'Sounds like he's got the perfect racket.'

'He sure does.'

'Maybe you should try a new business plan.' Terry pulled a face when I said it.

'C'mon Andy, you know I am too honest to do something like that.'

'Sure, sure, Terry, it was just a joke.'

'Andy, I know all the lawyer jokes, but seriously, most of us have integrity.'

'I know you do. It was just a joke.' Maybe this is why I have beer at lunch instead of Martinis. Terry's second was a distant memory, and he was getting a little too sensitive for my liking.

'So, Johnny O'Day isn't the best defense attorney out there,' I said to shift the topic a little.

'No, not really. I think he does it because he has to keep the lights on. He should stick to estates or tort law.'

We turned down the offer of dessert, though the apple torte sounded pretty good. By the time we had finished our coffees and I had put some of the judge's hard-earned money down on the table, something struck me as funny. Torte and tort. Fancy apple pie and the branch of the law that involved injuries, litigation and lawsuits. Lunch had been worth every penny that I had spent.

'Hey, man, do you think that O'Day has a current address on Raymond Lee Keith?'

'He should. O'Day is the type to get every last penny out of his clients. He'll know where to find Keith if he thinks the guy owes him a nickel.'

'Can you point me in the right direction to find O'Day?'

'Sure. Just don't beat him up or shoot him, OK? He's a member of the bar, after all.'

'I don't shoot everyone I meet.'

Terry just snorted and said he'd call me.

NINE

We shook hands in front of the restaurant, and I watched Terry for a few seconds as he walked back to the courthouse. He wasn't exactly unsteady on his feet; he was just walking like a man who had a little more than two Martinis. Maybe he had a taste before lunch, something to steady his nerves before his hearing? I didn't love thinking about it.

I turned and started back to my office. Terry had represented both Lee Raymond AKA Raymond Lee Keith and the late, gravity-challenged Lonnie Cusick. The two men were like a Venn diagram overlapping at my friend Terry McVicker. My recent history had taught me that I had a blind spot when it came to friends. On the other hand, why would Terry hire me to help the judge if he was the brains behind the blackmail scheme?

Johnny O'Day was also their lawyer, according to Terry . . . which, if he were trying to draw attention away from himself, another person with overlapping involvement with the two men, would make sense. Even if Terry was behind it all, I still had to check out O'Day. After all, sometimes things were just coincidences and friends were just friends. I had to trust somebody sometimes.

It was cold enough out that by the time I got to my office, the tips of my toes hurt and I was pretty sure that the tops of my ears had no feeling. My missing earlobe itched, and my nose was running slightly less than the leaky faucet in my bathroom. Normally, after a lunch like that, I would have been ready for a nap. The walk back to the office in the cold had countered the effects of the heavy lunch and two beers. That was the magic of Boston in January.

Inside, the office was warm and the clanking of the radiators was reassuring. I sat down at my desk and took out the yellow legal pad with the case notes on it and a felt-tip pen. I wrote down everything that had happened to date. I wrote out the names of the two lawyers as well as Lee Raymond and Lonnie Cusick. I doodled, drawing arrows back and forth. It didn't get me any closer to figuring out how to help the judge.

I picked up a pipe and packed it with a mixture from Dunhill's. It was called Durbar and had a lot of Turkish Latakia in it. It was strong and rich, giving off a cloud of nice-smelling smoke when I got the pipe drawing. I cracked the office window to let some of the smoke out. Then I picked up the phone and managed to get through to Danny Sullivan.

'Hey, Andy, how's the boy?' he asked out of habit when he came on the line. Danny was successful enough to have a secretary who was a very efficient layer between him and everything.

'Not bad. I met with your banker friend.'

'How'd it go?'

'It was educational.'

'Yeah, he called me earlier. He said he liked you and that it was an interesting conversation.'

'I agree. Listen, I was hoping to get your opinion on something?'

'Sure, what?'

'What do you think of Terry McVicker?'

'Good lawyer, good reputation. He used to be a "true believer" over at the Public Defender's Office. He's private, but he does a good job for his clients, and he wins a lot more than he loses. Why, are you looking to hire a defense attorney?'

'No, not right now.'

'He'd be a good choice if you were in the market.' That was high praise considering how few of Danny's clients ended up in jail, even though they richly deserved to be there.

'Good to know. Hey, do you know a guy named Johnny O'Day?'

'Sure, I do. He's in a different league from McVicker. Terry will knock himself out on a case. O'Day is the exact opposite. He shows up, does the bare minimum, maybe makes some noise in court so he seems like he is doing the job, but you know . . . in the end, he isn't really doing much for his clients except taking their money.'

'You don't like him much, do you?'

'No, I don't. He's a two-bit chiseler who gives my profession a bad name.'

'Your profession doesn't need any help in that regard.'

'You're one to talk.' It struck me that we had spent years not talking to each other yet fell into the same easy banter. I didn't have much time to reflect on it, because I heard the outer office door open, and then Brenda Watts was standing in my office. She didn't look happy.

'Hey, man, I have to go. Something's come up.' I hung up the phone and smiled at Watts with the pipe clenched in my teeth.

'Hello, Brenda.'

'Hello, Andy.'

'What brings you by the old office?'

'What are you up to?'

'Smoking a pipe, working on some case notes, nothing particularly special.' I casually flipped the pages closed on the legal pad and slipped it into the desk drawer. Watts took in every little movement, registering them in her mind. I was pretty sure that I knew how the fox felt running around the English countryside with the barking of the hounds behind him.

'Andy, don't be obtuse.'

'I am not even sure how to spell it, let alone be it.'

'Stop dodging. What are you playing at?'

'Not sure what you mean, Watts.'

'Today, you were walking around Copley Place with a prominent mobster and money launderer. A guy who has connections to a lot of people in the underworld. More than even your pal Danny Sullivan.' I didn't bother to ask how she knew that. I had met Brenda because back when Danny and I were friends, the Bureau had him under surveillance. She braced me one night in a bar trying to convince me to try to get Danny to roll. It didn't work out the way she wanted, but we became friends in spite of it.

'Oh, that. I needed financial advice. I am looking to invest the Roark family hundreds.'

'Bullshit. You don't even have that much in your bank account.'

'Now, that's just insulting. The VA sends the check first of every month.'

'So why were you in Copley Place, strolling and chatting with an underworld figure?'

'Does anyone actually say "underworld" anymore . . . that seems so dated. Like something from one of those old TV shows where they mention J. Edgar Hoover like he's some sort of hero.'

'To a lot of Americans, he was.'

'Sure, just ask Malcolm X and Dr King's families how they feel about him.'

'Stop trying to change the subject.'

'I was talking to him about a case.'

'He looking to hire you?'

'No. He comes with his own muscle.'

'Then, what?' Watts was tough, and I usually prefer to be straight with her. It was the best way to stay on her good side, but she was asking questions I couldn't answer.

'I was chasing down a lead in a case. He was there to assure me that he wasn't involved.'

'Why would he talk to you? You're not remotely in his league . . .' She paused and her eyes – very pretty eyes that missed nothing – flashed in anger. 'Danny Sullivan . . . you reached out to him, and he set it up. Jesus, I thought you'd put paid to that.'

'Like you said, the banker is out of my league.'

'Please tell me you aren't wrapped up with them.'

'Nope. I'm working a case. Nothing more.'

'What case?'

'It's a blackmail case. A possible lead required me to talk to Danny, and he arranged for me to talk to the money guy.'

'Who's being blackmailed?'

I shook my head from side to side. 'I can't tell you that.'

'Why not?'

'Because clients hire me and expect me to be discreet. They pay a premium for that discretion, and the minute I violate that, I might as well go sell insurance or something.' Also, if I told her that a judge was being blackmailed, she probably couldn't ignore it, and the FBI didn't care about anyone's reputation.

'Andy, if you get in bed with these guys, not only can't I help you but I won't.'

'Watts, I am not in bed with anybody.' Which wasn't exactly true where Ms Estrella was concerned, but I couldn't trust Watts not to pistol-whip me if I pissed her off too much.

'Ha! That'd be a first.' She stood up and walked to the door.

Being a gentleman of sorts, I followed her. At the outer office door, she said, 'I hope you know what you're doing.'

'Watts, you know better than that . . . I just make it up as I go along.' I smiled charmingly at her.

'I'm serious, Andy. If you're doing business with these guys, there's nothing I can do for you.' Clearly, my charming smile needed some work.

'I know, Watts.' I almost told her to trust me, but every time someone said that to me, they were lying. It didn't matter anyway, because she was out the office door before I could say anything else. I closed the door behind her and went back to the pipe and my case notes.

If the banker and his clients weren't worried about exposure from the case, then who would benefit from blackmailing the judge? Lee Raymond and his partner weren't asking for money, which didn't seem to be how blackmail was supposed to work. Without the banker in the picture, assuming he wasn't lying, that only left the defendants in the suit itself. It was cheaper to pay Lee Raymond and his pal than pay the settlement from the suit. Probably a lot cheaper.

I wanted to talk to O'Day. He was tied to both Lonnie Cusick and Lee Raymond. He was a criminal lawyer, but maybe he was connected to the lawsuit in some way. Everyone I had spoken to said that Raymond wasn't the brains behind the operation. I was pretty sure that the late Lonnie Cusick wasn't management material. Management doesn't hang around in cold, abandoned apartment buildings waiting to beat someone's head in with a baseball bat. O'Day was a lawyer, and that was a hell of a lot closer to management than guys like Raymond or Cusick.

I pulled out the Yellow Pages and turned to the L section. I found O'Day's number. He hadn't bothered to take out an ad, instead opting for just a simple line with his name and number. Even I have an ad in the Yellow Pages. It takes up a three-inch-by-three-inch top corner of a page. You have to be pretty cheap to be outdone by me.

His address was buried somewhere deep in the warren of streets over by the courthouse. I was betting that it wasn't much more than my two-room affair, except that a guy like O'Day probably had a secretary. I figured I was better off without one, and on the occasions when people have done things like booby-trap my office door with a hand grenade, I have felt validated in that point of view.

I picked up the phone and dialed Angela Estrella's number. She answered on the third ring, and I imagined her as being the type to unclip an earring before answering the phone. After we exchanged greetings, I used my keen interrogation skills to ask her what she was wearing, and we discussed that for a bit. I said, 'I met a very interesting man today.'

'Who?'

'A man who specializes in banking for people who can't deposit their money in regular banks.'

'A money launderer?'

'Yep. A very polite gentleman who once invested in NT and C on behalf of his mafia family.'

'Oh.'

'Not just NT and C but the trucking company, too.'

'That can't be a coincidence.'

'No, it wasn't.'

'Is he behind the blackmail?'

'Oddly enough, I don't think he is.'

'Why not?'

'I got the impression from him that it wouldn't be worth the risk to blackmail the judge. His business model seemed pretty sound and risk-averse.'

'Andy, he's a money launderer . . . a criminal.'

'I know, I know.'

'But you believed him when he told you he wasn't involved.'

'I did. I think that he's an honorable man, in his own way.'

'And a criminal.'

'They aren't necessarily mutually exclusive.' My friends Carney and Chris were both on the wrong side of the law, but they were honorable men.

'No, I guess not,' she said reluctantly. She was eager to protect the judge and have this thing over.

'I was wondering, do you know if a lawyer named Johnny O'Day is involved in the case?'

'Double Pay O'Day?' she asked with a laugh.

'Double Pay O'Day?'

'Sure, he's been kicking around the courts for years. I used to clerk in District Court and would see him there all the time. That's what the clerks used to call him.'

'And?'

'He is very grabby – none of the girls I know ever wanted to be stuck on an elevator or otherwise alone with him. He's not a very good lawyer either.'

'Why did you call him Double Pay O'Day?'

'He got suspended from practicing for six months. This was, like . . . ten years ago.'

'How come?'

'He had a scheme where he would bill some of his court-appointed clients, even though the Commonwealth was paying him.'

'Who would fall for that?'

'Usually, the clients who didn't speak English and didn't have green cards.'

'What happened?'

'One of the public defenders found out and made a complaint. Apparently, he had been doing it for years. He made a small pile of money. The Bar Association and the review board made him pay it back and then suspended his license for six months.'

'That's it?'

'He is friends with a couple of judges, plays golf with some more. He knows where a few bodies are buried. He got a slap on the wrist and was given a second chance.'

'I'm surprised he didn't get arrested.'

'None of the people he ripped off would go on the record. In the end, it was just the word of the PD, but she made such a stink that they had to do something. What is that the cops say – no complainant, no crime?'

'Something like that.'

'Well, there you go.'

Johnny O'Day was starting to look like management material to me. He didn't seem like the type to do the dirty work himself. No, he sounded like the type who wouldn't mind having a client do it. He certainly seemed to have an appetite for easy money and wasn't too picky about how he came by it. The problem was that I couldn't figure out how he would profit from it.

'Um, I don't suppose you'd like to have dinner sometime this week?'

'Silly me, I was beginning to think you only called to talk about the case. I would love to.'

We briefly talked about options. I thought about taking her to the Café Budapest, but that seemed like a little much for midweek. By the end of the discussion, I was somehow on the hook to make dinner for her at my place. I hung up feeling the twinge of mild excitement that comes at the beginning of any romance.

It was too early to call it a day and too late to go looking for Lee Raymond. Instead, I packed my case notes in my old postman's bag along with a couple of spare legal pads and some felt-tip markers. I wondered if I should throw in a flask of whiskey or a box of ammunition, but both seemed like overkill. Besides, this way I had enough room in the bag for books if I stopped by the Brattle Book Store, which, for those not in the know, is the best used bookstore in Boston, and, therefore, the world.

It had only gotten colder since I had walked to the office from Copley Place. Now my ears and the tip of my nose felt ready to fall off after a couple of blocks. Crossing the street and turning into the wind, my eyes began to water with the force of it. By the time I got to the Public Library, I was ready to get out of the wind. It was warm inside, and the heat hit me like opening a furnace door. My cheekbones, the tip of my nose and my ears all began to itch.

I made my way to the reference section. I sat down and took out my notes. NT and C probably had a lawyer on staff or contracted with one. My guess was that when they were hit with the lawsuit, they hired outside counsel. It was not out of the realm of possibility that Johnny O'Day knew the lawyers involved or that any of them had once been in criminal law and knew him. Or knew Lee Raymond and Lonnie Cusick, for that matter. Somehow, it made sense that O'Day and the criminal courts were at the center of this thing.

The problem that I had was one of scale. It might take me days to track down people at NT and C who might be behind the whole thing. I could start with the CEO or the shareholders, or was it the lawyers? That might be a half-dozen potential suspects. Lee Raymond was my best bet; I already knew he was involved and it would be easier to find him than untangle who at NT and C was directly involved. Plus, I could link him to Lonnie Cusick through Johnny O'Day.

I spent a couple of hours hunched over the table looking at Bar Association registers and lists of law school graduates, and comparing them to the list of lawyers involved in the suit that Angela Estrella had provided me with when I started the case. I was trying to cross-reference some sort of connection between them and Johnny O'Day. It was looking worse than the Red Sox's chances of winning the World Series.

O'Day had gone to Northeastern and then Suffolk for law school. There was nothing wrong with either, but they didn't compare with the NT and C lawyers, who all seemed to go to Ivy League schools for undergrad and either Harvard or Yale Law. O'Day worked in District Court or Superior Court doing marginal criminal defense work. The other lawyers represented companies that were in every home and garage in America. A couple had even worked on the Ford Pinto thing. None of them seemed to have done criminal work, much less cut-rate criminal work.

After a couple of fruitless hours, I packed everything into my bag and stepped back out into the cold. The sun was just dipping low over the brick and glass buildings of Boston. I lit a cigarette and headed for home. I was running out of ideas. I could follow O'Day around and see if he led me to Lee Raymond. Maybe I would get lucky and Raymond's PO might call me to tell me he had found him. Or I might get luckier yet and Raymond might just call me and arrange to meet.

The only other thing I could think of to check out were the photography clubs. There might be places that had access to darkrooms and enlargers. Lee Raymond might belong to one. Maybe someone might be able to point me in the right direction. I walked home in the fading light, contemplating dead ends and false starts. Or maybe I should see if Lonnie Cusick had a last known address.

He had to live somewhere. Wherever that was or whoever he was living with might be able to point me in the direction of Lee Raymond. Or there might even be a clue. You know, the type of thing they make such a big deal about in detective books and movies. Or maybe my brain was frozen from walking around without a hat.

Either way, it would be worth making a call to Devaney to see what he had to say. I would pay for it with tickets or drinks accompanied by his running commentary on what type of Irish I was. I wouldn't mind that he called me shanty Irish every chance he got – at least, I wouldn't mind so much – if he could at least admit that he was too. Instead of putting on airs, acting like his people were lace-curtain types. Both of us drank whiskey from round bottles, and there was no way around that.

I let myself into my apartment to the happy and warm sound of the steam pinging in the radiators. The rent was mercifully affordable, which was a rarity in Boston, and if you looked out the right window, there was a view of the Charles River through the alleyways. Its other chief advantage was that it was warm in winter. I had slowly made a place where I felt comfortable, amassing furniture and books over the years. And a cat. I couldn't forget the cat.

Once I had sloughed off my coat and put the Hi-Power away, I set about the business of feeding the cat. He came running into the kitchen when he heard the unmistakable sound of dinner: the can opener piercing the can of cat food. That done, I poured myself a glass of Powers and went to check the answering machine. The only message was from the same sergeant major who had been patiently stalking me, trying to get me to go to the reunion. Not even walking around in the cold had made me change my mind about that.

The next morning, after working out and an uninspiring breakfast of toast, yogurt and coffee, I called Devaney. I had been worried about losing my touch in terms of predicting his approach to me, and I needn't have. Devaney was consistent in his casual bigotry.

'Roark, you shanty Irish piece of trash. You calling around looking for another favor.'

'I was hoping you could do me a small one.'

'Your pasty Irish ass isn't in the Charles Street Jail. I call that a pretty big favor I already done.' Billy had a strange affectation where he tried to sound more street by butchering the Queen's

English. He felt that when the troops heard it, they'd ignore the fact that he had a degree from BU.

'That is true, and I am very glad not to be in the house of detention.'

'That's about the smartest thing you ever said. What do you want?'

'An address for Lonnie Cusick.'

'What are you gonna do, go and break in, snoop around?'

That was pretty much the plan. 'Sergeant Devaney, I would never . . .' I said with mock indignation, mostly at the fact that he thought that I would ever admit to potentially committing a crime.

'Naw, you're just gonna go down there and see if his family needs anything 'cause you're so concerned about them after tossing Lonnie to his death.'

'Lonnie lived with family?' I asked.

'No, according to his PO, he lived alone. He didn't have much family. An ex-wife, now remarried – guess she got sick of Lonnie using her as a punching bag. His mother passed a couple of years back. He's got a brother doing time at Walpole for a manslaughter thing. He's scheduled to get out in 1998 with time off for good behavior.'

'So, no family, then.'

'No.'

'Where'd he live again?'

'Over on Jenkins, by the Old Colony Projects.' He gave me the number.

'Thanks, Billy.'

'Stay out of trouble, I don't need the headache that keeping you out of jail is turning into.'

'Sure, Billy, sure. Thanks.' I hung up before he could make any more disparaging remarks.

It was a tough neighborhood. I should know. Billy, Danny Sullivan and I had grown up not far from there. While the streets and buildings may be the same, the neighborhood of the 1950s and 1960s was very different. It was rougher now. Where most of our disputes were settled with fists or bike chains, now it was guns. We fought over some sense of territorial, neighborhood pride; now it was about who had the right to sell drugs on a corner.

The Judge

It was a little before nine in the morning, and most of the criminal types would be asleep right now. I slipped my .38 into its holster on my waist and put on my peacoat. Having learned my lesson yesterday, I wore my wool watch cap too. I took my red tool chest from the closet. It was the metal kind that they sold at Sears. I took out a foot-long flat-tip screwdriver and dropped it, handle first, in the pocket of my coat. The last three inches stuck indiscreetly out of the pocket.

Outside, the Ford Breadbox started reluctantly in the cold, and it took a few minutes for the heat to come out of the vents in the dashboard. I steered the world's most anonymous vehicle through the streets of the city and thought that it was the perfect car for a spy. Maybe that was the chief difference between spies like George Smiley and James Bond – Smiley would have loved the Ford Breadbox. On the radio, Frankie Valli was telling me how his eyes felt about me. The mellow music oddly complemented the way the Breadbox slipped through the morning traffic.

By the time I made it to Jenkins Street, traffic was light; most of the workers were at work, and the school buses had dropped off their kids. I circled the block a couple of times and parked on Vinton Street, which was the next block over, heading away from the Projects. I made a mental note of the buildings in case I had to get out of there quickly. I could cut through driveways or backyards, hitting the fences to get back to the Breadbox, straight lines being the shortest distance between two points and all.

I got out and locked the car. I walked down Vinton toward Old Colony Avenue, thankful not only for the warmth of the watch cap, but also the fact that with it on and the collar of the peacoat turned up, I was much harder to identify. I find that helpful whenever I am getting ready to commit a felony like a B&E. I turned left on Old Colony and walked back up toward Jenkins. I walked past Rotary Liquors, which someone had told me was the headquarters for some notorious Southie gangsters.

I whistled a Taj Mahal song about changing while I walked. I turned onto Jenkins and crossed the street to be on the same side as Cusick's building. I ignored the front door, which I was certain would be locked with at least a deadbolt. His building was a three-story wooden tenement, the type with two-bedroom apartments on the first and second floors; the third floor would be home to a series of one-bedroom apartments. Cusick's flat was on the third floor.

When I got to the back door, I could see that the wood around the door jamb was crushed inward against the frame. The door had been jimmied open a lot. I put my gloved hand on the knob and rattled it. I felt the door rattle in its frame too. I turned the handle and was rewarded by finding it unlocked. I opened the door and went in with all the confidence of someone who lived there or at least was a regular visitor.

The building had the smells that I had come to associate with poverty. Rancid cooking oil, cooked meat of indeterminant origin, stale cigarette smoke and the faint smell of trash, all historically layered on top of each other for years. The walls had a darkish sheen to them, and the corners all seemed to be caked with an accumulation of dirt or dust. The back hallway was cluttered with bags and boxes pushed to one side against the interior walls. I gingerly went up the stairs until I was on the third floor. The fact that I had met the recently deceased Lonnie Cusick on a third-floor landing not unlike this one wasn't lost on me.

I stopped in front of his door and listened to the building, trying to hear sounds in his apartment or movement in any of the others. I slipped the screwdriver out of my pocket and fitted its flat head into the already loose door jamb. I pulled back on the handle with my body weight, and the door popped open. It seemed gunshot loud in the quiet hallway, and I listened, but nothing moved. That was something I learned in Vietnam, to stop and just listen.

I stepped into the apartment and wrinkled my nose. Cusick hadn't been much for keeping a clean apartment. Being dead for a couple of days hadn't helped matters. The door opened right into the kitchen, which had plates and dishes stacked in the sink. The stove looked like a small cityscape of pots and pans in lieu of buildings. Each one was still partially full of whatever had been cooked in it. I saw a small, skittery movement out of the corner of my eye. Cockroaches. Great.

That had been one of the worst things about being a cop: summer nights in the Projects where the cockroaches would roam with impunity. They were so big that I have seen them move shell casings in the scenes of shootings. We always did what we called 'the dance' – a sort of shuffling and slight hopping to minimize the time you were in contact with the ground. Holding still was to invite an unwanted hitchhiker.

I moved deeper into the apartment, regretting that I had ever set foot in it. I don't like roaches and would rather deal with rats, and I hate rats. I was grateful that it was a small apartment. There was a tiny bathroom that probably hadn't been cleaned since JFK was alive. Other than a prescription bottle of pills that weren't prescribed by a doctor, there wasn't much of interest. There was nothing in the toilet tank or hidden under the sink.

The small living area had a black-and-white TV, a Salvation Army couch and a coffee table that looked as though it had been to the wars and back. There were no pets, no books, no art and no plants. The apartment was the place where a lonely man with not much in the world flopped. It was better than a prison cell but only just.

The bedroom was tiny, with a single bed and a small three-drawer chest made of cardboard. Other than a straight razor and prison-issued underwear, there wasn't much to see. There was a narrow closet with a couple of sweatshirts and flannel shirts hanging up. The nicest thing in the place was a Starter team jacket for the Boston Celtics – Cusick's prized possession or a gift when he got out of Walpole.

Back in the living room, under empty beer cans, I found some unopened mail. Bills, a letter from the probation office and one from the Law Offices of Johnny O'Day, Esquire. The address on the bill from O'Day was the same as in the Yellow Pages. I had committed a B&E just to remind myself of how much I hated cockroaches and not much else.

I let myself out of the apartment, pulling the broken door shut behind me. When I was outside in the cold, crisp January air, I took a few deep breaths. I felt hot and itchy with a thousand tiny, unscratchable itches. That was how it always was going into apartments like that. I never knew what the term 'it made my skin crawl' meant until I first went to a crime scene in a roach palace.

I walked back to the Breadbox. No one shouted at me. No

one chased me, and there was no wail of sirens in the distance. I didn't have to hit the fence to get away. I just shook my head at taking risks to hit a dry hole. I hadn't learned anything about Cusick that I didn't already know, other than that he was a slob.

I drove back to my office listening to Creedence on the radio singing about the Green River, still feeling like I had to scratch every inch of my skin. I had a hunch and wanted to see if there was anything to it.

Once inside, with a pipe going and a cup of espresso in front of me, I called Joe Pinto. For once, he was at his desk.

'Roark, did you find our guy yet?' he asked after we had exchanged greetings.

'No, I hoped you would have found him and save me some leg work.'

'No such luck. What can I do for you?'

'I was wondering if you could tell me if Lonnie Cusick and Raymond Lee Keith were ever cell mates?'

'I don't think they were cellies. I'm not sure they were ever locked up together.'

'Oh, well, it was a long shot.' I welcomed the news. That meant that the only connection, the only part of the Venn diagram that they shared, was the lawyers. I was certain that Terry McVicker was on the up and up. We knew that O'Day wasn't. It gave me an idea of how to narrow my search. I would follow O'Day and see if he would lead me to Lee Raymond, but first I would have to talk with him. See if that would spook him into leading me to Lee Raymond. It wasn't much of a plan, but I didn't have anything else to work with right now.

TEN

I called O'Day's office and spoke to his secretary. She told me that O'Day wasn't taking new clients right now. I beseeched her . . . I didn't actually say, 'I beseech you, madam,' but words near enough. She wouldn't relent, but I did find out that he was in District Court and was expected back in the office at around four.

By the time I made it to Boston District Court, it was a little after eleven, and my skin had stopped feeling as if I wanted to take a Brillo pad to it. I managed to find a parking spot, which was some sort of miracle and meant that I shouldn't bother playing the Lotto because I had used up all my luck. Inside, I said hi to a couple of court officers who had been cops when I was on the force and had retired only to put on another uniform. At the clerk's office, I found out that O'Day was doing arraignments. The nice lady also told me what courtroom I could find him in.

I made my way up the stairs to the courtroom. The hallways were filled with the smoke from hundreds of people nervously smoking before their time in court or waiting to see what the outcome would be for a loved one who'd gotten in a jam. I slipped into the courtroom and took a seat in the back of the gallery. The courtroom had the rundown majesty of a British transatlantic liner, with dark wood paneling and railings, and wooden benches in two rows in the middle of the room.

The benches were arranged so that there was a walkway down the middle and one on each side. On the other side of the dark wooden railing with its swinging gate, to the immediate left, was the jury box, populated by three rows of eight individual dark-green leather seats. They were built for comfort, and more than one juror had nodded off in them. In front of the railing were the tables for the defense on the left and the prosecution to the right of the swinging wooden gates. In front of them was the witness stand, the bench where the judge sat in his black robe.

The stenographer sat at a small wooden table in front of the witness box, and the clerk of the court was on the side of the judge opposite the witness stand.

The courtroom was half full. Cops, mostly detectives, were sitting in the front two rows of wooden benches on the far left. They were there to do the low-level arraignments. The district attorneys were there to handle the low-level felonies; anything sexy like a murder was handled by a senior DA sent over from the head office. The public defender sat at the defense table behind a wall of files and forms. They handled most of the arraignments, as most people who got arrested couldn't afford a private attorney.

Most people when they think of court, think of *Perry Mason* or *12 Angry Men* . . . maybe *Inherit the Wind*. Long, drawn-out trials with fancy speeches and shocking evidence, dramatically presented. In some cases, that is true, but what they don't show the viewer is the business of the court . . . the first step in the legal process, the arraignment.

Arraignments in District Court are a volume business, turned out with a level of efficiency that Henry Ford would envy. The court officers bring the prisoners in, shackled to each other in pairs. They sit them in the jury box, usually in an older courtroom where the chairs are a bit faded. Their names are called, and usually one of the cops will get up, read the charges, a very brief version of the circumstances and the number of arrests that the prisoner has. They will also mention if that person is in violation of parole or a bail violator. The Commonwealth takes that sort of thing very seriously. The judge will ask the police what amount of bail they are looking for.

At this point, the defense attorney will either concede or argue. Even though most of the defense attorneys are regulars in the court and well known to the judge and the prosecutors, they still put their names on the record as a formality. That was how, after sitting in the gallery, I got a positive ID on Johnny O'Day who was representing, in that case, a gentleman accused of assaulting a police officer who was trying to arrest him for snatching a gold chain at Downtown Crossing T station.

O'Day had brown hair that was cut in keeping with the current trends. He was a little under six feet tall. O'Day could have been the second man with Raymond, but given the generic description I had to go on, so could half of the men in the Commonwealth. He favored suits from Brooks Brothers over Anderson-Little. Not that there was anything wrong with a good suit at an affordable price. He had hands with long, thin fingers that he gestured with when speaking, and the whole thing reminded me of two rather animated squids.

His client was granted bail but was a probation violator and had to go to another courtroom to address the violation.

I slipped out of the courtroom and waited in the hallway. I found a spot against the wall where I could see the door to the courtroom. I lit a Lucky Strike and waited, confident that with my long hair, lack of a shave and faded jeans, I looked like someone waiting for his moment in front of the judge.

A little before one o'clock, O'Day came out, talking to another lawyer. I overheard a lot of talk about golf and some about tennis, two things I know nothing about. Eavesdropping on the two lawyers, I wasn't in a great rush to take up either pastime. I watched them get on the elevator, and I took the stairs at a jog so I could be on the first floor when the elevator doors opened.

I spent the rest of the day tailing O'Day until I found myself in the Breadbox a couple of car lengths behind his car, battling rush-hour traffic. While mine was nothing anyone would look at twice, his was a different story. His was a decade-old Mercedes sedan the color of lobster bisque that someone had overzealously seasoned with paprika. The hubcaps were also aggressively bisque-colored which made me wonder about O'Day's taste. Out of habit, I wrote the license plate down in the small notebook I carried.

I followed the Bisquemobile through the surface streets until we hit the central artery and then into the gaping opening of the Callahan Tunnel. I stayed a few car lengths back as we drove north under Boston Harbor, finally emerging into East Boston. We followed Route 1A north at a crawl, as everyone else was trying to get out of the city too. The only good thing about the traffic was that it meant that I wasn't going to lose O'Day. Tailing someone at night was harder than during the day as a rule of thumb. Less natural light, the streetlights and the lights from oncoming traffic all conspire against keeping a decent standoff distance from the person you are following.

We followed the highway north past Logan Airport and Orient Heights Beach. On the radio, Dire Straits was singing 'Once Upon a Time in the West.' I could relate to the song. By the time we were passing by Revere Beach, Van Halen wasn't talking about love, and I was wondering if the gnawing in my stomach was too much coffee or not enough dinner.

By the time we were in Lynn, I was starving, and my stomach was rumbling. For reasons that I never understood, people of my dad's generation, whenever Lynn was mentioned, felt obligated to say, 'Lynn, Lynn, city of sin.' I wasn't aware of Lynn being any more sinful than any other town in the state, but I suspect that the damage was done, and it was culturally ingrained in all of us.

Route 1A gave way to surface streets and residential neighborhoods, and I hoped that O'Day couldn't tell one pair of headlights in his rearview mirror from another. When Route 1A veered to the northwest, we went northeast. Had we gone left, we would have ended up in the historic and infamous town of Salem. No witchcraft for O'Day tonight: he was heading into Marblehead.

Marblehead is a peninsula with an attached submunition peninsula that juts into the ocean. The town was overflowing with naval and fishing history. I had heard that it was the birthplace of Marine Corps Aviation. With lots of craggy cliffs, waterfront property and historic architecture, Marblehead was an expensive community to live in. That didn't fit with everything I had heard about O'Day. Then again, I hadn't expected him to drive a Mercedes Bisquemobile either. Either he was a better lawyer than everyone gave him credit for or he had some sort of scam going. A lucrative one, like blackmail.

We drove through the thicket of stately Colonial homes and manicured lawns under the dim streetlights. In summer, Marblehead was probably lush and vibrant – yacht clubs, beaches and boating. But January was not as kind, and the whole place seemed gray and a shadow of its summer self. A cruel wind was screaming in off the ocean. The wind shook the Breadbox as we made our way through neighborhoods with street names like Harbor Avenue or, my personal favorite, Ballast Lane. It was nice to see that in Marblehead something as underappreciated as ballast got its own street.

As we neared what I thought was the tip of the island, I wondered if O'Day had spotted me or at least was checking for a tail. I was hanging back and contemplated what I would do if he banged a uey or some other half-assed spy craft to see if he was being followed. Instead, he turned into the driveway of a large house that loomed over the ocean. I drove past and went around the curve, switching off my lights and parking by the side of the road twenty or thirty yards down.

I pulled on my watch cap and made sure that my peacoat was buttoned up. The wind snatched at the car door when I opened it. I left the car unlocked. I doubted very much that anyone in Marblehead was going to rifle through the Ford Breadbox looking for anything. I walked back toward the house that O'Day had pulled into.

If the town were holding auditions for a haunted house, O'Day's would be a strong contender. It was large, and the cedar shingles had weathered gray. The front lawn was bordered by a privet hedge that needed to be trimmed sometime last summer. There was an opening in the hedge and a brick path that led to the front door. I stopped at the opening to the driveway and looked to see if there were any infrared sensors that let the homeowner know when someone was coming down the driveway.

Satisfied that there was nothing, I started down the driveway. The front of the house was in darkness, but even at night, I got the impression that it hadn't been well maintained for some time. The trim might have been faded. I couldn't tell in the darkness, but I could see that it had the texture of peeling paint. As I got closer to the house, I could see light spilling out of the back of the house onto the garage. It was a two-car garage with the types of doors that opened outward instead of rolling up into the garage. I stopped to listen, straining my ears for the sounds of a dog. The last thing I wanted was Fido raising hell while I was in no position to explain why I was on someone's property.

I eased past the Bisquemobile whose engine was ticking as it cooled in the night air. I came to the corner of the house and saw light spilling out. I could smell the smoke from a fireplace and wondered if it was from this house or another. Every now and then, the wind would die down and I could hear people talking, but I couldn't make out any of the words.

I slid around the pools of light from the window, staying in the shadows as much as I could as I made my way to the corner of the garage so I could get a look at who was talking. I looked back into the kitchen from the shadows by the garage. I couldn't hear anything and was just happy to be in the shadows enough that I was sure I couldn't be seen.

O'Day was in an animated discussion with another man. O'Day's hands were dancing around as he gestured with them. Standing in front of O'Day, arms crossed, with a sour look on his face, was Lee Raymond.

Raymond had a drink in one hand, and I got the impression that he wasn't just visiting. The wind kicked up and caught the lid of one of the trashcans on the other side of the garage, sending it to the pavement with a loud crash. Then it gusted again, sending the trashcan over too with a louder bang.

Both O'Day and Raymond whipped their heads and stared out the window. I held still, and when they started to move, I pushed myself back into the darkness between the garage and the neighboring fence. I couldn't see them, but I heard the kitchen door open. I could hear someone moving, and a flashlight beam played across the fence a few feet in front of me. Then I heard a voice say, 'It's nothing. The wind knocked over a couple of trashcans. It's freezing out here.'

I heard the scraping of trashcans, then a few seconds later I heard the slamming of the kitchen door. I stayed still, precious heat leaching out of my body. It required discipline, and I had to clench my jaw to keep my teeth from chattering. I waited five minutes, flexing my fingers in my gloves to keep them from going numb. My grizzled earlobe throbbed, and I wasn't starting to fantasize about hot chocolate or Irish coffee. Nope, not at all. Not poor freezing me.

If I hadn't been so cold, I would have felt some sort of flush of victory. I was too cold to do much. I decided to beat a retreat to the heat of the car and home. I slowly eased out of the spot between the garage and the fence and crawled past the Bisquemobile until I felt safe enough to stand up and walk out to the street. I stopped long enough to note the number of the house.

By the time I got back to the Ford Breadbox, my toes were

numb and my cheekbones stung. I got in, and the car started with mild protest. Fortunately, the engine warmed up quickly after the drive up from the city. The heat started pouring from the floor vents after a few minutes of my teeth chattering.

I headed back to the city with more questions, but at least I had found a link between O'Day and Lee Raymond. It also explained why no one, including Raymond's parole officer, could find him. He was hiding out with his lawyer/co-conspirator. I would tell Joe Pinto where to find Raymond but only after I had a chance to do more digging. Something told me that Johnny O'Day couldn't afford a house, even a rundown one in Marblehead, much less a bisque-colored Mercedes.

My teeth stopped chattering by the time I was back on Route 1A. The traffic heading into the city was lighter now that the rush hour was over. It still wasn't moving fast, but it wasn't the stop-and-go nightmare it had been heading out of the city. By the time I was crossing back over the Mystic River into the city, the chill still hadn't seeped from my bones. I needed a drink and some sort of hot meal to set things right.

I stopped at Athena's on my way home. I was more than happy to sit at the counter, basking in the heat rolling off the pizza ovens while they prepared my chicken parmesan sub. Somehow, fried chicken cutlet, marinara and melted provolone all on a giant sub roll was what I was craving. Athena's, if you asked them, would rub the inside of the roll down with the garlic and butter mixture that they used on their garlic bread. I asked them to.

After a blissful ten minutes by the pizza ovens, my sub was ready, and I was on my way home. Once I had let myself into the apartment and attended to Sir Leominster's insistent pleas for food and attention, I was able to sit down with my dinner at the kitchen table. Fortunately, I also had a large glass of Powers whiskey to help get any residual chill out of my bones.

I also had my yellow legal pad of notes. Between bites of chicken parm and sips of whiskey, I added to my case notes. I also made a note to call Devaney in the morning. I was curious to see if the Bisquemobile was registered to Double Pay O'Day and, if not, then to whom? I was also curious to see who the real owner of the house was. Hopefully, that could be solved by a trip to the Public Library. If not, I would go to the assessor's office in Marblehead.

I was planning to head back to Marblehead in the morning to watch O'Day's house. I wanted to see what Lee Raymond was up to and tail him if he was moving around. Also, I might be up for my second B&E in as many days. There was nothing to say that they didn't develop the pictures there or at least have some sort of evidence in the house. I might be able to find something that I could use as counter-leverage against Raymond and O'Day to get them to back off the judge. It was the closest thing to a plan that I had in a long time.

After I finished the sub and the whiskey, I realized I was doodling more than working on my case notes. I poured a second large whiskey and made my way to the couch to see if there was anything worth watching on TV. TV56 was playing *Where Eagles Dare*. I love the movie, but I had spent too much time outside freezing tonight to watch Clint Eastwood and Richard Burton plunge into a river in Bavaria during the height of winter. Fortunately, the Movie Loft was showing *The Manchurian Candidate*, and that always gets my attention.

I watched the movie and thought about my plan for tomorrow during the commercials. I was going to head back to Marblehead. If I was going to do another B&E, I should probably bring something other than a big screwdriver. I had some lock picks somewhere that I didn't use much because, frankly, I wasn't that good at it. When you watch Magnum pick a lock on TV, he gets it done in seconds. That is great if you are dealing with a padlock, but door locks on an old house tend to be sticky, even with keys. It's that much worse closer to the ocean.

When the movie ended, I went to bed. I had the rough shape of a plan in my head, and I set the alarm for five. I didn't relish getting up that early and frankly had avoided it since leaving the Army, but in this case, there was no other way, especially if I wanted to beat the rush-hour traffic. It was funny to think that the traffic in Boston was so bad it was literally a factor in my investigation.

The next morning, I was up, dressed and on my way out of the city before the sun was up. I had my trusty .38 on my hip and in addition to all of my usual stuff, I had my custom B&E kit.

I had two small, hard rubber wedges, a two-inch-wide by four-inch-long strip of plastic cut from a soda bottle and a three-inch multi-purpose painter's tool, the type that has a rounded cut out in the blade with a scraper and point at one end. They were useful for jimmying locks, and the thick handle would still let me get a decent grip with gloved hands. I had a clipboard with some papers and a ballpoint pen on a chain attached to it. Lastly, I had a white New England Bell hard hat, complete with the telephone logo.

I also had a thermos of hot coffee, and a quick stop at the local French bakery that was open at this ungodly hour meant that I had two ham and cheese croissants for breakfast. They were made with good ham, and the best part was the bit of Gruyère cheese that leaked out and was cooked to a crisp. I had also brought an apple from home so that I could pretend that I was having a healthy breakfast. There's no reason that one should suffer while going on surveillance.

I made the drive up to Marblehead in a little over half an hour, which the night before took almost three times that. I eased on to O'Day's street as the morning sun was starting to climb over the chimneys that were pushing out steam from hard-working boilers. The first of the bright-yellow school buses were snaking their way slowly through the narrow streets, and I settled in behind one. It allowed me to slowly crawl by the house and confirm the Bisquemobile was still in the driveway.

I hadn't seen another car, but if Lee Raymond was flopping there and trying to stay out of sight from his PO, then he probably parked in the garage. I had been too cold and too concerned with not being seen last night to look and see if there was anything in the garage. I found a spot up the street from the house where I could park and observe the driveway.

I poured myself a cup of coffee and munched on a croissant. Flaky crumbs dropped all over the front of my peacoat, but it was a small price to pay. I had my notebook and pen in my outer pocket in case I saw another car drive away from the house or I had some other note-taking emergency.

I hated doing surveillance in places like this. In Boston, no one cared, and the people made a habit of not noticing anything unless you were breaking into their place. In places like

Marblehead, they called the cops and expected them to come quickly. I had called the Marblehead Police Department before I left Boston. I told them I was a private investigator working on a divorce case and would be in the area if they received any suspicious persons calls. I told the sleepy-sounding cop what I would be driving and its license number. It wouldn't do me much good if the cops decided that they didn't want my type around, but at least I could claim I was playing by the rules.

I could move around but there were only so many places I could see the house from. On top of that, even with the Ford Breadbox, with my long hair and lack of a clean shave, I looked shady by local standards. I was hoping that most people would be in the fog of early morning or distracted by their need to get to work.

More school buses came and went. There weren't as many people walking dogs as I would have expected, but that had probably as much to do with the availability of large yards as it did with the January weather.

I had been sitting in the Breadbox for an hour when I saw the Bisquemobile nose out of the driveway. O'Day was at the wheel and sitting next to him was Lee Raymond. Sometimes even I get lucky.

I waited in the Breadbox just in case they forgot something and headed back right away. Then I circled the block and pulled up right in front of the house, just like someone with legitimate business might. I turned the car off, got out, put the hard hat on my head, locked the car and, with the clipboard in hand, walked up the front path to the house. In daylight, the house looked even more rundown than it had the night before.

I knocked on the peeling paint of the front door. The mail slot had a brass flap that hadn't seen any polish in years, and the greenish-brown patina looked as if it had been there forever. I would have rung the doorbell, but there were just a couple of wires sticking out. I knocked again and made a production of looking at my clipboard and flipping through the papers I had clipped to it. I hoped I looked like a telephone company employee double-checking an invoice or a work order. Right, perfectly legitimate, nothing to see here, nosy neighbor.

The Judge

I walked across the lawn toward the driveway, appearing to look at my clipboard and shake my head. I was trying to act every bit like an irritated phone company employee, just trying to do his job. I was thankful for the high, overgrown hedges. The back door was up a short flight of steps around the corner from the driveway. I went up the steps and knocked on the door, pausing to listen for footsteps or a dog.

The door was as weathered as the rest of the house. I was probably in Vietnam the last time someone had painted the trim or replaced any of the cedar shingles. The back door opened to the kitchen. There was a keyhole in the doorknob and a deadbolt above it. I tried the knob. It was locked, but when I leaned my weight against the door, it gave a little. The door either hadn't been deadbolted or the deadbolt didn't work.

I leaned against the door and took a rubber wedge out of my pocket and pushed it between the door and the frame. In theory, the rubber would be firm enough to force some space between the door and frame but not so hard that it would damage the wood. No sense in telegraphing to O'Day that someone had broken in.

I took the painter's tool out of my coat and slipped it into the space that was made by the wedge. I toggled it back and forth against the jamb. After a few seconds, I felt it catch on the tongue of the lock, and the door popped open. I kicked the wedge into the kitchen as I stepped in. I closed the door behind me, picked up the wedge and listened for the telltale beeping of an alarm, a dog or someone moving around in the house.

The kitchen was large with avocado-colored appliances and dark wooden cabinetry. It smelled like last night's dinner of fried meat. There was a table and chairs at one end of it, and it was easily four times the size of my kitchen. Everything in it was dated, but it had all been expensive from high-end stores in Boston in the 1950s and 1960s. There were piles of newspapers and mail at one end of the table and dishes that needed doing in the double sink.

I put the clipboard down on the table by the pile of mail and picked up a couple of envelopes to see if there was anything interesting. They were mostly utility bills in the name of Hellen Whitman. There were also several envelopes from Publishers Clearing House.

The trashcan was overflowing with empty cans of food and empty beer bottles precariously perched on top. There were a couple of grease-stained cardboard buckets from America's favorite fried chicken franchise too. I would have been shocked if one of them was a devotee of Julia Child.

I wasn't shocked that O'Day and Lee Raymond weren't the neatest pair. That being said, they seemed like an unlikely set of roommates. Maybe O'Day's dedication to his clients had been underrated around the courthouse.

I moved slowly through the first floor, looking for clues. That is what we detectives say to make our B&Es seem more glamorous or less criminal.

The house was large, and the first floor had a formal dining room, a living room and a front room or parlor on one side. On the other side of the house was a large study and a small office. Except for the study, the rooms were all dusty with sheets covering all the furniture. The furniture in the study was big and old and tasteful. The fireplace was being used regularly, and there was a big pile of wood next to it. There was a desk and chair at the far end of the room. There was a large console TV, a Zenith, and a color one that sat squatly across from the couch. There were empty beer bottles on one of the end tables and an ashtray filled with cigarette butts. I went back out into the hallway.

There was a pile of mail on the floor by the mail slot, all in the same name, Hellen Whitman. I turned away from the pile. There were two bathrooms on the first floor. Powder rooms, actually – a toilet, a sink, a medicine cabinet and lots of fancy soaps from France that no one was actually supposed to wash with. They were the type of soaps that look more like candies.

I went upstairs and found several bedrooms, and all but two had the same deal with sheets covering the furniture. The other two were being lived in. One had a pile of clothes on a chair and another on the floor. By the look of the clothes – sweat suits, acid-washed blue jeans, Nike sneakers – that was Lee Raymond's room. On the bedside table, there was an open pack of smokes – Newports. I detested menthol cigarettes, but I knew a lot of guys in Vietnam who had smoked them. There was nothing lying around that indicated he was a blackmailer. He didn't keep much in the bureau drawers or the closet. The only thing of interest on the bureau was a pyramid of three packs of Newports. I guess he didn't want to run out.

The next room was more neatly kept. Suits, pressed shirts and ties hung in the closet. T-shirts, socks and underwear were in the bureau drawers. Some casual clothes too, but, again, nothing that screamed out about a blackmail operation. The bathrooms adjoining each of their rooms reflected the personality traits found in the bedrooms. One neat and one slovenly. After twenty minutes of careful searching, all I came up with was a baggie of weed. Not very good stuff at that.

I went downstairs quickly and stopped to listen. Nothing. The house was still empty, and a discreet check out of the windows showed the yard and driveway to be the same. Back in the kitchen, I found a couple of pantry doors and a door that led down into the dark cellar. There was no light switch that I could see. I took out my penlight and shined it down the rickety steps.

The penlight gave off enough light so that I could see the cellar. Off to my right was an area that seemed to hold a lot of boxes and broken furniture. The furniture that was broken was old but not necessarily antique. There was a lot of very dated wicker furniture, which was definitely for patio use. There was a set of croquet mallets that seemed to have been repurposed into an elaborate spiderweb construction site.

To my left were metal shelves with cans of food, mostly stew and Campbell's soup, although there were a couple of cans of escargot, deviled ham and smoked oysters too. There were also tins of sardines and metal tins of saltines. There was also a healthy-looking wine rack with rows of dusty bottles. The place had been well provisioned several years ago, judging by the dust.

I worked my way around the cellar, finding a bin of coal, a shovel rising from it like a gravestone, and next to that an old coal furnace that was giving off some nice heat. Not far from that was a quartet of three-speed bikes with flat tires, festooned with wisps of cobweb. Deeper in the darkness of the cellar, I found the washing machine and the dryer, both of which were as dated as the appliances upstairs.

Alongside the washing machine was a large slop sink, and next to that was a small closet or room. I opened the door and found a small bathroom. It had a sink and a toilet with a tank that was raised high over the bowl. There was a pull chain for a light, and I pulled it. I found myself bathed in red light from a single bare red bulb in the ceiling. Then I noticed the crude shelves that had been installed by someone who wasn't very skilled. There were trays on the shelves, a timer and bottles of different chemicals. It was a home darkroom, a handy thing for a blackmailer to have.

It was also very empty. There were no incriminating pictures or negatives lying around. The clothesline strung across the width of it had clothespins clipped to it, but no pictures hanging from them. There were no machines either. I don't know how big an enlarger was, but the space was too small to fit that type of thing. There was a wastebasket in the corner by the toilet. There was nothing in the trashcan, but the weak beam from my penlight caught something fluttering on the floor behind the toilet bowl.

It was a strip of photographic paper. I could make out a series of images on it, each a little paler than the last, as if they were fading slowly away from frame to frame. It was the test strip that Artie had told me about. In one of the frames, I could make out Lee Raymond, naked except for a gold chain. I had seen the picture before. It was one of the ones that the judge had handed over to me. That was what we in the business referred to as a clue.

I leaned further down and took a closer look behind the toilet and was rewarded for my efforts with another strip of photographic paper. They must have ended up there by someone carelessly tossing them at the wastebasket. I put them both in the inside pocket of my peacoat.

I froze. A floorboard creaked above me, and I reached up and pulled down on the chain, switching the red light off. If I had learned anything in Vietnam, it was when to be still, to be quiet, and when to act with speed and violence. This was a time to be still. Someone was walking around upstairs on the first floor.

I carefully stepped out of the darkroom and quietly closed the door behind me. I flicked on the penlight and kept carefully searching the cellar. After searching, slowly, trying not to bump into anything or make any noise, I found a door in the wall. It was secured to the wall with two stout bolts, leading me to believe it might lead to a bulkhead. I wasn't sure how long I wanted to wait in the cellar and chance Lee Raymond or O'Day coming downstairs and finding me. Or, worse, calling the cops. A B&E arrest was a great way to lose my license.

I turned around and made my way back to where I had seen some tools and a workbench. I hoped there would be some sort of oil on the bench. Hope wasn't the best course of action but it was better than a lot of options open to me right now. My bet was that the door to the bulkhead was as well maintained as everything else I had seen so far. I didn't want to make any unnecessary noise, especially the sound of metal scraping across metal, a screeching noise that would raise the dead.

In theory, I could just wait in the basement and hope that no one would venture down into it. Or I could knock them out, but adding assault to my B&E seemed like a bad idea. The problem with waiting was I had no idea how long it would be. I might have to wait well into the night until the blackmailers were asleep. Or I might want to have a way to get out of the cellar in a hurry.

On the workbench, I found a metal can of sewing machine oil. The can was the type that held eight ounces of oil and had a metal tip that stuck out of the top with a little plastic cap nestled on it. It felt about half full, but it would have to do. I took it back to the bolted door and popped the cap off. It went skittering away in the darkness of the basement. I squirted a few drops of oil on each bolt where they would rub against metal.

I switched off my light to save batteries, and then, starting with the bottom bolt, began to slowly work it back and forth, little by little, adding a touch more oil as I went. Slowly but surely, the bolt gave way and quietly slid home. I waited, holding my breath, listening for any sounds above me. It took me another five minutes to get the top bolt open quietly. I spent another few minutes waiting, quietly. Then I flicked on the light and shined it on the hinges while I oiled them too.

After another twenty minutes of carefully applying oil and working the hinges, the door swung quietly open. I was rewarded by the sight of a set of concrete steps heading up to a rusty, metal bulkhead, the type with two doors that close by overlapping. I was also treated to the sight of horror-movie cobwebs across the steps. The doors were secured by a big metal bolt that ran through an eye hole. I went to work with the oil on the bolt.

I brushed the cobwebs aside, instantly itchy where they touched my skin.

The cellar hadn't been warm by any stretch of the imagination, but the cold of January on the North Shore bit deep into the stairwell. I spread the oil on the bolt, but every few minutes I had to take a break back in the cellar. I kept at it for half an hour and took breaks as needed. It was slow, deliberate work. More than once, I thought of how much easier it would have been to just walk upstairs and fight my way out of the house. I was certain that, on their best days, neither O'Day nor Lee Raymond was in my league. Instead, I just stayed focused on the task of getting out quietly.

Suddenly, there were voices upstairs, but they were too soft to make out. I strained my ears and then heard a bit of music, then voices. It took me a few minutes to realize it was the big console TV that I had seen in the study. I had heard commercials, then garbled voices I couldn't make out.

I went back and oiled the hinges of the bulkhead. With the bolt shot, I was able to slowly push up on one of the doors partway. Satisfied that it would open quietly enough, I stepped back down and pulled the door to the cellar shut behind me. There was no point in making it too obvious that someone had been there. I carefully opened the bulkhead and slipped out, quietly lowering it back down behind me.

I emerged on the opposite side of the house from the driveway. I ducked below the windows until I was at the front of the house and then I casually walked down the path and out to the street. My stomach started to rumble, reminding me that I had finished the croissants and apple hours ago. I checked my watch and discovered that it was almost two in the afternoon. I had spent five hours in the house. No wonder I was starving. I was also cold and itching from the dust and the cobwebs.

I got to the Breadbox and unlocked it. I tossed the New England Bell hard hat in the back seat and started the car up. It took a good ten minutes for the heat to kick in and another ten before I felt anything like warm. I was so hungry that I spent the drive back to town ruminating about what I was going to eat. Was it going to be pizza or maybe Chinese? Seafood wouldn't be filling enough unless I got fish and chips. Or maybe I need to go to my favorite Brigham's for a patty melt? Or a Reuben . . . a Reuben and a pint of Guinness was just about the most perfect thing I could think of in that moment.

I was so consumed thinking about food that it didn't occur to me that I had left the clipboard and its blank papers sitting on the kitchen table by the pile of mail. Raymond and O'Day might not find the cellar door unbolted or might think that one of them had done it carelessly, but the clipboard would definitely tell them someone had been in their house. It might spook them, but it wasn't as though they didn't already know I was looking for Raymond. It was pretty obvious that O'Day was the other man in the hotel. I couldn't picture Lonnie Cusick working a sharpened pencil, much less a camera. Also, they had already taken a run at me with a shotgun and set me with Lonnie Cusick. I wondered if it was Cusick who shot my car. But then why not bring the shotgun with him to the abandoned building? That would have been a lot more effective than a baseball bat. Unless he dumped it somewhere after the cops showed up? Cusick wouldn't have been looking to go back to prison on a weapons charge. Either way, I was pretty sure they were already spooked. Hence, they shot my car and I was driving a Ford Breadbox as a loaner. At least now I had evidence, and I was starting to formulate a plan.

ELEVEN

In the end, lunch was two hotdogs and some coleslaw from a greasy spoon that was on the way to the office. While I was waiting for my food to make it from the grill to my spot at the lunch counter, I stepped into the phone booth at the back. I called Devaney, and after the usual insults about my ancestry, he agreed to run the plates from the Bisquemobile. He told me to call him back in ten minutes. I took fifteen so that I could do justice to my lunch and wash it down with a Coke.

Back in the phone booth, I pressed the handset to my ear and listened to Devaney while he went on at length about what a bullet his kid sister had dodged by not getting married to me. I didn't point out that we had been in high school and marriage wasn't an option.

'Billy, any chance you might get to the point and tell me about the plates you ran?'

'Sure, sure, anything for you. It's registered to a Hellen Whitman. DOB - 4/10/1910, died November of 1984.'

'Car's still registered?'

'Yep, on a 1974 Mercedes.' He then read off the address in Marblehead where I had just spent an uncomfortable few hours hiding in the basement.

'Thanks, Billy, I appreciate it.'

'You not marrying my sister is thanks enough,' he said, not unkindly, before hanging up the phone. Devaney had a sentimental side – who knew?

Instead of heading over to the office, a trip back to the Public Library was in order. I spent so much time in the place that I was beginning to think I should explore just using it as my office. I'd save a bundle on rent and utilities.

I was curious to see what I could find out about Hellen Whitman, and, more importantly, why Johnny O'Day was living in her house and driving her car. He seemed quite comfortable in both, and he certainly couldn't afford a house in Marblehead. Maybe he inherited them from her.

The reference section of the Boston Public Library was exactly where I had left it. I fed some quarters into the Xerox machine and made several copies of the test strips I found in the basement darkroom. I wasn't exactly sure what I was going to do with them, but it made sense to have copies. Then I settled in behind a microfilm machine with microfilm for the November/December issues of the *Boston Globe*. Something told me that Hellen Whitman was too classy to have an obituary in the *Herald*. I was pretty sure that I wasn't high-class enough to have an obituary in a supermarket flyer.

Hellen Whitman was the granddaughter of a confectioner who figured out how to mass-produce and, more importantly, package chocolates. She had inherited the house in Marblehead and a small pile of money that had been significantly reduced by the crash in 1929. It was still big enough to keep her in comfort for the rest of her life. She had married and had two sons. Her husband was killed in World War Two when the destroyer he was commanding was on the receiving end of a kamikaze attack. Both of her sons were killed valiantly leading their men in Korea. Neither had married or had children. Whitman never remarried, though she was socially active with the types of clubs and charities that the rich seemed to favor – flowers, horses, dogs and yacht clubs. When she died, she had no relatives, distant or otherwise, to claim her fortune. Interesting, too, was that she didn't have a will when she died.

When I had scribbled a few more pages of case notes and had a mild headache, it was time to go. As was usually the case, I had found an answer that had led me to more questions. If Hellen Whitman didn't have any living relatives, how was it that O'Day came to live in her house? Were he and Lee Raymond squatters? It made me want to investigate probate records, and to do that I would need help from someone who worked in the court. Fortunately, I was going to be seeing a very pretty, very smart clerk for dinner.

I stopped by my local Bread and Circus to buy the ingredients for dinner. I left with a decent size tenderloin of pork, new potatoes, spinach and a bunch of relatively fresh herbs. I also bought the makings of a salad and one of those green plastic baskets of strawberries. A small baguette and a quart of heavy cream also made their way into the shopping cart. By the time I made it home, first stopping at the liquor store for a bottle of both red and white wine, my wallet was a lot thinner than it had been at the start of the day.

Sir Leominster, when he was done meowing and rubbing up against my shins, hopped up on the table to investigate the groceries. I hung up my peacoat and started the oven. I stopped to change the batteries in my penlight which then went back into the pocket of my coat. Then I put a pot of water on the stove to boil.

I dug around the refrigerator and came up with a couple of carrots that still had a little snap left to them and an onion. I cut the onion into eighths and did the same with the carrots. They went into the bottom of a roasting pan with a couple of cloves of garlic, forming a bed for the tenderloin.

I unwrapped the pork tenderloin and carefully trimmed away any of the silver skin the butcher had missed. That done, I rubbed it with olive oil, salt, pepper and minced rosemary, placing it on the bed of vegetables in the roasting pan. I chopped some of the other almost-fresh herbs and threw them in too. I popped the tenderloin in the oven, and when the water came to a boil on the stove, I added the potatoes.

After ten minutes, I took the potatoes off the heat and strained them, putting them back in the pot with some ice and cold water. Once they had cooled down enough to handle, I rubbed them, removing the skins. When I had skinned the new potatoes, I opened the oven and added them to the roasting pan, around the tenderloin. I popped it all back into the oven after giving it a few shakes to coat the potatoes with the liquid in the pan.

Then it was time to shower the cobwebs away before Angela came over. It wasn't that I had worked up a sweat, but two days of cobwebs and cockroaches had left me feeling itchy. It wasn't the way to embark on a date with an attractive lady. Much less so with one that I liked.

When I had showered and dressed, I went back to the oven. I turned the tenderloin over and moved the potatoes around so that they'd brown evenly. The kitchen was overwhelmed with the wonderful smell of roasted pork loin with herbs. I set the table with mostly matching plates and wine glasses. I found some napkins and laid them out with silverware. I even managed to find a couple of candles. There wasn't much point in inviting her over for dinner and not trying to impress her.

I turned on the radio which was set to the local public radio station. The evening news was on, and President Reagan was promising to enlighten us about Libya's links to terrorism. The South Africans dealt with the ongoing strike at a platinum mine by firing 20,000 workers. I suspected that there wasn't an Afrikaner among them. Cory Aquino said that she was so anti-communist that if she beat Ferdinand Marcos in the election, she wouldn't have any communists in her cabinet. It made me want to vote for her. The only interesting thing here at home was that we had a new postmaster general.

By the time the news gave way to jazz, I had cut the baguette into pieces that went into a basket on the table next to the butter. I turned the oven off when the tenderloin was done. It would keep warm for a bit. The spinach wouldn't take more than a minute or two to sauté, and there was no point in jumping the gun on the world's most delicate leafy vegetable.

A little after seven, the intercom buzzed, and Angela's voice came through the tinny box telling me it was cold and to let her in. I pushed the button and buzzed her in. I gave the apartment one last quick glance to make sure everything looked good. Sir Leominster eyed me with suspicion, then yawned to let me know exactly how interesting he found all my machinations. What did he know? He'd never invited a lady cat over for dinner. I opened the door when I heard the tock-tocking of high heels on the landing.

'Hello.'

'Hi.'

We kissed in the hallway of my apartment for longer than was generally considered necessary for a polite greeting between friends. Then I took her coat and hung it up. She had a handbag that looked as if it could hold everything but the proverbial kitchen sink but was still smaller than a gym bag. Under her coat, she wore a dark cashmere sweater and expensive jeans, both of which accentuated her curves. I was not going to complain.

She wore high-heeled boots that came up to just below her knees. Diamonds sparkled in her earlobes, but they were dim compared to her smile.

'I brought a bottle of wine,' she said, handing me a bottle in brown paper.

'The more the merrier.'

'It smells wonderful in here.'

'Thank you. You look . . . fantastic.'

'Thanks . . . a girl tries.' I was rewarded by another smile that did her diamond earrings a disservice. She was wearing lipstick that was eye-catching but not loud.

'Can I get you a drink? Wine or something else?'

'Yes, please. A glass of wine.'

'Red or white?'

'White.'

After I had poured us each a glass, I pulled the tenderloin out of the oven to rest. Then, while sautéing the spinach with crushed garlic, a liberal dousing of black pepper and nutmeg, I told her about my adventures in Marblehead. When the spinach wilted and the tenderloin had rested, I sliced it into rounds, which went on a large plate that I pretend is a serving dish. The browned new potatoes went around it with the sautéed spinach at one end. I sprinkled some salt on the potatoes and spinach.

'So, you found them?' she said over the lip of her wine glass.

'Yes. I am not sure about how they ended up in the late Hellen Whitman's house or driving her car, but Lee Raymond and Johnny "Double Pay" O'Day are definitely living together. I was hoping you might be able to check around the court about the Whitman estate?'

'Sure, I can do that. That won't be hard to find.'

'I don't know if it will help, but it can't hurt.'

'No, it can't.'

'Probably another dinner in it for you.'

'Oh, I'm holding out for more than just dinner,' she said with a slight leer.

'That is good to know. It's important to have something to look forward to.' I put the platter down on the table.

'Oh, that looks good.'

'More wine?'

'Please.'

I poured more into each of our glasses.

'So, now what?' she asked.

'I thought we'd eat dinner and then maybe go to the couch and make out.'

'You're single-minded. I meant with the case.'

'Well, if I have to be single-minded about anything, making out seems like a good thing to be single-minded about. But to answer your question, now that I know where Lee Raymond is and who he's in league with, that is half the battle.'

'What's the other half?'

'Getting my hands on the pictures and negatives. It is not enough to know who they are; we have to take away their means to blackmail the judge.'

'What will you do? Go shake them down, beat it out of them, some sort of tough-guy approach?'

'Well, the test strips I found are a direct link to a criminal conspiracy. They aren't anonymous anymore. I thought I might go have a talk with Double Pay O'Day and see if the thought of prison scares him.'

'You know the judge will never testify.'

'I know. I would, in essence, be bluffing him.'

'And if he doesn't fall for it?'

'I plan to be persuasive. If he doesn't like the thought of prison, maybe he will panic, try to move the pictures and negatives. Might end up revealing their location so I can grab them up.'

'Then you'd swoop in and steal them, saving the judge and getting the girl?' she said with a gentle mocking tone and a bit of laughter like the tinkling of piano keys.

'Sure, it's as good a plan as any.'

'Is this how you go through life, just making things up as you go?'

'More or less. I mean, it hasn't failed me yet.' How one defines failure is subjective, but I'd like to think that I am right more often than I am wrong.

'Jesus,' she said, whistling in mock admiration, or maybe it was mock disbelief.

'It might not be the most detailed plan, but it is better than no plan.'

'Only just. You can't turn them over to the cops. You know that?'

'I don't have any intention of turning them over to anyone. I just want to make sure they can't keep blackmailing the judge.'

'And protect his secret?'

'And protect him, yes. That is what he hired me to do.' I didn't bother mentioning that there were some things that I wouldn't do. Nor did I mention that the judge, or Angela for that matter, might not agree with me about the best way to do it.

'Do you think they're working for someone at NT and C?'

'Probably not directly. I think they approached someone at NT and C and said something like "We can make your problem go away for enough money." Raymond and O'Day don't strike me as the types to share a source of leverage with anyone else.' We stopped talking about the case and moved on to those things that you talk about with someone new. Favorite things, old lovers, family, things like that. The slow unpeeling of memories and experiences, trying to get to know each other.

'Let me help you with the dishes.'

'No, you're my guest. It wouldn't be right.'

'I insist.'

'I rather thought the dishes could wait.'

'Oh, you had something else in mind.'

'I did.'

'Something involving your bed, no doubt.'

'That and a lot less clothes.' Smooth Roark, very smooth.

The next morning, I slept in. Angela had woken up early and dressed quickly. She had turned down my offer of breakfast and didn't even want coffee. She had to go to work and didn't have time. When she had dressed, she leaned over me in bed, smiled a million-watt smile and kissed me.

'We should do this again soon,' she said huskily.

'Do you have plans tonight?' I said eagerly.

'Let a girl get some rest,' she said, smiling from ear to ear.

I followed her to the door and kissed her again.

'I'll call you later when I can look up the Whitman probate matter,' she said.

'Thank you.'

She left and I went back to bed. The light outside the window was the blue-gray of dawn, and it was cold outside. That was a sure recipe for wanting to climb back under the covers. In bed, the pillow next to me smelled of her perfume and I fell asleep.

I woke up some time later with Sir Leominster meowing at me because I overslept, and he was hungry.

I fed the cat and then went to shower. I was in the middle of my coffee and toast when the phone rang. I picked it up and was treated to Angela's voice.

'Good morning, Mr Roark,' she said saucily.

'Good morning, Miss Estrella.'

'I found out about O'Day's connection to Hellen Whitman.'

'Do tell.'

'O'Day is registered as her attorney and the executor of her estate.'

'OK, do executors normally live in their dead clients' homes or drive their cars?'

'No, they don't. As a matter of fact, that is sort of against the rules.'

'But not against the law.'

'It would only be against the law if someone could prove that he was defrauding the estate.'

'Which would be a neat trick because Whitman didn't have any heirs.' No complainant, no crime.

'True, but it looks like O'Day filed the paperwork making himself the executor and controller of her estate the day before she died.'

'What?'

'Yes, very convenient for him.'

'Didn't she have a lawyer?'

'She did. He died in the fall of 1983.'

'I bet she didn't have a will.'

'She didn't, but apparently O'Day told one of the clerks that Whitman had a number of bequests that he was discharging on her behalf.'

'Sounds like a con job.' I stated the obvious; it's a talent of mine.

'It probably is, but it's hard to prove he is doing anything that is actually illegal.'

'No, but I am not sure he knows what we can and can't prove.'

'Good point.'

'Can you make copies of the paperwork? Anything with her signature.'

'You think he forged her signature?'

'I think that is a lot more likely than he was retained and filed paperwork as the executor of her estate the day before she died.'

'Sure, I'll make copies. Anything else?'

'Yeah, is there any way to see if he is a last-minute executor for anyone else's estate?'

'Sure, might take a bit longer but it shouldn't be any trouble.'

'Good. You know that "make it up as I go" plan that you were so worried about?'

'Yeah.'

'I think it's starting to take shape.'

'Oh, good. Here I was, worried that you'd just act impulsively,' she said with sarcasm that Watts would be proud of.

The subject shifted and we spent a few minutes telling each other how much fun we'd had the night before. After we had chatted for a couple of minutes in soft, romantic tones, we rang off.

I got out the yellow legal pads and updated my case notes. Then I sketched out some sort of plan of attack. By the time I'd finished my coffee, I had a good idea of what I was going to do. I dug out the Yellow Pages and started looking up names and addresses. There were a couple in Boston, a couple in Marblehead that I needed. When I finished, I sat back and smiled because I had a plan of sorts.

I spent the bulk of the next few days in the Ford Breadbox following Double Pay O'Day around. I had my Canon thirty-five-millimeter with a zoom lens and managed to get a bunch of good pictures of O'Day. There were a few of him going in and out of different banks. I was curious if the Whitman estate had accounts in any of them. I was also able to get a couple of pictures of Lee Raymond. It was nice to have pictures of him with his clothes on for a change. The real winners for me were the pictures I managed to get of Raymond and O'Day together.

During this time, I felt like I was only in my apartment to shower, change clothes and get some sleep. Sir Leominster viewed my time spent in the apartment through the lens of his need for food and my responsibility to rub him under his chin. The answering machine had messages from the sergeant major reminding me to send my check in so that I could attend the reunion. There was the occasional one or two from Angela. Lastly, Joe Pinto had gotten my home number somehow, but that wasn't surprising given he was a probation officer and his job often involved tracking people down.

Pinto's messages were essentially variations on the following theme: 'Roark, Joe Pinto from Probation and Parole. Have you made any headway finding Raymond Lee Keith? Call me, man. Let me know. My boss is all over me about this one.'

That was exactly why I didn't have a boss. I could sympathize with Pinto, but I wasn't ready to have Raymond violated. Also, there was no telling how that would impact the judge. I couldn't risk Raymond making a deal or O'Day getting spooked and upping the ante or doing something dumb. Nope, Pinto could wait. I needed Raymond to stay in play so that I could brace him and O'Day.

The next day, I decided to give the surveillance a break, which was convenient because Angela Estrella wanted to come by my office on her lunch break. Shortly after noon, she walked in with snowflakes melting on the shoulders of her camel-hair coat. She was carrying her large handbag and a brown paper bag.

'You travel light.' Maybe Watts was rubbing off on me.

'Shut up, I brought you lunch and the records you wanted about O'Day.'

'Thank you.'

'Here.' She handed me a thick manila envelope. It wasn't first-novel-manuscript thick but close enough.

'Let me guess, Mrs Whitman wasn't his first dubious executorship?'

'Nope, the first happened in 1979. All told, he's done it four other times.'

'Oh, you've been putting some work in on this.'

'Yes, did I do good?'

'You did indeed.'

'Then kiss me.' She didn't have to tell me twice. She stepped away. 'I brought lunch.'

'I am a lucky guy.' I watched as she pulled two bottles of Perrier from the bag, two wax paper squares that I assumed were sandwiches and two Styrofoam bowls with plastic lids. The bag also had oyster crackers, paper napkins and plastic spoons.

'BLTs and clam chowder. Nothing fancy.'

'It's great.' We sat using my desk as a table while we ate and talked.

'You said O'Day started doing this in 1979?'

'Yeah, he hadn't perfected it yet, and a cousin turned up out of the woodwork looking for his inheritance. O'Day coughed up the money and nothing happened. Then I did some digging and found four other instances where he became the last-minute executor of an estate. Usually, they have been small estates, not a lot of money, and he's flown under the radar.'

'So, the Whitman estate is a big step up for him?'

'It seems to be.'

'I would think he makes decent money as a lawyer. Why take the risk?'

'Maybe he thinks it's not a risk. Andy, if there's no family to complain, who would find out? He makes easy money for filing some paperwork. He makes OK money, but he's more of a bottom feeder. Plus he's probably still paying off his student loans from law school.'

'True, that makes sense, plus this time he's also ended up with a house in Marblehead and a Mercedes to go with it. Quite the upgrade for a guy like him.'

We finished our lunch talking about other more interesting things. Then Angela had to go back to work, leaving me with a kiss and a promise to call me later. I started the espresso machine and packed a pipe; both would help me focus. I was able to get the pipe lit and drawing nicely with one match, which was all you needed according to Raymond Chandler. Who was I to argue?

When I had a tiny cup of espresso in front of me, I opened the manila envelope that Angela had brought by. There were six sets of legal documents. I started to read one, but legal boilerplate should be used to treat insomnia. It was a struggle to get through a couple of pages.

The Judge

When my eyes started to grow heavy, I flipped to the pages that included the signatures. I folded the other pages over and laid each set of documents so that the signature pages were next to each other. I reached into my desk drawer and took out a large magnifying glass that an old girlfriend bought me as a joke.

I looked at O'Day's signature under the magnifying glass in each of the documents. Then I did the same with the clients' signatures. I went back and forth, letter by letter between them. I am no handwriting analysis expert – I wouldn't even pretend to be one – but there were similarities. O'Day made distinctive e's and a's, and they looked eerily similar to the ones in some of his clients' signatures. Probably just a coincidence. Not bloody likely.

O'Day was turning out to be a thief and a blackmailer. He wasn't the type who would welcome any attention, any focus on his activities. Lee Raymond was a con and a hustler. Neither one struck me as the tough-guy type, so it might be time to lean on them a little. Now, Vietnam-era me, Boston Police Department me would have done that with my fists or a blackjack. But I'd been on a self-improvement kick lately, trying to be a better person, so putting the work in on them wasn't the route I wanted to go. I had been reading Nietzsche and that whole 'beware when fighting dragons' thing was resonating a little too strongly.

I pulled the Yellow Pages open and flipped to the L's. I found the number I wanted and dialed. After a minute a man answered, 'Johnny O'Day, Esquire.'

'Mr O'Day, this is Bobby Bell King over at the *Boston Globe*,' I said with my best imitation of a Southern accent.

'Oh, Mr King, what can I do for you?'

'I'm writing an article about local businesses . . .' I trailed off. It wasn't much of a game of cat and mouse, but it was a start.

'That's great, but I am not sure how I can help.'

'Well, you see, I am writing about eccentric business owners.'

'Still not sure how I can help.'

'Well, I saw that you represent the estate of Hellen Whitman . . . you know, the candy heiress,' I said grandly.

'Yes, I do.'

'I was wondering, sir, about the codicil in her father's will?'

'What codicil?'

'Oh, apparently, old man Whitman was a bit of an eccentric, and if his children died without any heirs, the estate was supposed to be liquidated and all the money donated to the Hull Lifesaving Museum.'

'What?'

'Yes, I guess it was a pet project of his.'

'Mr King, I'm afraid I can't comment on that at this time. Good day.' He hung up abruptly.

I sat back, smiling at myself. I love stirring the pot. Once in Vietnam, when the practical joking was on the brink of getting out of hand, Sergeant Major Billy Justice pulled me aside.

'Now, young Sergeant Roark, you know I appreciate a good joke as much as the next man.'

'Yes, Sergeant Major.' Anyone else I might have made a wise-ass comment to, but not Sergeant Major Billy Justice. There might have been faster ways to get myself hurt, but I couldn't think of any.

'Your problem, Roark, is that you enjoy the shit too much. You like to antagonize people and you take things too far.'

'Sergeant Major, I . . .'

'Now, don't interrupt me, son. Sergeant Major's in a generous mood, dispensing wisdom and shit.' He waved his glass of Chivas almost like a conductor in front of his orchestra. He was slurring his words slightly, but it was a rare thing to see the sergeant major drunk.

'Yes, Sergeant Major.'

'You enjoy the shit too much. You lose focus on the periphery. That's gonna get you killed one of these days, young sergeant.'

It was only later, in my bunk, wondering why my hooch was spinning so violently, that it occurred to me that Billy Justice was worried about me. He was trying to tell me not to get killed on a mission because I was pushing my luck too hard. It was funny because you could do everything right and still get killed. That was just the nature of it.

Now, I packed up the paperwork that Angela had brought in my old postal carrier's bag. It went in there with my case notes and felt-tip pens. I shut the office window, turned off the lights and locked the door on my way out.

* * *

It was early afternoon, and the traffic was in my favor. I made the now familiar drive up to Marblehead, which at this time of day didn't take long. It was a pretty drive along the water with snow flurries spinning and twirling in the wind.

I parked in front of the Whitman house, listening to the engine ticking and watching the snow for a minute. Then I took out two business cards and a blue pen. Blue is the color that is most associated with the police. I wrote on the back of the cards. 'You want to talk to me first. Your partner will do anything to avoid prison.'

I got out of the car with the cards in one pocket of my peacoat. My .38 was in the other. I was trying to rattle cages, make people nervous. The problem with nervous people, especially felons, is that they are prone to overreacting. That was why my Maverick got shot up. I walked up the front walk, bold as brass, and knocked on the door, loudly, the way I used to when I was a cop. Well, almost – back then, you used your nightstick. You could tell apartments that the cops had been to a lot because the doors all had a series of small dents in them.

Not surprisingly, no one answered. If Lee Raymond was at home, he wouldn't want to talk to me. If he wasn't, that was OK too. I took one of the cards out of my pocket and pushed it through the mail slot. I didn't care who found it first, just as long as one of them did. Then I walked to the driveway and around the back of the house.

I knocked on the kitchen door and made a big show of looking through the windows. There was nothing moving inside. I knocked again and repeated my bit of theater for anyone watching. I would be disappointed if Marblehead was the only town in the Commonwealth without nosy neighbors. I slipped the second card between the door and the frame. One or both of them should get my card and the message. Hopefully, it would sow some seeds of doubt about each other's loyalty. Almost everyone is loyal until it comes time to pay the check or go to prison.

I walked back up the driveway toward the Ford Breadbox and home. There was a woman in her sixties bundled up against the cold walking an Irish Setter. She looked at me, and it registered very quickly that I didn't belong. I hadn't done much more to appear like a resident of Marblehead than wear my duck boots from Bean's. In towns like Marblehead, kids get issued Bean's duck boots as soon as they can walk. By the time they are teenagers, they walk around with them unlaced, jeans bloused into them like paratroopers, scraping their heels as they walk.

'Who are you?' she said with the air of someone used to telling servants and other commoners what to do. I was tempted to tell her to pound sand to see if her face would turn purple. The Irish Setter wagged its tail and sniffed my offered hand. If it were capable of it, the Irish Setter would have been suspicious of me, but Irish Setters are incapable of such emotions as suspicion.

'Chauncey, heel. We do not know this man. He could be any sort of common criminal.' I think that was for my benefit more than Chauncey's.

'Or even an uncommon one, for that matter.'

She did not look amused. 'I can set the police on you.'

'You could, but the fact of the matter is that I haven't broken any laws.'

'You were trespassing.'

'Well, if the homeowner or tenant wanted to make a complaint, I am sure the police would do their due diligence. But I was just trying to get in touch with the tenants.'

'Don't get smart with me, young man. I am well known in this town.'

'I'm sure you are,' I said, doing my best imitation of Groucho Marx's leer.

'Sir, I will not be propositioned! Of all the nerve!'

'I certainly don't have enough nerve for that. I'm afraid it's so much worse, madam. I'm a private investigator, working on a sordid case. Very scandalous – fidelity, infidelity, nouns, various verbs, all of it unsuitable for polite company.' I winked and walked off, feeling bad for Chauncey.

I got into the Breadbox and watched her staring at the car. Her lips were moving, and I was sure she was repeating my license plate to herself. I took another one of my cards and wrote the plate number on it. I handed it to her through the open window as I drove by. She looked at it as though I handed her a turd. Hopefully, Carney would have the Maverick back to me before I had to come back to Marblehead.

* * *

When I got back to Boston, it was that magical time when the streetlights come on but it isn't quite dark yet. Boston is, in its own way, a romantic city. Or maybe, at the beginning of a new relationship, I was viewing it that way. Who knows? Any romantic thoughts I had vanished at the sight of Joe Pinto getting out of a beat-up Ford sedan that made the Breadbox look good.

'Hey, Joe, whaddaya know?' I said, using the old greeting from my father's war.

'Hey, Roark. I'll tell you what I don't know.'

'What's that?'

'Where Raymond Lee Keith is.'

'Well, we have that in common at least.' I wasn't strictly lying; I didn't *exactly* know where he was.

'Bullshit. I think you know where he is but you aren't sharing information with me, his PO, for some reason.' He seemed a little angry.

'Is this the point where you threaten to haul me in and yank my license . . . because I've heard that one before.'

'Don't crack wise with me, mister. You wouldn't like me when I'm mad.'

'You might lose your temper? Do something you'd regret? I've been doing this for more than a minute and I have heard it all, so forgive me if I am not impressed. You lost your guy – you go find him. That's what the Commonwealth is paying you for.' The funny thing about cops, prison guards and POs is that they are so used to having control that they aren't used to it when you push back.

'What? Who the hell do you think you are?'

'A guy who's tired and hungry and not much in the mood to be berated by you or anyone else.'

I walked past him, and I could tell that he was contemplating taking a swing at me. He thought better of it and just said, 'Roark, c'mon, help me out. My boss is up my ass about this kid.'

'I'll call you if I hear anything, Joe.' I went up the steps, almost meaning it.

The next morning found me standing in a doorway across the street from a coffee shop near Government Center and, therefore, near the courts. It was a little before nine, and I had followed O'Day from his office to the coffee shop. I had planned to talk to him in the courthouse, but it was cold out. Seeing him inside with his coffee and Danish, reading the paper, made me irrationally angry at him.

I crossed the street and went inside where it was warm. He was sitting down by himself in a booth, which worked for me. It is hard to intimidate someone sitting on one of those revolving stools at the counter. It would be hard to resist the urge to spin around while making unpleasant conversation.

I sat down next to him and waited for him to lower his copy of the *Globe*. He said, without lowering the paper, 'Seat's taken.'

I ignored him and waited patiently. He lowered the paper and said, 'Look pal, I'm waiting for someone. Now, beat it,' in some sort of cheap imitation of a tough guy. Lately, it seems like everyone wanted to try to convince me of how tough they were.

'Save the tough-guy act, Johnny. I've known too many of them and you don't fit the bill.'

'Oh, yeah, pal.'

'Johnny, drop the act. We both know you aren't that tough.'

'How come you're so sure?'

'You are a blackmailer and thief – well, grave robber more like. It's been my experience that people like that, like you, aren't tough.'

I was rewarded by his face draining of color. I would have continued but the waitress came by.

'Get you some coffee, hon?' she asked.

'Please.'

When she left, Johnny said, 'You can't say that. I'll sue you for slander.'

'It's only slander if it isn't true. Plus, you will find that hard from inside a cell in Walpole.' The waitress came back with my coffee in one hand and the pot in another. She topped off O'Day's cup. She was really messing up my rhythm.

'You want something to eat, hon?'

'No, thanks. Coffee's fine.' She left, and I turned my attention back to O'Day. 'It's simple. I can prove that you are a blackmailer and that you have defrauded several people in violation of the laws of the Commonwealth of Massachusetts.'

'Bullshit, you can't prove anything because I haven't done anything.'

'Oh, you've been a very busy boy. Blackmailing people and stealing from the estates of people without heirs . . . it's a wonder you have time for your practice.'

'Knowing and proving are two different things, asshole. Plus, if there are no heirs to the estate, who is there to complain? Hypothetically, I mean.'

'Well, the late Hellen Whitman was a dog lover. Apparently, the ASPCA is confused as to why they haven't received the money she wrote that she was going to leave to them. Also, I am certain the Commonwealth, not to mention the Bar Association will not take kindly to you forging signatures on the documents that name you as the executor of her estate, among others.'

'You can't prove that.'

'The signatures are all filed with the clerk of the courts, going back to 1979. I don't have to be a handwriting analysis expert. The District Attorney will get one of those.'

'Oh.'

'I left my card at the Whitman house last night. Two cards to be exact. Here's the deal that I will make with you. It's the same one that I am going to take to Lee Raymond. It's very simple. Whichever one of you cooperates will get immunity.'

'Immunity . . .?'

'My guess is that Lee, having spent a significant portion of his life in prison, is in no rush to go back. You, on the other hand, are just dumb enough to think that you can finagle a way out of this. You can't. The only way out of this is to cooperate. I'll give you some time to think about it.' I stood up and dug my wallet out of my back pocket. I took a five-dollar bill out and dropped it on the table. 'Breakfast is on me. Might be your last Danish for a while, but I hear the oatmeal at Walpole isn't too bad.'

I walked outside, crossed the street and went around the corner to where Artie was waiting. He was just putting his Nikon and its telephoto lens away in a camera bag.

'Did you get anything usable?'

'Yes, some very nice shots of you sitting down, you and him talking, you paying for breakfast. All chummy and nice.'

'When do you think they'll be ready?'

'Give me an hour or two.'

'Thanks, Artie, I really appreciate it.'

'No, it was worth it to say that I was working on a real live case with a gumshoe.'

'Come on, I'll give you a ride back to the shop.'

Artie was true to his word. Two hours later, I was back in my office with two copies of each picture he'd described. They were in black and white and on glossy paper. They looked like something out of a real surveillance operation. I took out a sheet of typing paper and wrote on it in blue ink.

'I am going to make you the same offer: whichever one of you cooperates will get immunity from prosecution. The other eats the whole blackmail charge by himself. I don't think the lawyer likes the idea of going to Walpole. Do you? Call me.'

I took one of each picture and stuffed them along with my note in a manila envelope. I licked the flap, sealed the envelope, and bent the little metal tabs down. Then I wrote 'Raymond Lee Keith' on the outside of it. I doubted that either one of them was going to confess or turn over pictures, but I wanted them to be nervous. Nervous people make mistakes.

I put my hat and coat on and went down to the car. I made the now familiar drive to Marblehead in the Breadbox. Devo was on the radio, covering 'Satisfaction' by the Rolling Stones. I was of the highly controversial opinion that I liked their version just as much as the original. If nothing else, it was more fun to sing along to in the car.

The drive was pleasant enough when you weren't fighting traffic, and I made good time. I pulled up in front of the Whitman house. I noticed a curtain twitch in an upstairs window, but something told me Lee Raymond wasn't going to answer the front door. I knocked anyway. I knocked loudly again and waited for something to stir inside.

Not surprisingly, nothing did. I walked across the lawn and down the driveway to the back door. I knocked on that, but, again, no one was answering and nothing was moving inside. I pulled the storm door open and left the envelope between it and the thicker inner door. Then I walked down the driveway to my car. Sadly, the lady with the Irish Setter wasn't there to accost me today.

I drove back to town, wondering what was going through Lee Raymond's mind right now. I smiled to think about what the conversation in the Whitman house would be like when O'Day got home. I was starting to take pleasure in stirring the pot. I probably should have paid heed to Billy Justice's words of warning in Vietnam all those years ago.

TWELVE

The next morning was gray and cold, and it took a real effort to crawl out from under the covers. Any thoughts of going for a run that morning quickly evaporated when I looked outside. Instead, I settled for doing push-ups, sit-ups, flutter kicks and dips in the apartment. I was supposed to be reunited with my Ford Maverick today, which, after almost a week with the Breadbox, was something I was looking forward to.

After I had eaten, had coffee and showered, I dressed warmly. Outside, the air was cold and dry, and my breath came out in plumes of steam. The Breadbox started under protest and with a whining noise from the belts. I let the car warm up for a few minutes while I listened to The Cars on WBCN. When the engine stopped whining and heat began to trickle out of the vents, I pulled out of my parking spot, easing into traffic.

As I made my way to Carney's garage on Charles Street near the jail, I noticed a boxy car behind me. A Chrysler, one of the new ones that actually made the Breadbox look good. Not only was it ugly but it seemed to be going in the same direction I was, whatever turns I took. It isn't hard to tail someone; the art in it is tailing them and not getting made. My tail either wasn't very good or didn't care if I knew I was being followed.

There are a couple of schools of thought about being tailed. One comes from Hollywood, which would have you believe that you should do everything you can – run lights, drive the wrong way down one-way streets – to lose your tail. The other is that if you don't know who is tailing you, you might want to find out. Maybe even why they are tailing you.

Given that I had a few people to choose from, I wanted to know who was tailing me. For instance, given their interest in Danny Sullivan, it could be the FBI, but I ruled them out as they were usually pretty good at following people. They get classes on it and everything. It could be some Vietnamese gangsters who I made really mad at me last spring. You know, the blow-up-my-car kind of mad. Or it could be Lee Raymond or Johnny O'Day. No matter who was doing the following, it was in my best interest to find out who it was.

I made my way down Comm Ave. No self-respecting citizen of Boston refers to it by its full name, Commonwealth Avenue. It was morning commute time, so traffic was moving sluggishly between lights, and I had no trouble not losing my tail. I made sure that they didn't have to work too hard at it by using my turn signal, as though I had been born in the Midwest instead of Boston. I took a left onto Berkeley Street and then another left onto Boylston Street. If they didn't know better, they might have thought I was going to my office.

At Arlington, the Chrysler was four cars back and I slowed down for the green light. It turned yellow and I glided into the intersection as it turned red. I sped up and pulled out of view. When I drew level with the Four Seasons, I pulled in under the covered area where cars and taxis were supposed to pick up or drop off guests. I slid past the doors and waited, counting to sixty slowly. Then I edged out like I was going to pull out. A cab pulled in and let his fare out, then pulled up behind me. I waited, the cab beeped at me and, conveniently, the Chrysler that had been following drove past.

The cabby beeped again, and the driver of the Chrysler turned his head. It was the Commonwealth's hardest-working probation officer, Joe Pinto. I had to give him credit: he was serious about getting his man. I pulled out in the next break in traffic and took a left onto Charles Street when the traffic lights were in my favor. I drove the rest of the way to Carney's without Joe Pinto keeping me company, which was just as well as he was beginning to cramp my style.

I pulled into Carney's, parked the Breadbox in front of the office and went in. He was sitting behind his desk on the phone. He was smoking something that I couldn't dignify by calling it a cigar – even 'stogie' would be an act of generosity. He waved a hand at me. I put his key on the counter, and he covered the mouthpiece with a hand.

'It's parked on the street, on the block behind the shop. Good as new.' He tossed me the keys.

'Thanks,' I said, catching them one-handed. I knew better than to offer him money. Unless I was actually buying a car from him, he never charged me. He felt he owed me, and I felt that he'd paid me for the job I'd done. We had a lifelong commitment to agree to disagree.

He had made it clear that if I ever needed anything that I couldn't get anywhere else, he was to be the first and only stop. I was nervous to think of what he was offering. Carney made good money supplying guns and cars to serious criminal types. He catered to a very specific clientele, not the type of guys looking for a Saturday night special to knock over a liquor store.

When I found the Maverick, it didn't look as good as new, but it looked good enough. More importantly, the back windshield was intact. It was a small thing that made a lot of difference in January in Boston. I didn't survive Vietnam to die of hypothermia at home, much less so driving up to Marblehead.

It was nice to be behind the wheel of my own car again. It had more under the hood than the Breadbox did, but it had been a byproduct of the oil embargo. The Maverick's engine, fed by the Holley four-barreled carburetor, gave a throaty roar when I pushed down on the accelerator. I wasn't sure that I actually made the drive to Marblehead any faster, but it sure felt like it.

The Whitman house was where I left it, still looking like the least-loved house in Marblehead. When I rolled by the driveway, the Bisquemobile was gone. I had to imagine that my little talk with O'Day wasn't enough to convince him to miss a day of billable hours. I went around the block and parked on the same side of the street, a hundred yards back from the driveway.

I sat, waiting patiently, watching. The Irish Setter lady came out to walk her dog. I resisted the urge to make a face at her. I was pretty sure that she didn't have much of a sense of humor. I was also sure that the Irish Setter could do better. A little before eleven, a blue Peugeot station wagon pulled out of the driveway. It was a newer model than the Bisquemobile, and I imagined it was the workhorse of the Whitman estate. I waited for the Peugeot to make the turn at the end of the street, and then I pulled out and raced down to the stop sign. I turned left and followed it at a distance. I wasn't sure what had dragged Lee Raymond out into the light, but it seemed like an opportunity that I didn't want to miss.

I followed the French-made station wagon, with its distinctive curves and lines, back to town. At least Raymond was leading me back home. Or so I thought, because we ended up outside the Howard Johnson's in Quincy. I ended up in the parking lot. I snapped a couple of pictures of Raymond going into the orange-roofed beacon of hospitality. I waited a minute and then headed inside. Raymond was sitting in an orange upholstered booth, wearing one of those tracksuits with the stripes down the arms and legs, across from a clean-cut-looking guy in his late twenties. While Raymond was nervous, looking around a lot, the guy was calm, stirring his coffee slowly.

I sat down at the L-shaped counter at the small part of the L so that I was facing them but still partially obscured. The waitress came by, and I ordered a coffee and held the menu up as though I was looking at it instead of over it at Raymond and his friend. I felt like a cheap imitation of a Michael Caine spy movie.

The man sitting with Raymond said something and reached his hand under the table. He looked down at his lap and stuck something in the inside pocket of his jacket. He handed something to Raymond under the table and then Raymond leaned over, looking down at something between the wall and his hip.

I left my coffee on the counter with a dollar bill under the saucer and walked out of the restaurant. I went back to the Maverick and was able to get my Nikon out of the trunk and sit down inside as the man who met Raymond walked out. I got a bunch of decent photos of him and his car, a black Cadillac with New Hampshire plates. He got in and started it up. I panned back over to the windows where, through the telephoto lens, I could see Lee Raymond sitting sipping a coffee. A rumpled brown paper bag was on the seat next to him.

I got out of my car and jogged across the parking lot. This might be my best and only chance to brace Raymond. He was still sitting in the booth when I got inside the dining room. I wonder how long the man from New Hampshire had told him to sit there. I slid into the booth across from him.

'Hello, Raymond, or do you prefer Lee?' I wish I could say that his face drained of color the way that O'Day's had, but life in and out of prison had taught him not to give much away. He was handsome, more so in person, and I could see why the judge had been taken in. He looked fit, though prison does that to you. But he had the shifty eyes of someone for whom reading the room meant the difference between life and death. Or at least a mild shanking.

'Who are you?'

'My name's Roark. I'm the guy who's been trying to talk to you.'

'What do you want to talk to me about?'

'Trying to give you a chance to stay out of Walpole for the next ten to fifteen.' I wasn't sure how much time the Commonwealth put people in prison for blackmail, but ten to fifteen years sounded sufficiently scary.

'Yeah, for what?'

'Oh, let's see, violation of probation, extortion, conspiracy to commit fraud.' He wasn't looking too impressed. 'Oh, yeah, I guess we could add attempted murder.'

'Who'd I try to kill?'

'Me, when you shot at me in my car. We both know that O'Day has soft hands, and he isn't going to shoot at anyone with a sawed-off, and Cusick was too stupid to be trusted with anything more than a bat. That leaves you.' If it was Raymond and not Cusick who shot at me, he'd be just as eager not to get caught with the shotgun after attempting to massacre the Maverick.

'What do you want?'

'I told you I want to give you a chance to stay out of Walpole.'

'Why would you want to do that? You my new best friend?' he asked sarcastically.

'You have some pictures I want.'

'Why do you want 'em, these pictures of whatever.'

'That's my business. You want to keep playing dumb or should I call Joe Pinto?' This time his face paled.

'No, don't call him.'

'Good. Then listen to me carefully. You and O'Day are blackmailing a judge. I can't have that. I don't care who's paying you. I don't care what happens to you – go to prison, stay free, I don't care. But I care about stopping the blackmail. I have to believe that you care about not going to jail.'

'What do you have in mind?'

'I can prove – not just that I know – but can prove that you and O'Day are blackmailing the judge. I can also prove that O'Day has committed several acts of fraud. You know I already spoke to him. He's going to take a deal to stay out of jail, but he says you have the pictures and negatives of the judge.'

'Bullshit. He has all that. He keeps it in a safety deposit box at his bank.'

'Not all of it.' I pulled a copy of the test strip out of my pocket and slid it across to him. 'I have two test strips, found in the basement of your house. I bet there are fingerprints on them. You see where I am going with this?'

'Yeah.'

'You can make a deal or O'Day can. I don't care who gets me the pictures and negatives, you or him. First one who does is the one who doesn't go to jail.'

'But . . .'

'No buts. If you don't want me calling Joe Pinto, if you don't want to go back to prison, then be the first to get me what I want. Because you and I both know that if it comes down to saving his skin or going to jail, O'Day's going to sell you out.' I stared him dead in the face, and he reluctantly met my gaze. He was rattled: I could see it in his eyes.

'You've got my card. Call me when you have what I need. Don't wait too long because I made O'Day the same offer.'

'Can I go?'

'Sure, sure you can. It's a free country. If you aren't in prison.' I smiled cruelly at him.

'Yeah, don't I know it.' He got up, taking his brown paper shopping bag with him. It was crumpled, and he held it by the roll of paper on top, and something inside weighed heavily against the paper. He walked away, the bag swinging against his blue jean-clad thigh.

I wondered why Lee Raymond had bought a gun. Everything about the clandestine meeting, the exchange under the table, spoke of drugs or guns. But the weighted object in the bag could only mean it was a gun. He was taking a chance. With his record, getting picked up with a gun would mean serious time. Why was he getting one now? Was my campaign starting to get to him? Was he worried about his partner, O'Day?

I watched him walk to the Peugeot and drive off. I went out

to the Maverick and got in. I was smiling. The day was shaping up nicely. I had gotten my car back, and I got to put some real pressure on a blackmailer. If I had half a brain in my head, I would have listened to the nagging voice of Sergeant Major Billy Justice telling me not to think I was the smartest guy in the room.

I drove back to the office and was pleased to see that Joe Pinto wasn't waiting for me. Even better than that, there was no one lurking in the back where I park, and no one had booby-trapped my door. It was like the old joke – just because I was paranoid didn't mean I was wrong.

I spent the next couple of hours writing down in my notes what I had found out to date. I also added my actions toward and conversations with the blackmailers. The gem of an idea I had been kicking around was gelling and refining in my mind. I was putting pressure on the blackmailers, trying to drive a wedge between them. The stick part was shaping up nicely. I was kicking around the idea of introducing a carrot into the mix. At the end of the day, it wasn't about seeking justice but protecting the judge.

I picked up the phone and called Angela Estrella. After she picked up and we exchanged greetings, she said, 'What did I do to rate a call from you?'

'I was calling to see if you wanted to have dinner?'

'Dinner and . . .?'

'You mean besides me sharing my tales of investigative derring-do and progress on the case?' I said with mock innocence.

'Yes, I was hoping for something a little more bedroom-oriented.'

'I was thinking that was the after-dinner part.'

'Ooh, I like the sound of that. Do you want to come to my place?'

'Sure, what time?'

'Seven-ish?'

'Perfect, can I bring anything?'

'Do you know how to make a Martini?'

'I have it on good authority that I make perfect Martinis.'

'You're extra modest today.'

'I've had a breakthrough in the investigation. It tends to go to my head.'

'Isn't that what the Martinis are for?'

'That and to make me easier to take advantage of.' I was not good at flirting, but I was making a game effort.

'Something tells me that you don't need anything to make you easier.'

'Ha!'

'I'll see you at seven.'

'I'm already looking forward to it.'

'I'll bet you are.'

We rang off. I sat back, smiling. The day really was shaping up nicely. Also, there is nothing like the beginning of a new relationship. I had an ex-girlfriend who was of the opinion that the best part of the relationship was the first six months. Maybe that's why she broke up with me after five.

I packed up my case notes and put on my coat. I made my way down the front stairs to the street. I looked out the door, but I didn't see anyone waiting with ill intent. Outside, I walked down two blocks and turned right and then right again. I turned down the alley that led to my parking spot, where my car had been shot a few days before. Now that I was stirring the pot, threatening people with jail time, it made sense to exercise a little caution.

Neither O'Day nor Lee Raymond and his new gun were waiting for me in the alley. I got in the Maverick and pushed the radio buttons, fleeing commercials until I ended up on WROR where they were playing a Modern Lovers song that talked about Pablo Picasso and his Cadillac El Dorado. It was good music to ease my way through the afternoon traffic to.

I stopped at my local packie for a bottle of Stolichnaya, dry vermouth and a jar of olives with pimentos in them. I know it probably seems odd that I would buy Russian vodka, but the truth was that commie vodka was about the only part of the evil empire that I liked. I had promised a lady a perfect Martini. I wasn't going to be able to make that with cheap vodka.

At home, Sir Leominster was asleep on the couch in a shrinking patch of late-afternoon sunlight. Eventually, he stood up and stretched, yawning elaborately, then came over to me in the kitchen. He rubbed up against me, meowing, and I scratched him behind his ears. I decided to kill some time by reading about

Dien Bien Phu and generally lazing about. I'd had a busy couple of days and had earned a break.

Later, after a shower and a change of clothes, it was time to head over to Angela's apartment. Outside, under the streetlights, a few cars back from mine, I noticed the shape of a familiar Chrysler. I wondered if Joe Pinto was charging the Commonwealth overtime for all the time spent following me around. No wonder my taxes were so high. I thought about ditching him in traffic again, but doing it twice on the same day seemed cruel. After all, he was just trying to get his man, and I certainly wasn't doing anything to help him out.

I was standing on the cold, granite steps of Angela's brownstone a little after seven. I had to circle the block a couple of times before I found a parking spot. That was a hazard of living in Boston. I pushed the intercom button next to her name and stamped my feet, wondering if it was possible for one's ears to actually fall off from the cold.

She answered, and I cleverly said, 'It's me.'

The door buzzed and I stepped into the comparative warmth of the vestibule. By the time I made it to her door on the third floor, my feet weren't cold anymore, and it seemed unlikely that my ears were going to fall off.

She was waiting for me at her door. 'Hiya.'

'Hi.' I held up my brown paper shopping bag for her to see. 'The makings of a perfect Martini. I hope you have a shaker.'

'I do.' She kissed me by way of a real greeting. 'Come on in.'

Her apartment was still barracks-inspection neat. Nina Simone was playing on the stereo, and there was an actual fire in the fireplace. Not one of those logs made of paraffin and sawdust where you light the wrapper, but an honest-to-goodness pile of logs on fire.

'Let me take that.' She held out her hands for the paper bag. I handed her the bag and took my coat off. 'Just put that in the hall closet.'

'Sure.' Inside the closet was a baseball bat leaning against the door frame, handle side up. I found a hanger and hung my coat up. 'Do you play a lot of baseball?'

'No,' she laughed, 'that's just in case someone tries to break in. I thought about getting a gun, but I'm not sure I could kill someone.'

'Probably just as well you don't have one, then.'

'Make a Martini and tell me about what you did today.'

'Sure. Shaker?'

'In the kitchen, come on.'

I followed her, taking in the view of her in a white silk blouse and dark slacks. Her high heels clicked-clacked as she walked. She was wearing a strand of pearls at her throat and matching earrings. I might have to step up my fashion game. Her kitchen was through a swinging door, whereas mine just had empty hinges.

'It's right there,' she said, pointing to a metal shaker.

'Ice?'

'Tray's in the freezer.'

Getting to know your way around someone's kitchen was every bit as important a step in getting to know them as all the conversation. I took an ice tray out of the freezer, noting a pint of Häagen-Dazs ice cream and a bag of frozen peas as the only other things in residence. 'Glasses?'

'Here.' She reached into a cabinet and pulled out two Martini glasses.

I twisted the ice tray and dumped a few cubes into the shaker. I poured a dollop of dry vermouth over the cubes, put the lid on and gave it a few shakes. I took the lid off and poured out the vermouth. I pulled the strainer off and added in the vodka, replacing the strainer and lid. I then shook the whole thing vigorously until a thin sheen of frost coated the shaker. Then, and only then, I poured the Martinis. I topped them each with two olives that were impaled on tiny plastic swords. I handed hers to her.

'Madam,' I said with mock formality.

'You know you have a lot riding on this?'

'I do?'

'Yes, when a man offers to make the perfect Martini and doesn't deliver it, could potentially doom the relationship.'

'I do have other talents.'

'You might, but you did say perfect.'

'I did. Well, you should taste it. No point drawing things out.'

'Uh-uh.' She took a delicate sip. I waited, curious to see how far she was going to go with this. 'Oh, that is good.'

'I do try. Cheers.' We clinked glasses and each took a sip.

'Roark . . . I said it was good. I didn't say it was perfect.' She smiled wickedly at me, and I was pretty sure that I was paying the tab for my bravado.

'Give it some time, have a few more sips. It'll grow on you.'

'You mean I'll get tipsy, and you will take advantage of me?'

'That is exactly what I mean.'

'Now that is an excellent plan.' She smiled brightly.

'Be foolish not to have a plan.'

'Tell me about the case while I get dinner on the table.'

'Sure. I've started to put pressure on both O'Day and Raymond.' I explained about the evidence I found, the signatures on the documents that O'Day had forged. I told her about the pictures I had Artie take and brought her up to speed on my harassment campaign to drive a wedge between them. While I was telling her about my efforts, she took the lid off a large, orange-colored, enamel Dutch oven that was on the stove. I was immediately struck by the smell of saffron, herbs, white wine and seafood.

'Do you like paella?'

'Yes, I do.' That was a mastery of understatement and self-control. I love paella and was looking forward to it almost as much as the after-dinner events. Almost.

'Do you think it will work?' she asked.

'The paella? You'd have to get up pretty early in the morning to make a paella that wouldn't work with me.'

'No, your plan.' She smiled, pleased with the compliment.

'Well, I'm pretty sure neither of them wants to go to jail. I think something is working because I'm also pretty sure I witnessed Raymond buy a gun today. If I'm right, something's rattled him, because being a felon in possession of a firearm could land him in jail for several years.'

'Only if he gets caught with it,' she said, putting the pot on a blue, enameled metal trivet on the table. She put out two brightly embellished dishes that were either a shallow bowl or a deep plate.

'There's a good chance of it. His PO wants to violate him badly. He's following me around trying to find him.'

'Aren't you obligated to tell him? Why don't you make us two more Martinis.'

'Kind of murky on that one.' I raised my hand chest high,

palm to the floor and waggled it from side to side. I went to the shaker and did as I was told. 'He's technically not wanted – that I know of. Also, his PO can earn his own paycheck.'

'So, you think this pressure will work?' she said, using a large metal spoon to serve the beautiful rice dish onto our plates.

'I think it is the stick part of the carrot and the stick,' I said, refilling our Martini glasses.

'What's the carrot part?'

'I think the judge should offer them some money to buy the pictures and the negatives. They might be more inclined to walk away if they aren't walking away empty-handed.'

'I don't know. How much were you thinking? Cheers.' We carefully clinked glasses that were threatening to overflow.

'That's up to the judge. I wouldn't offer them more than twenty or thirty grand.'

'Would it make them go away?'

'They'd only get paid once I was sure we had all the pictures and negatives.'

'It might work,' she said doubtfully.

'I can't see any other way out of this, other than turning them over to the cops, and we both know that is not what the judge wants.'

I dug my fork into the steaming dish of saffron rice with chicken, chorizo, squid rings, shrimp and mussels in it. It tasted fantastic, and it took real effort to use my 'date' manners and not shovel it down like I was in an Army chow hall.

'How is it?' she asked, but judging by her grin, she knew how I felt.

'Fantastic. I love paella.'

'You've had it before?'

'Sure. I know I'm a boy from Southie, but I've traveled a little. Why, I've even been to New Beige and Fall Reeve,' I said, using the Anglo-Portuguese pronunciations of New Bedford and Fall River, both known for their large Portuguese populations.

'You? I was impressed that you'd made it out of Southie as far as Back Bay.'

'Me too.'

'You traveled to Vietnam. What was that like?'

'Hot and humid. I worked very closely with some of the locals, ate their food, spent time in their culture. That was cool.' I left out the part about going on missions with the Yards, fighting the NVA and then feeling guilty as hell about how we as a nation abandoned them when we pulled out of Vietnam.

'Did you eat the food?'

'Constantly. You can't befriend people of another culture, expect them to trust you, if you won't do something as basic as eat their food.'

Leading up to missions, we ate nothing but Vietnamese and Montagnard food so that we wouldn't smell different in the field. When we could, we ate the Project Indigenous Rations or PIRs, which were developed by Ben Baker for SOG. The foil-wrapped packets of dehydrated rice, vegetables and fish were neat because everything was identified by pictograms instead of words – a picture of a fish for fish-based meals, that type of thing. It was designed for both the Yards who might be illiterate and, in case of capture, to not offer the enemy proof that the American Army had been there.

'That makes sense. How was it? I imagine a lot of it was very different.'

'It was. Some was good, some was . . . well, tough.'

'Like what?'

'The Montagnards – the Yards for short – would make their version of the local fish sauce. They would trap the little fish from the rice paddies and leave them out in the sun to ferment. It smelled godawful.'

'But you ate it.'

'Yes.'

'Did you eat everything they offered you?'

'Yes. When I first got there and met the people I was going to be working with, they threw us a party. The new guys were the guests of honor. The Yards have this homebrewed rice wine, and you have to suck it down with a long straw. You have to drink a lot of it very quickly. It tasted foul, but I got a good drunk on.'

'Not as good as the perfect Martini?'

'No. Warm rice wine – not even close.'

'Was there anything you liked about it?'

'The Yards. I loved the Yards. Fierce, loyal and tough. Great fighters, they were more like an extended family. The beaches were beautiful, and the country was too, once you got away from the cities.' And the war . . . I loved the war. Loved my part in it, being an elite soldier, fighting a secret war, but I couldn't tell her any of that. She would have run for the hills.

Fortunately, instead of running for the hills or asking more questions about the war, she said, 'Wanna see my etchings?' I could fall for any girl who tried to seduce me with lines taken from a Philip Marlowe novel.

'I thought you'd never ask.'

The next morning, after saying goodbye properly, I headed home for a shower and to check on Sir Leominster. There were no new messages on the machine. I fed both the cat and me. I showered and dressed and took note of the grin on my face every time I passed a mirror. I was in a good mood, and, romantically, there was the possibility that this one might last more than a couple of dates.

The other advantage of being up early and out of Angela's apartment was that I was at the coffee shop that O'Day frequented before he got there. I stamped my feet in a different doorway than last time, and when I saw him walking up the street, I found myself smiling again. I was looking forward to making him squirm some more. It was a small taste of what the judge was going through.

I walked into the coffee shop just as he slid into a booth. He was learning, though. He was facing the door this time, and his face darkened when I walked in. I slid into the booth opposite him, half turning my body so that I was sitting against the wall and could watch the door too.

'Good morning, Johnny.'

'It was until you walked in,' he snipped at me.

'Geez, that's a crummy thing to say. After all, I'm trying to keep you out of prison.'

'You just threatened to send me to prison two days ago.'

'I wanted you to understand how serious I am and how serious this could be for you.'

'And now you want to offer me a way out.'

'Sure, the same one as yesterday. Turn over the pictures and the negatives. Walk away from the judge, and we'll call it even.'

'Ha. You're nuts. You must be smoking weed if you think I know what you're talking about.'

'Nope. Look, I'm not asking you to admit to anything. I'm not recording you. Nothing like that.'

'You're awfully confident, then.'

'I am.'

'Why?'

'Because I know what you don't.'

'What's that?'

'I know what cons are like. I know that Raymond doesn't want to go back to prison. I know that he doesn't want me to call his PO. I know that he bought a handgun yesterday . . . which means he can get jammed up and end up back inside Walpole instantly. If it comes to Walpole or giving you up . . . I know which he's going to pick. Do you?' I watched O'Day's face as he chewed over what I had said. He knit his eyebrows and chewed on his lower lip.

'You're bluffing.'

'Nope, I saw him buy the gun yesterday at the Howard Johnson's in Quincy. I took a bunch of pictures of him and the guy who sold it to him. License plates and everything. Then I went and sat down with Raymond. I had a nice cup of HoJo's coffee. Raymond and I talked. I told him that I was going to make him the same offer I made you. The first one that gives me the pictures and negatives, all of them, doesn't go to jail.'

'Bullshit!'

'Let me ask you a question?'

'What's that?' Gotta love anyone who answers a question with a question.

'He's been to prison and doesn't want to go back. You've never been to prison, but I imagine you really don't want to go. Who's going to be smart and make a deal first? You or him?'

'Screw you.'

'It doesn't matter to me. I'm just trying to help my client. It doesn't make a difference to me which one of you ends up joining the Walpole all-male non-voluntary dating society.'

'You're an asshole.'

'Probably, but at least I am not looking at prison time. Why don't you prove to me that you are as smart as you think you are? Make the deal first. You know how to get in touch with me.' I stood up and started to walk out but turned back. 'Hey, Johnny. Who do you think he bought the gun for? Is it for you or him?' I laughed, doing my best impression of a movie villain, and walked out for real.

I walked to my office, smoking a Lucky and contemplating the direction that the case was moving in. One of them would turn on the other. I was exerting pressure and slowly ramping it up. At a minimum, it should make them sloppy. I would love to be a fly on the wall for any conversation in the Whitman house tonight.

I got back to my office and was happy to see that Joe Pinto and his boxy Chrysler weren't lurking. It was nice to see that he had stopped, however briefly, following me around. Hopefully, he had embarked on his own self-improvement plan and was trying to find his guy. It would make me happy to see my tax dollars going to good use instead of doing his work for him.

Inside, there were no blinking lights on the answering machine, which meant that the sergeant major was probably regrouping in his assault on my lack of interest in going to the reunion. After hanging up my coat and stuffing my wool hat in the pocket, I turned the espresso machine on and readied it to make me a cup of the lifesaving stuff. I packed my pipe and managed to get it lit with two matches.

When the espresso was in the cup and my pipe was drawing nicely, I killed some time by updating my case notes. It was a habit left over from the Army, constantly updating intelligence and information. It also helped me keep the details of my cases fresh in my mind. Losing track of little details could be deadly, and I had spent most of my adult life trying not to get killed.

Shortly after eleven, my phone rang. I picked up the handset and said, 'Hello.'

'Mr Roark, it's Ambrose Messer.'

'Good morning, Your Honor.'

'Angela said that you needed to speak to me?' It is funny how 'talk' turns to 'speak' with the right breeding.

'Yes, sir.' I defaulted to the formal deference of the Army and treated him like an officer. 'As I'm sure Miss Estrella told you, I have found the people responsible for your current situation.'

'She did.'

'I have enough evidence to have them arrested and, I believe, convicted. I know that isn't what you want, but I think that is still the best way of dealing with them.'

'It is not what I want. I can see why you would think so.'

'I figured you would say something like that. I do have another idea.'

'Go on.'

'Arrest and jail time are the stick of the carrot-and-stick approach.'

'What are you proposing for the carrot?'

'If you offer to buy the pictures and negatives from them.'

'How can we be sure that they won't try to extort me again later?'

'While I can't guarantee it, I think that the threat of jail, and the fact that you have proof of not one but two crimes they've committed, is probably leverage enough. I think that the chance to make some money might be enough to convince them to be smart about things.'

'I don't want to get involved in anything that would result in . . .' He trailed off.

'Exposure. Yes, sir, I understand. I think this will be enough. Lee Raymond's parole officer is breathing down his neck, which means he's most vulnerable. As for his co-conspirator, Johnny O'Day, I believe that I can prove that he has been forging documents and defrauding either estates or the Commonwealth. He seems like someone who very much wants to avoid going to prison.'

'I know him.'

'O'Day?'

'Yes, he's been before me a few times as a judge. When he was new to the bar, I was still practicing and would see him around the courts. I don't think he was terribly successful.'

'Are you friends?'

'We were friendly but not friends.'

'I see.'

'Professional acquaintances. The legal community is fairly small, and we'd run into each other at work, social functions, golfing, those sorts of things.'

'I understand.' That was another nice thing about being a PI: we didn't have a set. We didn't have to be professionally nice to one another. There wasn't a lot of small talk and ass-kissing in my line of work, and our social ladder only led downward. The last time I had been golfing was at an Air Force base in Thailand on a weird trip when I was a Covey Rider.

'What do you think I should offer them to buy the, uh . . . materials?'

'I should think that no more than thirty thousand dollars should do it. It's better than nothing and much, much better than jail.'

'I can see that. OK, negotiate on my behalf. I can go up to forty thousand dollars if need be. Anything more than that will draw too much attention from my wife.'

'Sure. I'm assuming you will need a couple of days to get the money together.' Being able to lay my hands on forty thousand without drawing any attention was a luxury I've never had.

'Good. Thank you, Mr Roark.'

'You're welcome, sir.'

'And Mr Roark?'

'Sir.'

'Do be careful. I know you are used to taking risks and probably don't think much of it. After all, that is part of your profession, but I don't want you or anyone else to get hurt.'

'Yes, sir.' He hung up and I listened to the dial tone for a few seconds, thinking about what he had said.

I was certain that he was sincere about my not getting hurt. I was also pretty sure that he was asking me not to hurt Lee Raymond. Sentimental, but he was probably a more noble type than me. If I was being totally honest with myself, I wanted to give both Raymond and O'Day a beating the likes of which they'd never forget, the type that would land them in Mass General.

In my mind, I could justify it a hundred different ways but, in the end, they were scum. They were blackmailing a decent man, who, in spite of their blackmail, still didn't want them hurt. The result of their blackmail would mean that a bunch of people who were hurt by a biggish company that had cut corners would be cheated out of the compensation they were due. People's lives had been irreparably harmed, and these two were trying to make a profit from it. I wanted to let old Andy, Vietnam Andy, have a few minutes with them, but in the end, that wouldn't do much to help the judge.

Now I had to figure out how to offer Raymond and O'Day their lifeline. Was it better to offer it to them together using the reasonable-uncle act? Or was it better to float it to each of them individually and see if their natural greed would lead them to try to double-cross each other? There was a reason why the divide-and-conquer strategy is effective. Instead of a united enemy, I would be facing two separate actors, each doubting the other as much as they were worried about me.

I decided to stick with the classics. First, though, I would give them a night to stew over everything that I had done to date. I wanted to spend some time and effort seeing if I could shore up the case against O'Day involving his fraud. Maybe someone, somewhere, had gotten screwed out of an inheritance because of his machinations. Or maybe a local charity did. It was unlikely that no one had been hurt by his scheme. The world was just too small and there was too much money involved.

I spent the rest of the day at the library. Eventually, they were going to charge me rent or declare me dependent on their taxes. It was the only place that I could think of, though, that might have information about the people involved in O'Day's estate pilfering.

I spent two hours hunched over the microfiche machine going through the *Globe* and the other local papers. When I was done, I had a headache behind my eyes and a crick in my neck, and my back hurt. I also had three names of people who worked for the deceased. I made a list on my legal pad and then went off to check the phonebooks.

The Yellow Pages are imposing. They are inches thick and look as if they could stop a bullet. But there are as many advertisements for businesses as there are listings of phone numbers. The less sexy, more pedestrian White Pages are usually a quarter or a third of the size. There are no flashy ads or drawings, just alphabetized listings, accompanied by a street address. The White Pages were one of a PI's best tools. You could find an address if you had the right name.

I made out all right. For one of the names on my list, I had two possibilities, both in Boston. Thankfully, there were not a lot of Kapchinskys in Boston. For the second, I had four possibles, because for some reason O'Leary was a common name in the greater Boston Metro area. Go figure. The last name was Franks – Harold Franks – and there were a surprising number of them – five – and all in the suburbs or neighboring cities. Someday I will accept the little oddities the universe sends my way.

When I had made my list of names and addresses, I packed everything into my postman's bag and bundled up against the January weather. I walked home thinking not about the case but rather about Angela Estrella. My luck with women the last year or so had bordered on bad to disastrous. She was smart and pretty, and we seemed to enjoy the time we spent together. I was cautiously optimistic.

I stopped at the market on the way home for steak, a couple of russet potatoes and some broccoli. Even though it wasn't yet five, it was almost dark and chilly. That made me want something more than salad and yogurt to eat. Nope, steak, baked potato and a vegetable so that I could pretend that I was eating something healthy too. If nothing else, it would soak up the whiskey. Besides, I had a full day of driving ahead of me in the morning. Then I would have to decide how to offer the blackmailers their unjust reward.

The next day I was up reasonably early by private eye standards. I drove out to Braintree. Braintree isn't known for much more than the South Shore shopping plaza and its giant T station. It wasn't that the station was especially big; it was the parking garage that went with it. The station is convenient for people coming from outside of the city who don't want to drive through Boston's infamous traffic jams. The mall is nice enough if you are looking to be parted from your hard-earned cash.

Harold Franks, when I tracked down the one I was looking for of the five, lived in Weymouth, not far from Weymouth Landing. He lived in a small Cape-style house and turned out to be a pleasant man in his early sixties with hair that was brown flecked with gray. He wore horn-rimmed glasses, which no one under sixty wore anymore.

'Mr Franks?' I asked.

'Yes.'

'My name is Andy Roark. I'm a private investigator.' I held out my license for him to see.

'You're here to ask about Johnny O'Day?'

'Yes, I am. How did you know?'

'I've been waiting for six years for someone to come ask me about that no-good son of a bitch.'

'That's a long time.'

'It is. You'd better come in. There's coffee on.'

'Thank you.' I followed him into his home and into the kitchen.

'How do you take it?'

'Black.'

He poured me a cup from what looked like a fresh pot. I muttered a silent prayer of thanks that it wasn't from a can of flavored instant crap.

'What do you want to know, Mr Roark?'

'Why don't you tell me from the beginning?'

'Sure, sure. I got out of the Navy in 1974. I had done twenty-five years as a machinist's mate. I was single and had a pension. I bought this house and spent time fixing it up, but I was bored. A buddy of mine from the American Legion told me about a friend of his mother's who couldn't drive anymore. Poor thing couldn't see worth a damn. So I started driving her around.

'One day, she asked me for a favor – I can't remember what. Fix something around the house or run some errands for her. She started asking for more favors, and pretty soon it felt like I was practically living at her house. I wasn't making a lot of money, but I didn't need much. Look at me, I'm a simple guy with simple tastes. I like Miller High Life, not champagne.

'She wasn't in good health when I first met her, and it only went downhill from there. She would tell me all the time how she didn't have any family left. There was no one to leave her stuff to. She'd say it all the time, then she started telling me how she was going to leave it to me. She told me she had written a letter leaving everything to me.

'I didn't think anything of it. You know, she was a lonely old lady, and I just thought she was talking. I didn't take it seriously. Then she got sick, and she says that she wrote it all down, how the house and the bank accounts all should go to me. Still, I didn't take it too seriously, you know?

'Then, one day, she tells me she talked to a lawyer and made out her will. She said that I would get everything. After she died, I waited to hear from the lawyer, and I waited. I came by the house, but the locks had been changed and there was a "for sale" sign in the yard. I called the real estate agent, and he gave me the name of the lawyer. Your pal.'

'Johnny O'Day.' I know the punchlines to all the knock-knock jokes.

'Yep, the very one. I called him and asked what was going on. I told him that the old lady said that she told me she was going to leave me everything. He said that she had died without a will. That she had named him executor but that she hadn't left any instructions. He said that, according to the law, he was supposed to sell everything and put it all in a bank account, along with her savings.

'So, I know I shouldn't have done it, but I was mad, and I broke into the house one night. All the furniture was still there. It took me ten minutes, but I found the letter in her desk drawer. She left me the house and her savings, which was twelve thousand dollars.'

'Let me guess, you went and confronted him.'

'Yes. I went to his office with the letter. I showed it to the little weasel. You know what he did?'

'No, what?'

'He laughed at me. He told me that the letter wasn't notarized, so it didn't count for anything in court. Well, not in probate court. He said that if he called the police, it would be used as evidence of my committing a B and E. He said that's a felony and I'd do time for it. I wanted to punch him in the face, but he told me to leave or he'd call the police and make a complaint about breaking into her house. What could I do? He beat me. Between her savings and the house, I was out thirty grand or so.'

'I don't blame you for being mad.'

'You know the funny thing, Mr Roark?'

'What's that?'

'When she was telling me about the house and the money, I didn't want it, you know? But then after she died and there was no one, I started thinking about it. Not greedy like, but more like I had won some money. Like on a Lotto ticket or something.'

'I do know what you mean.'

'Does that help, Mr Roark?'

'It does, but it will help me really stick it to him if you'd write your story down for me,' I said, taking a legal pad and blue felt-tip pen out of my bag. I slid them across the table to him.

'Sure. I'd love to jam that weasel up.'

Half an hour and another cup of coffee later, he was done. I thanked him and got back in the Maverick.

I never found the O'Leary I was looking for, but in Boston that was like not finding the tree for the forest.

Back in Boston, however, I found Mrs Kapchinsky. Her story was remarkably similar, except instead of being a caregiver, she worked at the local ASPCA. They had been promised the donation of a woman's estate. They had corresponded about it, but when the time came, the lawyer hired to deal with the estate said that there was nothing to indicate how the estate was to be disposed of. The property was liquidated, and the money went into an account.

I was willing to bet that O'Day had been living off those accounts for years. It was a pretty good scam if you were a lawyer. File the paperwork just before someone dies without heirs or a will, or shortly after if you don't mind a little forgery. He ends up controlling the money; there are no relatives to come looking for it and no one could make a legitimate legal claim to it. It was, for all intents and purposes, his money, except that it was unethical as hell. After Mrs Kapchinsky wrote out her version, I thanked her and headed back home. It had been a long day of driving and talking to people, and a whiskey was in order.

I got up early the next day, and after breakfast, I went to the office. I spent the day typing up everything that I had found out about O'Day and his scam. Then I typed up everything I had learned about Lee Raymond. Lastly, I typed up my case notes to date. In case I got hit by a bus or accidentally got shot thirty-seven times, I wanted to make sure that the judge would have a copy of what I had found out.

It took all morning to type up, but it looked professional, and more importantly, everything was laid out in some sort of coherent manner. I added the photos I had taken and copies of the test strips that I had found in the basement of the Whitman house. I put everything in a big manila envelope, and, grabbing my coat, I headed to the local printers to make copies of it all.

Leaving my office, I noticed a familiar Chrysler was trailing behind me. Joe Pinto was becoming a nuisance. I steered the Maverick through the series of one-way streets and cramped alleys without making any effort to shake Pinto. If he wanted to watch me Xerox, then he was welcome to. It wasn't going to help him find his man.

I made the copies and put one in an envelope on which I wrote Angela Estrella's name and address. I put a copy in another manila envelope – that would go to my bank to go in the safety deposit box – and I put another set of copies in an unmarked envelope. I would put the last copy in my office safe. It took me an hour or so to make my way to the bank and take care of things there. I lost another half-hour of my life waiting in line at the post office. Then back to my office, the whole time with Joe Pinto in tow.

Once back in my office, I made an espresso and pulled the phone over. First, I called Angela. She didn't have much time to talk, so I told her to expect a package in the mail. It gave me small comfort to know that if some misfortune befell me, at least the judge would have the leverage he'd need to keep Raymond and O'Day in check.

Next, I dialed O'Day's office. He answered, 'Johnny O'Day.'
'It's Roark.'
'What do you want?' he asked with a mouth full of vinegar.
'I would like to meet with you and Raymond.'
'Why would we do that?'
'Simple. Because neither of you wants to spend the next fifteen years in Walpole.'
'You can't prove anything.'
'I'll do one better than that, counselor. I will bring my proof to you – what you lawyers call discovery. Then I have a business proposal for you.'
'Where and when?'
'Tomorrow. Let's make it someplace nice and public so that

your pal Raymond doesn't get any stupid ideas about using his new gun. Let's say Quincy Market at noon. The Orange Julius stand.'

'Aren't you supposed to say something like "come alone and unarmed"?'

'No, that's usually what the extortionist says in the movies. I don't care who you bring or how many guns, just as long as you bring Raymond.'

'Is this some sort of trap?'

'It will be crowded and loud. Even if I wanted to wear a wire, and I don't, it would be too loud to get anything on tape.' The whole point was to get them to walk away from the blackmail and not to land the whole thing in court.

'Crowded?'

'Yes, it will be lunchtime – lots of people from Government Center looking to get a quick bite to eat, talking and otherwise making a racket.' I also wanted to discourage them from getting stupid and trying to take what I had by force. It would only lead to one of them getting hurt or shot, and that would bring the cops into it. Devaney likes me well enough but not so much that he'd squash a shooting for me.

'OK, we'll be there.'

'Good.'

He hung up and I put the handset down in the cradle. I smiled to myself in my darkening office. I was starting to say and do things more and more like some TV movie tough guy. Setting up rendezvous in public places and talking about wearing a wire. Jesus, my life took a wrong turn somewhere.

On the plus side, according to the paper, *Blade Runner* was on the Movie Loft tonight, so that would give me something to look forward to. I loved the mix of science fiction and film noir that was *Blade Runner*. The story was great, but at the heart of it, it was a classic missing person's story, just with more shooting.

I was at Quincy Market by eleven-thirty. I was pretty sure that they wouldn't try anything stupid, but I didn't want to take the chance and overestimate these two. I had walked from my apartment, and whenever possible made sure I was walking against the flow of traffic on one-way streets.

The last thing I needed was over-eager, under-talented probation officer Joe Pinto showing up and putting Raymond in handcuffs before I could make sure the judge was safe. To that end, I cut through the Public Garden and the adjoining Common and then headed down to Government Center. I walked down into the brick expanse of Government Center Plaza and wondered what they had been smoking when they had come up with the design. The only advantage was that there was no way for Joe Pinto to follow me in his Chrysler. That would mean he'd have to follow me on foot, and I was pretty sure he'd be just as bad at that.

It wasn't that I thought that Joe Pinto was bad at his job. I was sure that he was a pretty good parole officer. I just didn't think that he was very good at *my* job. Who knows, maybe Raymond was smarter than the average ex-con or at least smarter than Joe Pinto.

I went down the many steps of the plaza and crossed Congress Street. I strode into the wide expanse of Dock Square. In the good weather, spring and summer, they have tables and umbrellas set up so you can eat in Dock Square. Being January and almost on the water, the weather was not nice enough to eat in the square unless you were looking for a side order of frostbite with your meal.

I cut to my right, walked down Chatham Street and boxed around the whole area via Commercial and Clinton Streets. I didn't see any sign of Joe Pinto, or the blackmailers. I was hoping that they had run out of prison friends like Lonnie Cusick. I took the opportunity of being outside in the almost-fresh air to light up a Lucky. It helped cover up the stench of low tide in Boston Harbor.

Satisfied that I wasn't being followed and that nobody was lurking in the shadows, I decided it was OK to go inside. Adding to Boston's indefinable charm, I dropped my cigarette and ground it underfoot. I walked up the granite steps, between the Doric columns and into the Roman-style entrance.

The building dates back to the 1820s when it was essentially a large indoor vegetable and food market. Back then, there would have been stalls for the individual vendors. In the early 1970s, it was starting to show its age and was closed. The city managed to squeeze two million dollars out of the Feds to clean the joint up and restore its original exterior. They traded the vegetable stalls for restaurants and food stalls, and it was a hit with the locals and tourists alike. For the thousands of office workers in Government Center and the nearby buildings, it offered a variety of different foods for lunch that wouldn't decimate their bank accounts. For the tourists, it also offered an actual piece of Boston history.

I walked inside the two-story building, which was a little over five hundred feet long. There was a dome in the center with its ornate reliefs. The center under the dome serves as a seating area with tables and has the same communal vibe as Durgin-Park but without the waitresses who talk to you like they're trying to pick a fight. I stopped and bought a cup of coffee from a stall that claimed to have the best pastries and coffee in Boston.

I made my way down the long central corridor and found a place to lean against the wall that was out of the way but still allowed me a good view of the Orange Julius stand. Fortunately, I didn't have to wait very long. They walked in and over to the Orange Julius stand, each as different from the other as could be. O'Day was wearing a black wool coat over his conservative blue suit. Raymond was wearing a tracksuit with stripes down the side – this time it was green – and unlaced work boots. He topped it off with a Celtics team jacket, which in this town was practically a uniform item. I waited, watching them, watching to see if anyone was watching them too. I watched them buy a couple of the frothy orange drinks and then I walked over to them.

'Roark,' O'Day said. Raymond just nodded coolly at me, which was fine by me. It was preferable to some cheap tough-guy talk.

'Let's grab a table and talk.' I wasn't there to waste their time either.

They followed me with their orange concoctions. I'd never had an Orange Julius, and as long as I had coffee and whiskey in my life, I didn't see the need. We found a table and sat down.

'OK, Roark, we're here. Talk.' I had to lean in to hear O'Day over the dull roar of the lunchtime crowd. I couldn't have recorded a conversation with them even if I had wanted to.

'I've talked to you both, but let's go over it again. You guys are blackmailing Ambrose Messer; you want him to throw a case that he is presiding over or you will make public some compromising pictures of him and Raymond here.'

O'Day pulled a face but Raymond just sat back against his seatback, arms crossed, face impassive, his eyes scanning the hall. Like a lot of ex-cons, he always had an eye out for trouble.

'We're not admitting anything,' O'Day, ever the lawyer, said.

'You don't have to.' I reached inside my peacoat. O'Day flinched, thinking I was going for a gun. Raymond's eyes just took it all in. He had spent years in Walpole, watching out for people looking to hurt him. He knew I wasn't going to draw down on them. Instead, I pulled out a large manila envelope containing copies of the relevant parts of the case so far.

'What's this?' O'Day asked.

'Open it. I'll explain. The first paperclipped stack of papers is all about your blackmail scheme. It should give you a good idea of what I can prove.' Which was everything.

'And the second one?' O'Day asked.

'Well, O'Day, that's all about your particular scam. The one where you make yourself the executor of heirless estates and then loot them. I have found two people who will testify under oath that they had been told they'd inherit and that there was no mention of a lawyer until you showed up. In fact, in a couple of cases, it looks like you became the executor postmortem. That's a pretty neat trick.'

'That doesn't prove anything,' he said hotly.

'I can compare the signatures of all of your so-called clients. An expert will testify that you forged all the documents in which you were retained. I am a hundred percent certain that the fraud unit of the state police would be interested in that. What do you think?'

'You still can't prove anything.'

'Well, that is where you're wrong, but even if you weren't, I don't have to prove anything.'

'Why not, smart guy?'

'Because of him,' I said, jerking my chin at Raymond. 'He doesn't have to be convicted of anything. He can be charged, and that would be enough to violate him. Something tells me that his parole officer is all over him.'

'Yeah, he's an asshole.' Raymond didn't say much, which was a nice change compared to his literal partner in crime.

'So what?' O'Day asked, making me wonder if he got his law degree by mail order.

'So are you willing to take the chance that Raymond here won't give you up to make a better deal for himself? I'm betting that Raymond isn't in a rush to go back to Walpole. Are you, Raymond?'

'You have no idea,' he said slowly, for emphasis.

'So, you see, this is where we are. Raymond can easily be violated, sending him back to jail. He can implicate you, but even if he didn't, I'm betting that you can get jammed up with your little scheme. Even if you don't do jail time, I'd be willing to bet that you'd get disbarred awfully fast.'

'So, what are you proposing? A trade? Our pictures for your so-called evidence? It'd just be easier to have someone whack you.' So much for the lack of tough-guy talk.

'You could, but a lot of people have tried. I am still here, and they aren't.' That was the problem with tough-guy talk: it bred more tough-guy talk.

'You don't know the type of people I know.'

'O'Day, let's skip over the part where I say something pithy to show you how unimpressed I am and get back on track.'

'Let it go. You aren't going to intimidate him. Stop wasting everyone's time.' Raymond didn't say a lot, but when he did, he made sense.

'So, what do you want, we swap pictures and stuff, and we tell you who put us up to it?'

'No. That's your copy. Your only copy. My client has no interest in seeing either of you get arrested, but he isn't going to give up his leverage.'

'What, then?'

'You give me the pictures and the negatives. You tell me who put you up to it. I give you thirty thousand dollars in cash. We keep our evidence in case you get any funny ideas that you can have the money and keep blackmailing him.'

'Thirty isn't much. We were getting a lot more than that if this works out,' Raymond said, making me wonder who was the actual brains of the operation.

'Sure. The problem is that it isn't working out. Because if O'Day doesn't like the thought of going to jail, I am sure that whoever's paying you two likes that idea even less. At least this way, you walk away with something, and you don't go to jail. I hear it's hard to spend money there anyway.'

'Fifty.'

'Fifty what, Raymond?'

'Fifty thou.'

'Nope, thirty. That's the offer.' I smiled like a used-car salesman or maybe a shark.

'Fifty gives us twenty-five apiece.'

'How you split it is your business.'

'C'mon, Roark. Don't be an asshole. It's not your money, and the judge has plenty of it.' O'Day was showing off his stellar negotiating skills.

'Why don't you tell me how you figured how you were going to blackmail the judge?'

'I had heard rumors when I first started out, when he was still practicing,' O'Day said. 'I knew a guy who knew a guy, that type of thing. A couple of years ago I was at a gallery opening, must have been '83 or '84 and the judge was there.'

'Let me guess, the same gallery where Raymond here was working?'

'Yup. His Honor was discreet, but I picked up on it. He couldn't take his eyes off old Raymond here. Then I heard about the NT and C case and a lightbulb went off. I made a couple of calls and offered to make their problems go away. They didn't care how, just as long as it was discreet.' A real criminal genius.

'You sent Raymond to Florida?'

'I went with him. Someone had to take pictures.'

'You're a photographer?'

'I took some classes in college and belong to a club,' he said with unexpected pride, as though it didn't make him a dirtbag.

'A real Ansel Adams. You found a way to earn from your passion. They say when you love your job, it doesn't feel like work.'

If he noticed my sarcasm, he didn't let on. 'After we made the first contact, after we were sure the judge was game, it was simple after that.' He smiled and I idly wondered if my punching him in the face would ruin the deal. I decided not to risk it. 'After that, it was easy. Ray and I would pick a hotel, get two adjoining rooms. Ray would call the judge while I set up the cameras. They'd do their thing, and I would immortalize it in black and white. Pretty slick, huh?'

'Yeah. How much were you going to get paid?'

'A hundred grand.'

'Each?' He nodded. 'Not bad.' Considering Raymond was doing the hard part. 'Did it bother you?'

'Bother me?'

'Yes, you've known the judge for years. He's a decent man, a well-respected man.'

'No, it didn't bother me.' He sneered. 'Decent man. He's a degenerate and he was cheating on his wife. He acts so high and mighty, like he's some moral authority. Like he's better than me. Like he never had to hustle to pay the bills. No, screw him! He brought this on himself – of course I didn't feel bad for someone like him.'

My urge to punch O'Day in his bigoted face was almost overpowering. Instead, I steered the conversation back to the money. We haggled, and I let O'Day talk me up to forty thousand dollars. He was beaming with self-satisfaction. After all, he had won a minor victory.

'OK, give me a couple of days, and we can set up some sort of meeting to do the exchange.'

'You could come to our house,' O'Day offered, almost as though he was inviting me over to hang out.

'Naw, I'll pass. We'll come up with someplace we all feel comfortable.' It didn't seem like a good idea. That, and I noticed that Raymond had been watching me, not saying much. I got the feeling he was calculating how hard it would be to bump me off and get rid of the body. You'd be surprised how often I got that look. I thought about that as I walked out of Quincy Market, and I kept thinking about it all the way back to my office. It was good to know who was the lion and who was the hyena.

THIRTEEN

'He actually said that? What an asshole.'
'It took a lot of self-control not to knock his teeth out.' We were sitting up in bed, backs to the headboard, in the wreckage of bedding and discarded clothes. Angela's right leg was casually draped over my left, a gesture that I found both intimate and pleasantly possessive.

'I don't know how you managed it.'
'It didn't seem like it would help the judge.'
'No, but I bet it would have been satisfying.'
'True.' She rubbed her heel against my shin.
'I can't believe that the judge agreed to pay them.'
'It makes sense. The carrot-and-stick approach doesn't work if you're missing either one.'
'Still, it sticks in my throat.'
'I know.'
'Plus, O'Day's a bigot and an asshole.'
'I know that too.'
'Look at you – it must be nice to have all the answers.'
'Well, most of them,' I said modestly.
'You know you can't trust them. They'll try and double-cross you. There's too much money at stake for them not to.'
'I'd be disappointed if they didn't try.'
'Ha. You should go make us another round of Martinis.'
'Gladly.'

I went to the kitchen and got the makings for the Martinis. Sir Leominster jumped up on the counter, meowing at me as though he disapproved of the earlier events. Judgmental little bastard. I poured the vermouth over the ice cubes, gave the shaker a few shakes, then dumped it out. I poured in the vodka, capped the shaker and shook it until it was coated with frost. I poured the contents into two Martini glasses, which I carefully carried into the bedroom.

'Thank you,' she said, taking her glass and demurely sipping from it. I put mine down on the bedside table and got into bed next to her. 'Andy, why do you do it?'

'My dad told me knowing how to make the perfect Martini would help me impress women.'

'It does. But no. Why are you a private investigator? I get the feeling that you're smart enough to have done a lot of different things.'

'You mean instead of a job with crappy hours and long stretches between paying clients?'

'That and the danger. Since I've known you, you've been shot at once, fought with a guy who was trying to assault you with a baseball bat. You've clearly been hurt before,' she said digging a manicured fingernail into the scar on my thigh.

'Well, to be fair, a lot of that stuff I picked up in Vietnam.'

'Let me guess . . .'

'I heard that chicks dig scars.'

'No, seriously, why do you do it?'

'Oh, I don't know. A bunch of reasons, I guess.'

'Such as?'

'Well, for one, people like the judge – they need help. They have the type of problems that not just anyone can help with.'

'OK, I can see that.'

'That's part of it, but I guess if I was being totally honest . . .'

'Always a good idea with me,' she interrupted.

'I spent three years in Vietnam. I'd been in the Army for five years. I got home. I tried the cops, but it didn't work. I knew that I couldn't work a regular job, a nine-to-five in an office. I'd never cut it.'

'So, being a PI, occasionally getting hurt – that's the answer?'

'It seemed to be the best answer.'

'Did you have other options?'

'Sure, lots of guys stayed in the Army, a lot of guys went to work for the CIA, and I knew a few guys who went off to be mercenaries in Africa and South/Central America.'

'Not for you?'

'All those options still involved following orders or having a boss. At least doing this, I have a measure of freedom.'

'And you get to meet sexy and intelligent women.'

'I do. I do.'

The Judge

'You're going to make me spill my Martini.'
'I hope so.'

The next day was Saturday. After Angela had left, I showered and dressed. I got in the Maverick and steered it toward Route 3, heading south of the city. As I was weaving my way through the streets of Back Bay, I caught sight of a familiar Chrysler behind me. I had to give Joe Pinto credit: he was persistent. His timing sucked; he hadn't once been on my tail when I could have led him to his man. Be that as it may, I didn't want him following me to the judge's house in Duxbury.

There was no traffic to help me out on a Saturday morning in January. Instead, I got on the highway, hitting the on-ramp hard, merging into traffic and hammering down on the accelerator. The Maverick's engine gave off a throaty growl, and I was pleased to see Joe Pinto's Chrysler grow smaller in my rearview mirror. When I couldn't see him anymore, I slowed down and got off at the next exit.

I made my way south on the surface streets, moving slowly through the traffic lights and intersections of Boston's southern bedroom communities. The good people of suburbia were out and about, bundled up against the cold. Their weekend rituals were a mystery to me. I probably had more in common with the Montagnards I served with in Vietnam than I did with the average American suburbanite.

The further from Boston I got, the more the cars changed. Fords and Chevys gave way to boxy Volvos and stylish Mercedes. When I turned into Duxbury, I began to wonder if the only cars on the road made in Detroit besides mine were the cop cars. I turned into the judge's driveway and followed it up to the main house, which looked even more impressive during the day.

I had been mildly shocked when he had told me to come to his house Saturday afternoon, given all the subterfuge that had gotten me there on New Year's Eve. This time, instead of the front door, I went around to the side door by the kitchen. I rang the bell, and after a few minutes, Messer opened the door.

'Hello, Roark.'
'Sir.'
He was wearing faded jeans, well-broken-in boat shoes and a

cardigan that had recently been ambushed by some moths. I had never seen the judge in anything but a suit, and I wasn't quite prepared for the sight of him unshaven and dressed down.

'Come in. My wife is out for the day.'

'I see. That certainly cuts down on any awkward questions.'

'Yes, exactly.' He smiled a pained smile.

'I can't say as I blame you. Besides, discretion is part of the service.'

His smile widened, shedding the pained look as it went. 'Let's go to the office.'

I followed him back to the large office I had been in several nights before. He went to the large desk and opened one of the drawers. He took out four stacks of banded one-hundred-dollar bills. Each band had '$10,000' printed on it.

'Do you want me to sign something? A receipt?' I asked.

'No, Mr Roark, I think that might be awkward to explain if my wife found it.'

'I understand.' I picked up the bundles of cash, secreting them in the pockets of my coat.

'When are you meeting them?'

'Tomorrow.'

'Will it be dangerous?'

'The potential is there, but the idea is that this is easy money, which is better than no money.'

'What if they try to take it from you . . . with force.'

'Well, there's always a risk of that. I am hoping it doesn't come to that. I've taken the precaution of mailing the evidence against Raymond and O'Day to Angela Estrella. I have a copy for you and there is one in my safety deposit box.' I took a manila envelope out and handed it to him.

'Thank you.'

'If something happens to me, you will have something to use as leverage. I know you trust Angela, so that is why I sent her a copy.'

'You're right. I trust her implicitly.'

'Good.'

'Mr Roark, I know you might not have any choice in the matter but . . . if you can avoid hurting Lee.'

'I'll try, but that will mostly be up to him.'

'I know, but I had to ask. There's no fool like an old fool.'
'Sir, in all the time I've been doing this, I have learned something.'
'What's that, Mr Roark?'
'We don't get to pick who we care about or who we fall in love with.'
'Yes,' he sighed. 'It would be much easier if we could choose.'
'Probably, but it is beyond our control.'
'You might be right,' he said, clearly believing in his mind that I wasn't.
'I'll call you when it's done and let you know how everything turned out.'
'Thank you, Mr Roark. Take care of yourself.'
'That is the plan, sir.' I said it as though I actually had a plan. It was never a good idea to give the client a reason to doubt you. I wasn't a hundred percent sure that Raymond or O'Day wouldn't get greedy or stupid.

I drove home via the highway. It was nice to get out of Duxbury. I had grown up in a working-class neighborhood and never really felt comfortable in places like Duxbury where a lot of the houses had quarter boards above the doors and were named like old-time sailing ships. The fact that I lived in Back Bay and – at the right angle out of the right window – had a view of the Charles River was as far up the economic ladder as I was going to climb.

Back in my apartment, I went to the closet, moved the panel on magnets and unlocked the gun locker. I put the judge's forty thousand dollars inside and locked it all up. The last thing I needed was a junkie to break in and make the score of his life. I am pretty sure no one would believe me anyway.

I spent the rest of the day lazing about. I smoked a pipe of good tobacco with a fair amount of Latakia in it. I finished the book about Dien Bien Phu and even caught the last twenty minutes of a Godzilla film on Creature Double Feature on TV 56. Sir Leominster spent most of the day lazing next to me on the couch.

O'Day called late afternoon and suggested that we meet at a location in Southie, down by the harbor. He gave me a street address, and I was pretty sure it was an old warehouse. I told him I would be there, and then, after hanging up, my mind turned to food.

Dinner involved roasting chicken breasts in the pan while cooking penne. I blanched some broccoli in the pasta water right before straining the pasta. I chopped up the broccoli, sliced the cooked chicken and stirred it in with the penne in a big bowl. I added a couple of tablespoons of pesto sauce from a jar and mixed it all together.

While doing that and sipping whiskey, I started making plans for Sunday. Ideally, we'd meet and exchange the money for the pictures and negatives. We'd all head our separate ways and that would be that. A nice simple plan. You know what the problem is when you have a plan? Nothing ever goes according to plan. Nothing.

I slept in Sunday morning. I fed the cat and made breakfast, still thinking about the meet with the blackmailers. I made myself a cup of strong coffee, and while eating scrambled eggs and bacon and wheat toast, I listened to the classical radio station and read the *Boston Sunday Globe*.

I showered and dressed for the weather, which had turned colder overnight. It was supposed to be a balmy twenty-two degrees, dropping down to single digits at night. New England in January is not for the weak. But we didn't run around in grass skirts and coconut shells either. For me, it was jeans and a dark wool commando sweater, wool socks and boots.

Sitting at the kitchen table with a section of the *Globe* spread out on it, I cleaned and oiled both my Colt Lightweight Commander and my .38 snubnose. Both guns were nickel-plated, but the Colt had stag horn grips compared to the revolver's slim wooden ones. An old friend of mine once described the Colt as 'something a Tu Do Street pimp would carry.' Tu Do Street in Saigon was the Vietnamese version of the Combat Zone but times a hundred.

I reassembled the Commander and made sure it functioned, then slid fourteen of the thick .45ACP rounds into the two magazines. I kept an extra loose round to top off one of the magazines when I charged the gun. It was methodical and mindless work. It was also familiar and comforting, a pre-mission routine. I brushed the lint out of the revolver's barrel and chambers. I put a thin coat of oil on it and pushed five hollow-point rounds into its cylinder.

When I was done, I put the .45 in a leather tanker holster with a strap over my collarbone that lay flat across my chest with the muzzle facing the floor. The loop at the bottom of the holster threaded through my belt and there was a leather strap over the handle. It wasn't the fastest draw, but it would do for my needs. The spare magazine went into my left pants pocket. I had fifteen rounds of .45 ammunition if I needed it.

I threw the oil-soaked paper in the trash and then found a brown paper shopping bag and dropped the cash in it. The cat rubbed up against my shins and I reached down to scratch him between the ears. Then I put on my peacoat, absentmindedly dropping the revolver in a pocket. I pulled on my watch cap and went down to my car. There were snowflakes floating on the breeze, like moths at night.

I hadn't been exactly honest with the judge, or Angela for that matter. When I said that we were going to meet someplace safe, someplace public, I was at best naïve, at worst disingenuous.

The truth is, I would have been shocked if they had suggested someplace public. This would be a chance to make forty grand and to keep blackmailing the judge. Of course they'd try to double-cross me. They'd be shitty criminals if they didn't. That was one consistent thing in an inconsistent world – criminals will do criminal stuff.

I piloted the Maverick through the quiet Sunday streets. The Pats were playing the Miami Dolphins at four. I couldn't tell you when the rivalry between the Dolphins and the New England Patriots started. Like the Capulets and the Montagues, no one even cared anymore about the origin of the rivalry. As this was a big game – whichever team won would be in the Superbowl – there were going to be a lot of fans glued to TVs and more still at parties watching the game.

Fortunately, I was never much of a football fan. I love the Bruins, and few things can compare to sipping a cold beer while watching the Sox play at Fenway. If there was a chance to catch a good fight on TV or ringside, then I'm there. The upside of the game was that the streets were almost deserted. I felt a little bit like Charlton Heston in the opening of *The Omega Man*.

I slowly went from Back Bay, back in time, toward my youth in Southie. Lots of the dads worked down here in the same warehouses and factories that I was driving past. Lots of the guys who I grew up with had gotten jobs there too, only to find that there was little future in the dying industries of Boston. More of the factories were closing as jobs moved south or overseas. The ones that still had jobs were clinging to industries that were on the endangered species list. Even worse, they clung to a dying way of life and the illusion that the American dream could still be had on the wages of semi- or unskilled labor.

I parked a block up from the warehouse in an alleyway. I got out, taking the big screwdriver, the key to the city, with me. I walked down to the building which had a faded 'For Sale or Lease' sign prominently displayed. The front door was unlocked. I went around back to check the rear door, which was locked but not bolted. I was pretty sure that there was no alarm.

It should have been bolted shut from the inside. There was no sense inviting thieves in to strip the carcass of the building. After a couple of tries, the back door yielded to my efforts with the screwdriver. I waited, listening, to see if anyone heard the faint popping of the door, then I went inside. I was in a corridor that had offices on either side of the passage for about twenty feet. The hallway was cluttered, and what little light there was came in the form of late-afternoon sun through the slats in the drawn shades of the office. It was the type of place where the windows had chicken wire embedded in the glass.

I moved carefully down the corridor, feeling my way, moving slowly. It was funny how often the skills I had perfected as an SOG man in Vietnam were pressed into service in my civilian life. I followed the hallway, passing darkened offices, until I was at the edge of a large warehouse. I could see O'Day and Raymond ahead of me in the large expanse of the warehouse floor.

O'Day was fidgety, as though he'd had too much coffee or just enough blow. Raymond was sitting on a crate, hands inside the big pockets of his green satin Celtics jacket. I had to respect his hometown pride. There's nothing worse than someone who isn't committed to the hometown sports teams. I've even heard rumors of New York Knicks fans up here. Scandalous.

'Hello, boys,' I said, stepping out of the corridor.

O'Day wheeled around, like a shaky gunfighter, his hand

gripping something in his waistband. Raymond turned slowly, taking everything in, then he stood up, hands in his pockets.

'Jesus, Roark. You fucking startled me,' O'Day said. 'That's not a good idea with a guy like me. I might have plugged you.' Yep, O'Day definitely had some Bolivian bravery coursing through his nostrils. If the situation had been different, he would have been laughable, but I was far more worried about being killed by an amateur than a pro.

'I have the money,' I said, holding up the bag with my left hand. My coat flapped open, and there was no way they couldn't see the shiny automatic with its pale grips nestled in its holster against my chest.

'You're armed?' Coke definitely wasn't making O'Day any brighter.

'Yes, Johnny.'

'I've got a gun too,' he said as though it mattered to anyone but him.

'Good for you.' As my eyes were adjusting, I could see the unmistakable butt of a German Luger. A relic of the Great War. A museum piece but still deadly, especially in the hands of a coked-up amateur. It might be sixty or seventy years old, but it still held eight rounds of nine-millimeter.

'Did you bring the pictures and negatives?' I asked.

'There's been a change of plan,' said a voice from somewhere to my left, behind a pile of boxes.

'I'm sorry, Andy,' Angela said. 'He came to my apartment. He has a gun.'

'That's right, Andy. I have a gun, and don't think for a minute I won't shoot your girlfriend,' Joe Pinto said.

'Hey, Joe.' I didn't finish the famous Jimmy Hendrix line, as it seemed too much like tempting fate. 'You here to bring your man Raymond in?'

'Nope, that's not the plan.'

'What's the plan, Joe?'

'I'm going to come over there and you're going to hand me – very carefully hand me – your gun,' he said, slowly and deliberately. He was the exact opposite of O'Day.

'Let me guess, or you'll shoot the girl.'

'Good boy, you figured it out.'

'I've seen this movie a few times.'

He shuffled closer to me, pushing Angela in front of him. Her face was contorted, and it occurred to me that he must be pushing the muzzle of a gun into her back. I can say from experience it hurts a lot more than you would think.

'You OK, doll?' I asked, doing my best Bogie imitation, which is pretty lousy.

'I've had better days, and don't call me doll.' She smiled but without much conviction. I have to admit that if I were her, I might not have a lot of faith in me right now. Pinto was close now.

'Roark, take out your gun and toss it on the floor.'

'No.'

'What? I'll fucking blow her spine out.'

'Andy, this isn't the best time to clown around,' Angela said coolly.

'Joe, this is a single action forty-five, and if I toss it on the floor, it's liable to go off. None of us want that.'

'OK, what then?'

'I'll put it down and step back away from it.'

'Do it.'

'Sure.' I did as I said I would, carefully placing the pistol on the floor. 'Joe, why are you here if you aren't here to bust Raymond?'

'You think these two have the brains or the balls to pull off a job like this?' he said gesturing to Raymond and O'Day.

'You might have a point there. How did you come up with it? You don't strike me as the type who follows lawsuits for fun.'

'I've been Ray's PO for years. O'Day used to pay me not to violate his clients. Fifty bucks here and fifty there, that type of thing.'

'Is that how Lonnie Cusick ended up trying to beat my head in?'

'Yep. Lonnie wasn't bright, but he was available.' Pinto smiled wryly.

'Bright enough to take a shot at me?'

'Lonnie, no. That was Raymond here. I wouldn't have trusted Lonnie with a sawed-off.' Raymond smiled slightly at having been appreciated more than Lonnie. It doesn't take much for some people.

'Makes sense. Go on.'

'The money?'

'Sure, here.' I held the bag out, but he had a gun in one hand and Angela's arm in the other. He pushed her into my arms and took the money. He gestured for us to move back with his gun. It was a Smith and Wesson Model 15 with a short barrel. A good gun. A lot of cops carried them.

'So how did you find out about the lawsuit and the judge?'

'O'Day. He heard about it. We were having some drinks after he paid me for helping out another client of his. He's full of get-rich-quick schemes.'

'So, the two of you cooked it up?'

'Sure. I knew how to convince Ray, and we were off and running. A real partnership.'

'Split three ways?' I asked, almost innocently.

'Sure, that's a partnership.'

'Bullshit,' I said harshly. 'You're worried that these two were going to take the deal. Leave you in the cold rather than go to jail.'

'You're full of it, Roark,' he spat back.

'He's got to kill me and the girl,' I said to the lawyer and his client. 'He's looking at life in prison for kidnapping her. You think he's going to split all the money with you and worry that you might give him up later when you get jammed up? I don't. Not when he can use two more bullets and walk away with all the money.'

'You're so full of it, Roark,' O'Day chimed in.

'Really, Johnny? He's holding forty thousand dollars. That's not a bad score if he doesn't have to split it. He doesn't need you anymore. All you are is a liability. You know the old saying – one guy can keep a secret, maybe two, but three end up in jail.'

'Bullshit, Roark. I said we're a partnership.' Pinto's voice rose a plaintive octave or two.

'Partners!' I scoffed. 'You probably treat these two like garbage.' I stood close to Angela, my left hand on her shoulder, my right, slipping into the pocket of my coat. 'They don't have the brains or balls,' I imitated Pinto. I curled my fingers around the butt of the revolver. I would have to pull Angela down and out of the way, draw and shoot Pinto first.

'Fuck that guy!' Raymond pulled a flat Spanish automatic out of his pocket and started shooting at Pinto, hitting him in the chest. Pinto winced as each small caliber round hit him to the cadence of popping noises as the rounds went off. He managed to squeeze off a round that caught Raymond under the chin and popped out the top of his skull. Raymond dropped like a puppet who suddenly had his strings cut.

O'Day screamed and pivoted toward Pinto with his German museum piece of pistol. His face was already lined up in the sights of my revolver.

'Drop it, O'Day!' I shouted.

His coked-up brain was working on overdrive. He saw my gun pointing at him as he fumbled with his own, and he thought better of it. He slowly put it down on the floor, holding one hand out in supplication. 'OK, Roark. Don't shoot. Don't shoot.'

'Johnny, I'm going to give you one chance to get out of this. One chance to not go to jail, and one chance only. But if you lie to me, try to trick me, you're going to Walpole. Get me?'

'Yes.'

'Good. Where are the pictures and negatives?'

'Back at the house.'

'Where at the house?'

'They're in a Maxwell House coffee can, one of the big ones. Under the kitchen sink.'

'OK, we're going to go get it.'

'And then?'

'Then I don't care. You can fuck off then for all I care.'

'What about the queer judge? How do I know he won't hold this against me? I'll still see him in court. He always acts like he is so much better than everyone. Fucking degenerate.'

I started to answer but never had the chance. There was a bright orange flash to my left, a loud explosion, and my ears started ringing. Oh, and a .38 special round from Pinto's revolver blew a neat hole between O'Day's eyes.

I turned and looked disbelievingly at Angela, the revolver now hanging at her side in one gloved hand. January in Boston was cold and almost everyone wore gloves, a seasonal advantage if you are going to murder someone. I was saying something. I eventually heard my voice, through the roaring of the surf, say, 'There was no need to kill him.'

'Why the hell does he get to live? He would have kept squeezing the judge. Maybe not right away, but he would never have let him go.'

'But . . .'

'Fuck him, he doesn't deserve to live, to go on to hurt more people.' She turned to me. 'Tell the cops what you want. I'm glad that asshole is dead.' She tossed me the gun and turned and walked away. I stood there, flatfooted. My brain was trying to wrap itself around what I had just witnessed.

Eventually, I went off to find a phone. I called Devaney at home. He was definitely not happy with me. 'Andy, it's the fucking playoff game. We might be in the fucking Super Bowl.'

'Joe Pinto's been murdered. I have two other dead bodies too. You need to send someone.'

'You shanty Irish pain in the ass! Where are you?'

I told him.

'Andy, you all right?'

'Sure, Billy, sure.' There was no explaining it.

I made one more short phone call.

When the cops came, the money and my .45 were locked in the trunk of my car. I walked them through how Joe Pinto, Probation Officer for the Commonwealth, had been helping me with a case. I'd been hired by Judge Ambrose Messer to investigate a corrupt lawyer, who was cheating estates by falsifying paperwork and declaring himself the executor so that he could raid the coffers. The lawyer had a partner, an ex-con that Pinto was looking for on a violation.

We tracked them to a warehouse by the harbor. When we confronted them, the lawyer drew down on Pinto, who shot him. The ex-con didn't want to go back to Walpole and shot Pinto, who managed to shoot him with his last dying breath. I told them that Joe Pinto was a hero and that he saved my life. I told the story to the Uniform cops who were pissed about being in a freezing warehouse with three dead bodies instead of being able to sneak off somewhere to watch the game.

They took me to headquarters and sat me down at an uncomfortable table in an uncomfortable interrogation room. The box. Then I sat in the box and told the detectives. Then I wrote it out.

By the time I got home, Pats fans had been thrilled for a couple of hours that they were going to the Super Bowl with Chicago. I called the judge at home again and woke him up. My first call to him had been simple. 'Listen to me. If you want to protect Angela Estrella, tell the cops when they call you that you hired me to investigate O'Day for his estate plundering.'

This time, I told him the full story of what happened in the warehouse. He listened and there was a sharp intake of breath, but he agreed it was best to say that he hired me to investigate O'Day. I told him that I wished it had worked out differently, and maybe I meant it. He told me to send him a bill. I was sure he meant it.

Two nights after that, I drove up to Marblehead in the wee hours of the morning. I broke into a certain house and took a coffee can from under the sink. I burned the contents in the fireplace and left. A few days later, Joe Pinto was posthumously given a hero's burial by the Commonwealth.

After a week, I started wondering if I should call Angela. Maybe I should check on her, see how she was doing. I hadn't had a Martini in a while, and it wasn't the same drinking them alone.